Cue the Battered Wife

'Eve woke with a start. "Go back to that slide of the adult bird." She sat up, suddenly interested. The image was a classic scene – but it wasn't the birds that alerted Eve. "That's a hand!" she cried.'

Vivien Reid's life is transformed the day she meets Rupert Lasco. A celebrated mountaineer and travel writer, she has been used to calling the shots – until the day her publisher decides to drop her from the list. Rupert persuades her that fighting back is the only answer. A former editor himself, he offers to help her start a new career – as a crime novelist.

At Vivien's home in the wilds of Scotland, however, her staff welcome Rupert warily. But no one's antagonism can match that of Vivien's neighbour and former climbing partner, Alastair Semple. And when Rupert and Vivien marry, Alastair's resentment turns to venomous obsession.

Tensions mount between the Lasco and Semple households to explode on a night of impending storm. The inhabitants of the remote community wake to the beauty of the Highlands under snow – and the awareness that one of their number is missing. With threats and cunning the cover-up starts. People conceal the truth from the police – and even from each other – until a bird-watcher photographing eagles feeding their young unwittingly records evidence of a savage death. Up till then had it been the perfect murder?

By the same author:

LADY WITH A COOL EYE
DEVIANT DEATH
THE CORPSE ROAD
MISS PINK AT THE EDGE OF THE WORLD
HARD OPTION
OVER THE SEA TO DEATH
A SHORT TIME TO LIVE
PERSONS UNKNOWN
THE BUCKSKIN GIRL
DIE LIKE A DOG
LAST CHANCE COUNTRY
GRIZZLY TRAIL
SNARE
THE STONE HAWK
RAGE
THE RAPTOR ZONE
PIT BULL
VERONICA'S SISTERS
THE OUTSIDE EDGE

Non-fiction:

SPACE BELOW MY FEET
TWO STAR RED
ON MY HOME GROUND
SURVIVAL COUNT
HARD ROAD WEST
THE STORM SEEKERS

Cue the Battered Wife

Gwen Moffat

**MACMILLAN
LONDON**

First published 1994 by Macmillan London Limited

a division of Pan Macmillan Publishers Limited
Cavaye Place London SW10 9PG
and Basingstoke

Associated companies throughout the world

ISBN 0-333-61424-0

Copyright © Gwen Moffat

The right of Gwen Moffat to be identified as the
author of this work has been asserted by her in accordance
with the Copyright, Designs and Patents Act 1988.

All rights reserved. No reproduction, copy or transmission
of this publication may be made without written permission.
No paragraph of this publication may be reproduced, copied or
transmitted save with written permission or in accordance with
the provisions of the Copyright Act 1956 (as amended). Any
person who does any unauthorised act in relation to
this publication may be liable to criminal prosecution
and civil claims for damages.

9 8 7 6 5 4 3 2 1

A CIP catalogue record for this book is available from
the British Library

Phototypeset by Intype, London
Printed by Mackays of Chatham, PLC, Chatham, Kent.

Introduction

'It's not dark enough,' Paul Mason said. 'Justin, you're nearest. Pull the curtains together.'

Justin got up and blundered past the furniture to the window. The sliver of light from the street lamp disappeared.

'Glorious country,' Eve said brightly, stifling a yawn. She really did appreciate her husband's slides but running a house, a family and a busy medical practice didn't leave a woman much energy in the evenings. On the sofa beside her Ben whispered unctuously, 'I should be doing my homework, you know.'

'It's Friday,' she whispered back. 'Do it tomorrow—'

'And this is looking up the glen towards the site of the eyrie,' Paul was saying, the bright red arrow of his torch settling on a shadowed crag with a few pale spots high in the gullies.

'There's snow!' Justin exclaimed. 'What's the skiing like, Dad?'

'I've no idea. I was a long way from the Cairngorms. Now this is a grey wagtail.'

'We have those,' Ben said, kicking the sofa.

'No, we have yellow wagtails.'

'It's the same thing—'

Eve nudged her younger son harder than she'd intended. She wondered why Paul didn't show the boys slides of bridges being built; they were always clamouring to be taken to see his work in progress. She presumed that bird-watching was a reaction to the bustle of a civil engineering project: all that dust and noise and people... She wondered why she didn't find bird-watching an attractive antidote to disease, and people, and logistics. She couldn't hear the dish-washer; was it working? She had switched it on – no, the boys had been squabbling in the passage... She woke with a start.

'You snore,' Ben said, giggling.

'What do eagles eat?' Justin was asking.

'Rabbits,' Paul told him. 'Dead lambs, all kinds of carrion; they're scavengers, like buzzards, but they take nestlings too, and grouse, ducks, anything really.'

'Go back!' Eve exclaimed.

'What?'

'Go back to that slide of the adult bird.' She sat up, suddenly interested. 'Are you focused properly?'

Paul fiddled with the remote control. The image was a classic scene but one that everyone was accustomed to from television so the boys gave their father little credit for a still picture of a golden eagle presenting a piece of meat to a downy chick. But it wasn't the birds that alerted Eve.

'That's a hand!' she cried. 'Beside that second chick, see? Give me the torch.'

The red arrow fastened on something pale and spiky.

'It's part of a ribcage, dear. Rabbit.' Paul peered. 'Perhaps it's a grouse's wing.'

'It's a hand, Dad.' Ben had no idea but it made for a bit of excitement.

'Not a whole hand maybe.' Eve had advanced to the side of the screen. She stooped, then stepped back. 'It's the phalanges: a thumb and two fingers. It's much too big for rabbit's ribs or a wing. It's human, darling. What *have* you uncovered?'

EIGHTEEN MONTHS EARLIER

Chapter 1

The pass was clear but above it the slope was in cloud and plastered with snow; there would be cornices above the northern gullies. Vivien glanced to her left down the glen; it was below the snowline and patches of deer grass glowed where they caught the light. It was three o'clock: half an hour to go before sunset, a thousand feet to the summit – but the snow was good and hard – a thousand feet down the west ridge and she'd come out below the cloud but into twilight, and then there were two miles of a wicked little stalker's path that traced the edge of gorges where you could come to grief in the dark as easily as on a cliff. She had a torch but the batteries were low. She'd look great, sitting by the lochan: Vivien Reid, high-altitude explorer, stuck on a mountain at the back of her own house, waiting for the moon to rise. She grinned and started up the slope, her crampons biting into snow that had scarcely softened all day.

There were no tracks; no one had been here since the last big storm before Christmas but then few people came to this area at any time, let alone in the depths of winter. The climbers went to Ben Nevis and Glen Coe, and the massif was too remote for most walkers; only the odd fanatic would venture out to bag isolated Garsven above Loch Alder.

Something moved ahead of her, a shape more solid than the mist. Her pace slowed but she maintained her rhythm. Now she saw a black line, a hint of red, and she could distinguish the outline of a ptarmigan and hear the scratch of its claws on the surface. The bird walked ahead of her, alert but not alarmed. The weather would hold, she thought, if the ptarmigan stayed high.

Beyond the bird, half-right, the snow had a dense, unshadowed appearance as if immensely deep. She had come to the cornices. She diverged leftwards, feeling more secure as she encountered masked boulders: a nuisance to negotiate but safer than those sinister eaves poised above the gullies.

The light was fading fast, in fact it was already dusk in the cloud. She could still read the compass although she didn't really need it until she reached the summit, and you knew when you'd reached the top because there was nothing higher. Her guts contracted suddenly as imagination took flight and visualized the four ridges that converged on the peak. Darkness, cloud, and four ways down – and only one of them correct.

She swallowed and went on walking, edging right to try to find smoother ground but resisting the temptation to tread those swelling crests now so obvious against the grey void. She stopped and put her compass round her neck so she couldn't drop it. Hikers walked with compasses round their necks: hikers and idiots who didn't know which ridge was which on their own mountain. If she continued to walk on this bearing she could walk right past the cairn, but she had to come down the correct ridge – surely? It was on the same bearing.

She was panting a little now, short of breath. At thirty-five, in her prime, she was short of breath? A heart attack? God, it was dark – but she could still see the compass. She walked on, her ankle gave a sharp twinge and she gasped. Sod you, she thought viciously; people had come down, alone, crawling, dragging a broken leg; there's nothing wrong with that ankle, it's playing up.

She tripped and put out her hands to save herself. Her ice axe gave a muffled chink. She pawed up something solid and saw a vertical shape like a frozen man. Stuck in the summit cairn was the post she had planted there herself, an old rusty fence post now plumed with frost feathers.

She trampled the snow about the cairn; if anything happened on the descent the searchers would know she was between here and home. The twinge in the ankle had been a warning; she'd been wearing crampons for a long time today, and zigzagging up steep slopes put a heavy strain on the ankles. She nursed her body down the initial drop as if it were a tired horse. It was her way of looking after herself, alone at the end of the day above the snow-line. At one point there was a soft sweep of air above her head and the resident eagle passed like a shadow through the gloom. She grinned; they knew each other. Such huge and long-lived birds had to have high intelligence. He'd recognized her, she was sure of it, and she revelled in the feeling of kinship, particularly in this place.

The transition from cloud to clear went unnoticed for a moment. She was descending on a long diagonal facing north, into the mountains, and everything was white, then she turned, changing her axe-hand, and stopped. Wisps of cloud like blanket fluff were fringed with pink against a sky of pale jade. The real sunset was round the corner to the west but she didn't mind that; the focus of attention lay at the far end of the burn that gleamed intermittently in the bottom. Between that and the loch that shone like a sheet of tinted glass were her house and woods.

She dropped down into the corrie where the lochan was frozen and indistinguishable from the snow-covered screes except for its regularity. A white hare got up and went lolloping across the ice, leaving no track. The cloud still hung solid at three thousand feet and there was no sound, no light except the afterglow. There was no sigh of wind in the high rocks, no croak of raven or ptarmigan, nothing. The eagle had gone.

She looked down the glen, feeling a sudden chill, as if there were wilderness ahead of her as well as behind, and then she tensed. A light showed by the loch, faded, went out and reappeared, finally vanished. She waited. A fainter light appeared and she nodded. Flora's timing was perfect. She'd just returned from town and before she unloaded the car she'd run upstairs and switched on a light as a welcome. Vivien took off her pack and found her head-torch. No way was she going to risk a fall into the burn on the home stretch.

Flora Gunn came plunging downstairs to find Danny Paton unloading the car, jostled by the animals; the dogs eager for bones, the younger cats infected by the general excitement. At Alder Lodge they shopped once a month and the return from Inverness held something of the air of a supply ship dropping anchor in the bay.

'Get that door closed sharp,' Flora fussed as they carried boxes into the kitchen. 'You're letting all the heat out of the house. You can put the car away, and get these dogs out from under my feet; look, there are the bones, you can have two just. And wipe the grease off your hands before you touch that steering wheel!' she shouted as he went out, Thomas the collie dancing ahead, her own little cairn yapping hysterically.

By the time Danny came back the tea was made and his pint mug waiting for him. 'Going to be a hard frost again,' he said, pulling off his woolly hat and sitting down. 'Any sign of her?' He knew Flora would have looked when she switched on the top light.

'I couldn't see her, but then she said her batteries were low.'

'She's mad. What time did she set out?'

'I dropped her at eleven.'

There was a pause. 'Cloud's down,' he said.

'She'll be below it by now.' Flora was indulgent. He did his best to hide his concern but he couldn't fool her. He adored Vivien. She had brought him back from a lecture engagement: 'Found him in Edinburgh,' she'd said, as if he were a stray dog. They'd been frantic for a man to cope with emergencies, like mending the deer fence, or adjusting the water system when the burn dropped below the level of the intake pipe, or handling the chain saw. Vivien and Flora hated the chain saw. Danny didn't talk about his past but they suspected he'd been a drifter; whatever it was he'd found his niche at Alder, and since he fitted it so well, as handyman and gardener, no one asked questions, least of all Flora who had landed the perfect job herself. Prior to working for Vivien she had nursed her mother through multiple sclerosis, years of service that ended only with her mother's death.

It was when she had been caring for her mother that Flora discovered the pleasures of writing: short stories and poems, never published, and she started to wonder if there were some job that might reconcile her love of words with her facility for looking after people. It was only three weeks after her mother's death that she saw an advertisement in the *Lady* for a secretary to a woman in the northern Highlands, and a box number. She couldn't believe it when, having written, she got a reply from Vivien Reid, the explorer and travel writer. She took the post and very quickly became indispensable, cleaning up Vivien's careless scripts, learning to operate the word processor, arranging lectures, even cooking, at least until Vivien found a housekeeper.

Working at Alder Flora felt as if she were brushed with glamour, and how else could you feel, involved with this woman who led expeditions to the Himalayas and the Andes, who had climbed Mount McKinley on a long weekend, who dressed like a bag-lady in the Highlands and a fashion plate in a TV studio, and who was always – or almost always – cool and beautiful, and who didn't give a damn for anyone except her staff?

'She's careless.' Danny was still worrying. 'That stalker's path, it goes awful close to the edge. It's bad enough in summer but tonight: all icy, and a weak torch . . . ' He trailed off and looked up at her. He had pale grey eyes and very long lashes. Today his hair was tied back in a pony tail with a red bow.

'She's all right,' Flora said comfortably. 'She can take care of herself in the mountains. It's around people she's impulsive.'

He looked surprised and he finished his tea thoughtfully. He padded upstairs in his stocking feet and after a few moments the *Polovtsian Dances* blasted through the house. Flora smiled. Living at Alder was like having a family without the bother of a husband and all that sex business.

'I guessed there was a call,' Vivien said, entering the kitchen as Flora replaced the phone, making a fuss of the dogs. 'I could hear *Prince Igor* as I came out of the wood and then it was suddenly cut off.' She turned and went along the passage to the foot of the stairs. 'Shut the bathroom window, Danny!' she shouted. 'It would be just our luck,' she said, coming back, 'to have a pipe burst when we've re-decorated the back room. Who called?' She went to feel the teapot but Flora pounced and tipped the contents in the sink.

'I'll make a fresh pot. It was Daisy.' Daisy Chedwin was Vivien's publisher. 'Will you call her back? If I'd known you were so close I'd have asked her to hold on.'

'It's not some problem about Australia?'

'I didn't ask. Evidently it wasn't something I could handle. Shall I call her back for you?'

'You get on with supper. Smells good, what is it?'

'Conchiglie and a seafood sauce. Clam chowder to start?'

'Delicious. Did everything go all right in town?'

'So-so. No watercress or sweet potatoes—' But Vivien was moving to the cupboard where they kept the spare bottle of Scotch, coming back with glasses. She wasn't interested in food until it reached the table; the query had been courtesy only. 'How was your day?' Flora asked.

'Fine. I'll tell you after I've got this call out of the way.' She sounded peevish. Flora hesitated, thinking how – workmanlike – she looked in the high stained gaiters and heavy breeches. She went to the stove as Vivien took the phone off the hook and at that moment Borodin blasted their ears. She dashed for the stairs.

When she'd shouted at Danny to turn the player down because Vivien was on the phone she drew the curtains in the bedrooms and took her time over it. By the time she returned to the kitchen the call was finished and Vivien was puzzled, inclined to be angry.

'Plan's changed,' she grunted. 'That bastard's not coming over from New York.'

'Leavitt? But he – well, he doesn't need to; he knows your books, he knows your reputation. It was only a courtesy visit – wasn't it?'

Vivien's mouth turned down. She was sulking but she still looked beautiful even though the day's strain had made her eyes sink in their sockets as they always did after a hard day on the hill. She tossed down her Scotch and reached for a mug of tea.

'You don't have to go to London then?' Flora was determinedly cheerful.

'I do. Daisy still wants to see me. I suppose she needs to; there's a lot of money riding on the Australian trip and there's always some problem with TV people – although she didn't mention television.' She blinked, staring at the table.

Flora lowered herself into a chair. 'You're not all that keen on this trip, are you?'

Vivien looked up, her mouth tightening. 'We–ll: driving round Australia, for God's sake! Where's the climbing? Where are the mountains? It's just a matter of me circumnavigating a continent: a gimmick.'

'So!' Flora beamed. 'If it falls through, go and climb mountains; you can take your pick. You always wanted to go to the Karakoram.'

'Who says it's going to fall through!' Vivien glared, then shrugged. 'All that time and energy wasted on logistics,' she grumbled, although Flora had been responsible for much of that. 'Changing course at this point is a bit more complex than changing destinations between package tours. But it can't have fallen through: Daisy would have said. No, I'll bet Leavitt's pulled out – but so what? There are plenty more American TV channels to choose from – although I wouldn't mind' – she looked mischievous – 'but then we couldn't have a housekeeper or the new bathroom.' She sighed dramatically. 'We all have to make sacrifices. I'll go to

Australia and do what it takes to keep the wolf from—' She checked at the sound of a shout. The dogs rushed noisily into the passage. 'In the kitchen, Alastair,' she called, and bent to unzip her gaiters. Flora got up and went to the cupboard for another mug.

The man who entered the room, pushing the dogs aside, was thickset and dark. He came in casually, quite at home, staring at Vivien, ignoring Flora as she poured the tea. 'Had a good day?' he asked.

'Great.' She dropped a gaiter and started on the other. 'The snow's hard as iron.'

'Why didn't you call me? We could have done an ice climb.'

'There wasn't time; I didn't leave the road till eleven. That's too late for a decent route.'

'I could have come with you—'

'Hell, Alastair, you don't need me to hold your hand!' She was grinning. 'Sit down, man; help yourself to a dram. I'm not going to call you every time I feel like popping up Garsven on the spur of the moment.'

He pulled out a chair and Flora placed the mug and a glass in front of him. Her eyes were dancing; there was always drama when these two got together. Alastair Semple poured himself a dram and pushed his hair back nervously. He drank half the Scotch and sat back, enjoying it. Vivien was unlacing her boots.

'You know the dangers,' he said pointedly.

'You are telling me the dangers?'

There was only the slightest emphasis on the pronouns but he heard it and stuck to his guns.

'You're too damn careless.'

Her eyes widened but before she could speak Flora said loudly, 'If you're going to take a bath then I'll have to hold supper back.'

Vivien stared at her uncertainly, muttered, 'I'll go up in a minute,' jerked her head at Alastair and walked out. He got up and followed. Flora stared after them, longing to hear the rest of it.

He followed Vivien to the drawing room at the front of the house. She pushed the door to behind him and turned. 'Even if I am careless,' she grated, 'I'm competent. Who the hell do you think you are?'

He was astonished. 'What's got into you? You know you're always taking risks—'

'Calculated risks—'

'Alone, you've only got to sprain your ankle—'

'Oh, come on! I was *walking*.'

'Aye, and how big are the cornices?'

She sighed and slumped down on a sofa. He sat opposite her. 'You're worse than a mother,' she said gloomily. 'I expect to have freedom on my own territory. I've got the others trained, now I have to cope with you.' The anger faded before fatigue.

'I know you better than they do,' he said and then, politely, smiling with sudden charm, 'Will you take a dram?'

Her eyebrows rose. 'You're the host now? OK, I'll take another; I'm not climbing tomorrow.'

'Yes, you are.' He was firm. 'You're coming out tomorrow, we're going to the Ben.'

'Oh yes? And what are you going to take me up?'

He grinned as he handed her a drink. 'You're going to take me up Zero Gully.'

She laughed. 'You don't know what you're talking about! We might look at Green Gully if the weather holds – but not tomorrow. I'm going to London.'

'You can't!' He was incredulous. 'I've been living for this: here we've had three days of perfect conditions and for two of 'em I was away buying fresh stock, then the first day I'm free you clear off on your own, and now you say you're going to London! You can go to London any time. Leave it till the thaw. We'll go to the Ben first thing tomorrow and stay there a few days, a week even. We're both free now, think of all the stuff we haven't done there! Come on, Viv, what's so pressing about London anyway?' He was suddenly suspicious.

'Australia,' she said. 'I've had a call from Daisy.'

'And that's another thing!' It was an old bone of contention.

'It's good money, you idiot; I can't run this place on air.'

'And it's dangerous too – worse than climbing alone. You don't know those dangers.'

'Oh, give over.'

'You don't know the first thing about cars: how they work. Oh, you can change a wheel and a plug, that kind of thing; what happens when you break down in the middle of a desert and there's no one – let alone a good mechanic – nearer'n a hundred miles, eh?'

'I'll have back-up. There's the camera crew. It'll only *look* like a solo trip.'

'Take me.'

She regarded him with resignation tinged with amusement. She said nothing, she couldn't be bothered. He pushed it, smiling, boyish now.

'I'm good with cars, you know that. We can climb: on sea cliffs, on anything; there's bound to be inland crags. It will give the film human interest.'

'You're mad,' she said with finality, dismissing the subject. 'All the same' – she was thoughtful – 'you're right about the conditions here. I'll come back in a couple of days, then we can go to the Ben. How's that?'

He was alert and happy again. 'Promise?'

'Not really. Something may come up in London.'

His elation was switched off like a light. 'If you make a prior commitment to me—'

'For God's sake!' Her patience snapped. 'You don't own me!'

Their eyes locked; she was furious, he teetered on the edge of a response which he just managed to suppress, knowing she was no longer in a mood to take it as a joke.

He stood up. 'Thanks for the drink,' he said shortly. 'I'll expect you when I see you – providing nothing more important turns up.' The sarcasm was laid on with a trowel.

He stalked out. Vivien grimaced as the front door slammed. After a moment Flora came in, wiping her hands on her apron. 'That fire all right?' she asked chirpily but her attention was on her employer.

Vivien stared at the flames. 'He *is* possessive,' she murmured, and went on, speaking her thoughts aloud: 'But then I'm all he's got – I mean, I'm the only climber for miles around; there's just the two of us. It's understandable.'

'He'd be lost without you,' Flora said.

'Other people seem to manage though. It wouldn't bother me if there was no one else to climb with.'

'Different styles.'

'I suppose. He's timid. Well' – as Flora stared – 'not much sense of adventure, you know? No, you don't.' She tried again. 'He needs direction.'

'I think he's a very masculine man,' Flora said, a little heatedly. 'Even a bit too much so.'

Vivien shrugged. 'I was talking about climbing.'

They stared at each other, both at a loss. 'I'm tired,' Vivien exclaimed, as if in justification.

'You go and have your bath. Supper will be ready in twenty minutes. You've got a long day ahead of you tomorrow.'

Chapter 2

'I'm glad that's not real skins,' Daisy Chedwin said grimly, staring at Vivien's purple coat trimmed with fake fur. Vivien slipped out of it and tried not to stare in her turn. Daisy was overweight and flaunted it, today in a red tunic and orange pants, but to compensate she had a rich chocolate voice: a cross between Marilyn Horne and the best of British theatre.

'So Leavitt's backed out,' Vivien said, sitting down.

'Not exactly.' Daisy could be circumspect when she tried. 'That's putting too fine a point on it. There's a merger pending, or so I understand, and everything's at sixes and sevens. Presumably there'll be a shake-up of directors. Once we know who's who we can try again, possibly with a slightly different angle—'

'You're waffling, Daisy.' Vivien was equable. 'It's immaterial; there are plenty more fish in the sea... The question now is: do we stay with the Australian project, or settle for something more in my line?' Her eyes gleamed. 'I've been thinking about the eastern Karakoram; there's masses of unclimbed stuff over twenty thousand feet: off the beaten track, inaccessible, unspoiled communities in the valleys—'

'Sounds great.' There was no enthusiasm in the tone. 'But it's a difficult time,' Daisy muttered and then, brightly, 'Of course things will pick up soon, we're bumping along the bottom at the moment; the big firms will ride out the recession, but this isn't quite the right moment for a mountaineering book that needs a big advance. And as for television' – she spread her hands – 'forget it; that's even worse.'

'You mean you want me to stay with Australia?' Vivien's jaw set, prepared for argument.

'I'm afraid Leavitt was our last resort there.' Daisy wouldn't meet her eye.

Vivien blinked. 'Australia's out – finished? The film *and* the book?' Her voice rose. 'And you don't want a book on the Karakoram?'

'It's a very competitive market—'

'I know that.' Vivien was dismissive. She paused, let her breath go and went on carefully, 'So what *do* you want me to do?'

Daisy seemed at a loss. 'If you could come up with something different . . . .'

'I've never been to the Karakoram. How different do you want it?' The tone was loaded with sarcasm.

'Publishers are flooded with manuscripts on the Himalayas, Everest, K20. There have to be hundreds of people climbing there and they all think they can write about it. And only a tenth of them reach print,' she added quickly as Vivien gaped. 'And half of those are remaindered. Perhaps – if you could pay for a trip yourself, or find a sponsor—' she raised an eyebrow.

'Are you telling me that I wouldn't get an advance – for *anything*; that I'm washed up? That's ridiculous – look at the reviews I get!'

'Reviews don't sell books. This will blow over; you head our list in the outdoor department. There's nothing wrong with your writing, it's the recession; everybody's marking time, just hanging on till the economic climate improves. It's only a hiccup; people will always want to read adventure stories.'

'This doesn't make sense. Climbing books are still being published. I had a list only last week from Northern Lights, *and* they're bringing out new editions of old books.'

'The kind of advance you'd get from Northern Lights wouldn't pay your air fare to Kashmir. One way.'

Vivien shook her head in bewilderment. She looked devastated. 'Well, what do you want?' she repeated. 'Something different? Canoeing: following a river – the Amazon, the Indus – no, I couldn't manage the white water. Suppose I do a horse trip: a long ride like that guy who rode from Cape Horn to Washington.'

'That's the point; it's been done.'

'Not by a woman. All right, I'll ride across Australia.'

'Someone did it on a camel.'

'Asia then: Siberia.'

'You've got to have a hell of an advance for the back-up.'

'Oh, for God's sake!'

'There *is* something,' Daisy said quietly. 'You know Annie Staubach?' She was suddenly busy with a file, biting her lips, fiddling with a pen. 'Staubach: took an expedition to your part of the world.'

'Kulu. I haven't been to Kulu and I don't know Staubach.'

'There was an avalanche. It carried away a tent with two women in it and she went back to rescue the survivors.'

Vivien was silent, anticipating something unpleasant, even more unpleasant than what she'd heard already.

'She did a magnificent job,' Daisy was saying, 'but then you're all alike, you hard women climbers – ' she faltered as she registered the silence from the other side of her desk. 'It's a sensational story,' she insisted: 'the hard climb, the accident, the futile attempts at rescue – and then trouble with the porters.'

'With their wives actually.'

'Oh? I understood all the porters were men.'

'That was the point. When the expedition returned to the valley and the village women discovered that the climbers had been sleeping with their husbands, the girls were stoned.'

Daisy hesitated then decided to ignore this for the moment. 'Staubach's written a book,' she went on. Vivien said nothing, deliberately contemptuous. She'd always had good relations with her porters, and she took the wives along anyway. Sherpa women carried as well as the men: not so much, but they did it more cheerfully.

'She can't write,' Daisy was saying. 'That is, she's shaky on grammar, occasionally a bit kitsch, but the material's there and it's superb; you could lick it into shape in no time.'

Now the silence was charged. After a while Vivien said coldly, 'You want me to do an editing job on this – book?'

'No, we could do that ourselves. But it needs – polishing: the expert's touch to eliminate solecisms, technical errors, to er—'

'Ghost it.'

'No, Staubach wouldn't wear that. How about a joint venture: put both your names to the book? She should be flattered.'

Vivien stood up and walked to the window. She found herself looking down on a construction site and she became aware of the jingling of a pneumatic drill. They were on the fifth floor and she could look through a chasm between roofs towards the river. She liked being high. Then she saw her face staring back from the glass, a patrician face with hooded eyes, a strong nose and generous mouth: the street kid who made it through grammar school and the jobs that no one else would do to the top. To be pushed off the top by a charlatan.

'The money won't be bad,' Daisy said to her back. 'Tide you over till something more suitable comes along.'

She turned, close to tears and seething with rage. 'Staubach,' she said, 'took a badly equipped expedition to a mountain that was too big and too hard for any of those women, including herself; the most she'd ever done was to be pulled up the Matterhorn by her husband. She misjudged the weather in the Himalayas and she pushed a couple of incompetent, *more* incompetent women to the top in deteriorating conditions so that they were stranded in a series of storms and then, when they tried to retreat from the highest camp, they took a stupid short-cut. It wasn't that an avalanche fell on their tent, it fell in the gully they were descending where even a layman would have known there'd be avalanche snow after storms. Staubach went up alone, without any kind of probe, and came back and said they were under the snow – buried deep. She couldn't have known where they were without probing for them. And that's just the technical mistakes. And you want me to put my name to this book.'

'It's a great story, Vivien; it doesn't matter about the mistakes. In fact—'

'It matters to me.'

'Look at it from a professional point of view. You're an established author—'

'I'm a mountaineer, and I'm respected. If I put my name to this trash I'll lose all vestige of credibility.'

'We don't publish trash in this firm.'

'Wrong tense; you didn't publish trash.' She came back to the desk and picked up her briefcase. Her eyes were blazing. 'You had integrity, Daisy. I thought you liked my stuff because it was honest; now you're going in for sex and violence and mistakes in climbing. You're exploiting a stupid, irresponsible woman.'

'Rubbish. There's no mileage in successful expeditions; the reader doesn't care whether you get to the top or what the view looks like, he doesn't *want* it to go right; it's the failures that sell books, and the more sensational the better. People want the human touch.'

'Like Sherpa women stoning nymphos who've been screwing the porters—'

'There's no need to be crude—'

'You could have fooled me. The human touch? Porno-climbing.'

'Fashions change, even in climbing books.'

'Oh no, don't give me that. *I* write climbing books, not Staubach. And my books are popular.'

There was a tense silence then, 'Were popular,' Daisy said softly.

Vivien smoothed her gloves. 'Some deal,' she said viciously: 'dropping a climber in exchange for a camp-follower.'

'There's no question of dropping you. I offered you a job: to pull a book together, to make something of it.'

'An editor's job.'

'Perhaps you should think in those terms now. A lot of people don't have jobs at all.'

'Is that a threat?'

Daisy brought her fist down on the desk, started to speak – and thought better of it. After a moment she said tightly, 'Sleep on it. It's better than nothing. You're going to need money to run Alder Lodge. In these times you have to learn to compromise—'

'The only difference between your job and walking the streets is that I wouldn't get AIDS from consorting with Staubach. On second thoughts—'

'You'd work well together. You'll strike sparks off each other.'

'Then I'll leave her to you.' Vivien bared her teeth. 'You're going to be sorry.'

Cursing herself for that appalling exit line as much as the whole bloody exchange, she stalked out of the office. In the corridor she was only vaguely aware of other people: faces turned towards her, startled or avid; someone in a tweedy coat plunging to a doorway, phones ringing. She realized that the row must have been overheard. 'Hold it!' she shouted as the lift doors started to close, and walked in and turned her back on the occupants.

On the ground floor she strode through the reception area and out on to the pavement, breaking into a yell as an empty cab passed down the other side of the street. She stepped off the kerb, there was a squeal of brakes and she stepped back, shaking. The driver of the car that had nearly run her down lowered his window and said coldly, 'Better go and see a doctor, darling.'

'Up yours!' she snapped, and gave him a stiff finger in case there was any doubt about it. The taxi had disappeared. She glanced up and down the street, realized that she had no idea what to do, had nowhere to go until her train left at nine o'clock, felt the tears sting, and snorted like an angry horse. People were skirting her carefully but she felt pressure: hands were on her arms and a man said companionably, 'How does a large Scotch sound?'

'Fuck off!'

'When I've put you in a cab. I have to get you away from the premises before you go back and throttle someone.'

She turned and glanced behind him. 'Daisy sent you to see me off?' She'd seen him before: a background figure from some department with which she'd had no dealings. Fiction? He had deep brown eyes not much above her own level, a wide body in a long Harris overcoat, thinning pepper-and-salt hair, an old-fashioned radio voice.

'Who are you?'

'I'm head of Security.'

He waved, a cab slid to a stop and he handed her in, saying something she didn't catch to the driver. He got in and she sat in her corner and continued her survey. Nice suit, expensive brogues, old but polished. He returned her study with interest.

'I'm Rupert Lasco.'

'Where are you taking me?'

'You're being abducted.'

She guessed him to be about fifty, too old to be the company clown; if he'd been detailed to give her an expensive lunch, Daisy's judgement was even worse than she'd already demonstrated. Any more schoolboy humour and she'd walk out on him. Abducted! She should be so lucky. Eight hours to go before the train left. Shopping as displacement activity: presents for Flora and Danny – Christ, how long would she have a home? At one stroke, in an hour she'd joined the ranks of the unemployed.

'Plotting murder?' came that honeyed voice. 'What method would you choose?'

Was he on her side? 'I feel violent,' she admitted, glowering at people bunched like zombies at a pedestrian crossing. 'I know how terrorists feel when they plant bombs.'

'Forget Staubach. You're in a different league.'

'Staubach! It's Daisy driving me up the wall.' She glared at him.

'I suppose everyone along that corridor heard us.'

'It was great! Like listening to lionesses fighting.'

Her lips twitched and she looked away. 'What makes you think I'm going to like the place you're taking me to?' she asked coldly.

He raised an eyebrow. 'I like it.'

The arrogance was a goad. 'You know my tastes?'

'We'll have a drink' – placatingly – 'and then we'll come back to the West End. You only have to say the word.'

She eyed him warily, suspecting a plot to persuade her to reconsider Staubach. She gave him a faint smile; she'd have a very expensive lunch, ditch him and spend the rest of the afternoon shopping.

She didn't know where they were. The cab dropped them at a pub called the Prospect of Whitby and she drank a schooner of sherry quickly before going to the lavatory to repair her make-up in preparation for the return to the West End. When she came back to the bar he'd disappeared and she wandered out on a balcony to find herself above the river. No one else was there, it was too cold for Londoners; she wrapped her coat round herself, snuggled into the furry collar and looked glumly at the water. A police launch was slipping downstream past a line of – barges? Lighters? A siren sounded on one long mournful note like a wild bird. Distant buildings held a sheen in their stone that made them appear insubstantial.

She paced a few steps and came back, staring at water, stone and sky, and the police launch fading at the head of its widening wash. She felt the ghost of the feeling that she had before a hard climb: eager, excited and cold, but the cold was more exciting than heat. A cold passion? Rubbish, it was the sherry on an empty stomach.

Rupert emerged and stood beside her. 'Do murderers still throw their victims in the river?' she asked. 'Or is that old-fashioned?'

'It's still done; it's so easy to disguise a murder as accident or suicide where a river's concerned; at least, that's how the killer's mind works. Did the victim fall or was he pushed? Murder's even simpler in countries where there are crocodiles. Or sharks. There was an Australian case where a shark was caught and they found a human arm in its stomach. It had been amputated with a saw.'

Her jaw dropped. 'You're like a Hammer film.'

But she was laughing as they went inside and she wasn't unduly put out to find that he'd ordered sandwiches. As they ate he talked about crime on the river and she was fascinated. At length, feeling she needed to walk off an indecent amount of sherry, she asked him to drop her at a park on his way back to the office. He demurred; he had other plans.

'Aren't you going back to work?' she asked, and then, suspicion returning: 'Or are you working now? Is this your job: buttering up authors like me?'

'There aren't any authors like you.' He regarded her gravely. 'But certainly Daisy did have the idea that I might exert my charm to restrain you from stamping off to Secker or whoever. She's not thick; she knew initially you'd be upset about the Staubach book, and she doesn't want to lose you.'

'She's lost me. Why did she make that ridiculous – no, insulting suggestion? And how do you know her attitude?'

'I'm supposed to be your editor. We're meant to be discussing the Staubach manuscript.'

'When do we start?' She was seething again and about to trample him into the ground. She looked round for the barman to tell him to summon a taxi.

'We don't,' he was saying. 'I'm on your side. But Daisy's right when she says there's a market for the Staubach story. Though it does need a writer to knock it into shape.' He raised a hand as she made to interrupt. 'Not you. Staubach's a bimbo trading on her sex, conning the public that she can climb, but you' – for a moment he seemed lost, then he beamed – 'you're a mountaineer' – he emphasized it – 'and a superb writer.'

'I understood that I headed Chedwin's list in that department.' She was stuffy, expecting instant agreement.

'Luxury goods, dear. Mountaineering books, climbing, climbers: they're superfluous in these hard times – travel as well, actually, although less so. People may be able to identify with expatriates in a villa in Provence but not with a human fly on an ice-wall.'

He held her eye. 'Is that really true?' she asked. 'Is that what you think?'

'I don't think, I know. I know how the man feels on the Clapham omnibus.'

She wasn't listening. 'It isn't the loss of self-esteem that hurts,' she told him. 'It's that my life can be ordered by someone like Daisy. She holds the purse strings. I have a household – a little community in the mountains, and we're all dependent on Daisy Chedwin. This is shattering; it's like living in a police state. I'm a serf.'

'She has a torture chamber in the basement. At least you escaped that by storming out. Now drink up; I have something to show you.'

He took her to the National Gallery, chivvying her past a kaleidoscope of colour that made the senses reel, past immobile and disapproving guards to stop in front of a tall ship with naked masts, palely splendid above a squat vessel whose chimney belched flames and soot. The sun was setting below a fiery sky and there was a glimpse of buildings that glowed like a fairy city on the shore. All the colours were reflected in tranquil water and except for the sunset there was an echo of the vista from the pub balcony.

'Why did he have to spoil it?' she asked. 'Putting that dirty little tug in front of the ship? It looks deliberate, like vandals destroying perfection. It's cruel.'

'She's the *Téméraire*. She fought at Trafalgar and now she's being towed to the scrap-yard to be broken up.'

She looked from him to the canvas and now she saw the poignancy: the nobility of that tall ghost ship, the juxtaposition of the tug.

'The buoys mark the channel,' he went on. 'She's being reversed on the same line she took on her maiden voyage.'

'On her way to the scrap-yard,' she repeated, and looked doleful.

He was with her immediately. 'You haven't reached your peak yet. The common denominator is beauty. I love her.'

He said it so sweetly that she was dumbfounded, and then he was walking away.

He led her out of the building, buying cards of the *Téméraire* for her, and conducted her through the maelstrom of Trafalgar Square and under Admiralty Arch to St James's Park where they drifted to an empty seat and sat in the pale sunshine and talked. He told her about Turner and she, by way of Highland sunsets, was led to enthuse about Alder Lodge and how she'd bought it cheap from her impoverished neighbour and done it up as the profits came in from lectures and books and television. Ever since she started climbing, she told him, she'd had this dream of a home in the Highlands and a community of like-minded people. Vaguely she'd thought they might farm because there was no other work

– not, that is, until she carved a remunerative career out of climbing. 'And now I've got the house,' she said, 'and the people and the animals, and I'm going to lose it all.'

'What about your family?' he asked. She had never publicized her private life.

'No money there, if that's what you mean. I'm a bastard, and my mother married when I was sixteen. My step-father's all right, so's Mum, but we're not close, and I had no siblings – to my knowledge.' She grinned at that. 'It would be unusual for a man to father only one bastard, wouldn't it? My mother wanted me to be a journalist; English was my subject at school, but reporting's not my style. I went to work in a book store, met a climber, and that was when life started for me: the Big Bang.'

She stopped, afraid of boring him, but he was fascinated, urging her to elaborate on the details of those early days when she had hitch-hiked round Europe with a rucksack that contained little more than her rope and a sleeping bag. She had slept in barns and under boulders when it rained, and would do any kind of work for a wage or a meal: gardening, decorating, labouring on farms. And then suddenly, dramatically, a career opened up for her.

She had taken a job as junior instructor at a mountain school in the Cairngorms, and had been selected to accompany an expedition to Greenland. The leader broke his leg high on a mountain and she took over, supervising his evacuation and getting all the members out in one piece. Her written report was instrumental in her being asked to be the climbing leader on an expedition to Patagonia. Daisy Chedwin had commissioned her to write the book of the expedition and, at the age of twenty-six, she was away.

'And then there was television,' Rupert observed. 'And the lectures. You couldn't go wrong.'

'I'm glad you didn't say I was lucky,' she said tartly. 'People do and I'm touchy about it. I worked damn hard. It wasn't just a matter of being young and photogenic. I wasn't even a good leader, that came with experience: learning as I went along, particularly on the expeditions. I was lucky in one respect: I didn't lose any members of my expeditions.' Not like some, she thought, but she was no longer bothered about Staubach. Her mind jumped to the future, disregarding links, fastening on the salient points. 'I can't work,' she muttered, 'not without Flora's contribution; she does all the logistics: the correspondence, the arrangements, all the part I hate. How can I afford to pay her? But then how many people will want me to lecture when I don't go on trips? The books paid for the trips; it's all connected: books, lectures, expeditions, an integrated construction. Pull out one brick and the lot collapses.' She turned to him, tired now, looking ravaged in the light of the low sun.

He took her hand. 'You got to the top. What more do you want?'

'To stay there of course. To keep my home.'

'You're on a plateau. Tell me, do you really like writing expedition books, and television studios and lecture halls – oh yes, and long flights?'

'It's a job. We all have to do it: the celebrity mountaineers. Look at what I've achieved with the money.'

'Chicken feed.'

'*What!* The job or the money?'

He stood up and pulled her to her feet. 'Quick, we don't have much time. We can just make it if we dash—'

Protesting loudly, she was hustled through the late-afternoon strollers, scattering fat ducks, running across the grass – back under the arch and across the square to an entrance and a lift that deposited them at an open door beyond which people sipped from champagne glasses, the nearest turning sharp glances on the new arrivals. Eyebrows were raised, one or two women smiled uncertainly.

'There's a crime conference in progress,' he told her as, having surrendered their coats, he guided her through the crowd. 'And firms are giving parties, promoting their products. At a guess this is Veuve Clicquot.' He took two drinks from a tray and they came to a halt before a wall of plate-glass. They were very high – for a building: perhaps two hundred feet, and the sense of exposure was stunning. Below them the river showed here and there as it looped through the city, while westward the sun was poised like a persimmon above a band of cloud, and the sky was splashed with red.

'What are you trying to do?' she asked. 'You've been involving me with Turner and the river since lunch-time. There's something going on.'

'I have ulterior motives.'

'Obviously. You have to tell me some time so why not now when I'm in a receptive mood?'

'I'm wooing you.'

She smiled warily. The party was warming up. Close by a man said loudly, 'That was the common assumption, but he was pardoned on the premise that he didn't kill the child. He was innocent of the charge for which he was convicted and hanged.'

A hubbub of protest broke out. Vivien looked at Rupert. 'Timothy Evans?' he hazarded. 'Hanged for the wrong murder?'

She wrinkled her nose. 'That was a sordid business. Distasteful.'

'Isn't all murder?'

'Not at all. Lucan – ' She shrugged. 'Upper-class certainly but crude and stupid—'

'Not to speak of the nanny's plight.'

She ignored that. 'The main point of interest was – what happened to him? That kind of chap doesn't commit suicide. Disappearances fascinate me more than murder.'

'Because there's no body. That's what makes it sordid: the body.' He accepted more champagne from a girl with a face like a smooth brown mask and the eyes of a deer.

'You could be right,' she admitted, her eyes following the waitress as she moved like water through the chattering crowd. 'Reducing something alive and beautiful to a mess of meat and shattered bones: there's an enormity to that, even worse than putting down an animal. You assume a terrible responsibility when you decide to kill.'

'Most murders aren't premeditated.'

'We're not talking about those: drunken brawls, what the police call "domestics"; they're closer to manslaughter. Although a man who says he didn't mean to do it usually means he can't control himself . . . He's no loss to society; you'd put down a vicious dog . . . But the person who plots a murder over a period of time is a different kettle of fish altogether. What must his mind be like?'

'Someone said all murderers are mad.'

'Oh, not at all. Think of it: plotting how to approach your victim without alerting him, how to dispose of the body, the cover-up – that chap knows exactly what he's doing, and that it's criminal.'

'Broadmoor's full of them,' came a clear voice at her shoulder.

Vivien turned to see a small girl in a neat grey suit and glasses, her hair cut short with a heavy fringe. She looked like a sixth former applying for an interview at a library.

'A successful plea of insanity doesn't mean they're mad,' she informed Vivien. 'Just that their counsel is superior to the prosecution's. We haven't met. I'm June Hexham.'

'Meet Vivien Reid,' Rupert said. 'My guest.'

'I know,' Ms Hexham said, sparkling at her. 'Are you about to convert? Is Rupert instructing you? But why you, Rupert? Did you switch to crime?'

'I've always been into crime, sweetie. As for my presence here: I stole an invitation and I needed a drink before braving the tube.'

'I see.' Cool eyes appraised them — calculating whether he's my editor or my lover, thought Vivien — and Ms Hexham smiled and moved on, dismissing them. Rupert's eyes narrowed.

'What was that about converting?' Vivien asked. 'And what does she have to do with crime?' She turned back to the view, seeing that the light had faded but the afterglow still coloured half the world above a void pricked with a myriad jewels. In a patch of empty sky Venus hung like an ice chip.

'She writes,' Rupert said drily, ignoring the first question. 'Four books a year, give or take a couple.'

'Christ! How does she do it?'

'Word processors and the lure of money.'

'What kind of — oh, crime books!' She swung round and surveyed the gathering. 'These are crime *writers*?'

'What did you think?'

'Reporters, I suppose, and police. I didn't think. Four books in a year. Is that what you have to produce to earn a living in fiction?'

'What she has to. The popular chaps work at a more leisurely pace and live very comfortably, thank you: second homes in Spain, the Channel Islands, British Columbia, you name it. The best of them are millionaires. Even June Hexham can afford an Escada suit.'

She looked down at her ruffled blouse. 'This didn't come from Marks and Spencer.'

'It could have. You'd make anything look as if it came from — let me guess: Calvin Klein?'

'Near enough.' It was Katherine Hamnett and had set her back a tidy sum, but she'd bought it and the purple coat to meet the

American producer... She studied the crowd. 'Are all these people crime writers?'

'Mostly, with spouses. There's the odd publisher and agent, and I see a huddle of CID chaps over there, in the corner.'

'Daisy isn't here.'

'No, she couldn't be bothered.'

'But she does publish crime.'

'I don't think she's interested, otherwise she'd have suggested that you go over, as it were.'

'Change to crime? Don't be daft.'

'But you're made for it' – he was grinning impishly, clowning again – 'menace, violence, mysterious disappearances... in mountain country: the Himalayas, Alps, Andes. The research would be a holiday all the time, as they say, and who else can write about mountains like you? All that's needed is an injection of drama and you'd take off like a rocket. Now' – suddenly he was serious – 'we have to get down to brass tacks. The question is: early supper and a show, or a show now and the Ivy later – and then what kind of show? Opera, movie, Shakespeare? And what do you want to eat, because we should book a table: fish, fowl or Angus steak? Ethnic, posh or Alf's diner?

Chapter 3

Vivien didn't return to Scotland that evening. Rupert found her a room in a small hotel in Kensington and after saying goodnight he went out into the street without another word. She had been surprised and suspicious. If she accepted his assurances that she was the wrong person to collaborate with Staubach, what was it he wanted? There are no free lunches, she thought; he has to be after something. Was it possible that this was an old-fashioned courtship? 'I'm wooing you,' he'd said. The trouble was she couldn't tell when he was clowning and when serious although, pondering her time spent with him so far, she was amused. His attentiveness distracted her – and she needed distraction. Tomorrow she must start to think about the future. Perhaps he would have ideas, but he was out of work too.

He had confessed that he'd been made redundant only recently, had just happened to be in the office that day and, having always admired her work, had seized his chance – most audaciously, he admitted – and followed her when she stormed out of Daisy's office. So why had he claimed to be the editor of Staubach's book? she asked. To lull her suspicions; she had to think he was an employee at Chedwin, had a professional, and therefore respectable, interest in her when really what he was after was her body.

When she phoned Flora from her room she was bubbling with laughter; she'd met a man, she said, and no, she couldn't say when she'd be back. Australia? Australia was off. The Karakoram? That too. What was she going to do now? She didn't know; suddenly she hated Flora, was overwhelmed by despair. 'I'll call you,' she said, and hung up, forgetting to ask after Danny and the animals.

What Vivien didn't know was that losing his job had plunged Rupert into a state of boredom that was fast deteriorating to misery. His speciality was crime novels but when, years ago, his firm had been taken over by Chedwin Daisy already had a young ambitious crime editor and Rupert found himself dealing with mainstream fiction, where he was competent and no more. He worked hard, trying to compensate for the lack of flair by fast turnover, trying to keep up with his younger colleagues, but his heart wasn't in it. As he approached fifty he considered himself burned out and when Daisy introduced the subject of early retirement he put up no opposition. He had a small private income and he owned a house in Notting Hill; with his pension he wouldn't be destitute and, as Daisy pointed out, he'd been in publishing all his working life, he knew the trade backwards; he could become an agent.

He had left Chedwin announcing that he would consider his options but he knew that if he didn't make a positive move immediately the rot would set in. He didn't consider becoming an agent; at his age he hadn't the drive to build up unknown writers, and he didn't need the money. He had no incentive to work. Nothing inspired enthusiasm. Not even Vivien Reid. When Daisy telephoned and asked for one last favour, as she put it: to take Vivien to lunch and smooth ruffled feathers after an anticipated battle over the Staubach book, she reminded him that he'd always admired Vivien's writing. A better incentive, had she known it, was that he'd always admired the woman, secretly and from a distance. That didn't mean much now except that lunch with anyone was a small event in an otherwise empty day. He allowed himself to be persuaded and agreed to be on hand at the crucial moment.

'But why me?' he'd asked.

'She's very feminine,' Daisy said. 'And you're a charmer. A dose of masculine flattery will do wonders for hurt pride. She has to learn to cooperate, Rupert, and in this instance that means collaboration. Staubach's exciting, she could be sensational, but she can't write. Vivien can; they'll make a great team. Get her to see it that way.'

Rupert, listening to the altercation in Daisy's office, knew that Daisy had got it wrong, and his admiration for Vivien took a new turn. He applauded her fight for survival where he had accepted redundancy without a murmur, and her fury sent a shiver down his spine. The violence of it fascinated him, perhaps because it was the antithesis of his own personality. Even without his promise to Daisy he would now have been looking for a way to get closer to this woman, and as she went down in the lift he was taking the stairs three at a time, like a youth embarking on an adventure. Or a love affair.

Crime came later, but not much later: at the Prospect of Whitby in fact, and it changed a situation which, for Rupert, had started with his first reading of one of her books, the first sight of her. There had been hero-worship – he felt cheated if he missed a sight of her on one of her infrequent visits to the office – and finally there was this day when, after hours in her company, he went to bed quietly exulting. At some point today: in the taxi, on the balcony, before the *Téméraire*, he had fallen in love. 'I am in thrall,' he thought deliciously, and turned to consider the hard facts.

He was fifteen years her senior and the case was classic: the old man and the young girl – well, a much younger woman. And yet, looked at rationally, it was the most natural thing in the world; older men were experienced and well-mannered and had to be preferable to her contemporaries: raw, callow, casual. But there was a problem; the relationship was one-sided. All that concerned her was her house and her career: in essence – money. He wasn't rich enough to buy her affections. So he came back to the subject of crime novels, which were a career, which could make money; they had the potential. The germ of the idea had occurred to him at the pub when he realized that this woman, who could certainly write, had an interest in crime that might be channelled productively. It was an impulse that made him take her to the Veuve Clicquot party and there the idea crystallized, although he'd introduced it merely as an amusing scenario. He didn't mention crime again that evening and, seeing that she was deliberately avoiding the subject, he was thrilled. She might not be considering it but she hadn't forgotten it either.

If he could start her in this new direction: guide her, support, encourage, she'd need him beside her, metaphorically if not literally. Propinquity might work; if he could sell a novel for her, she could keep her house, her self-esteem would be restored, she might mistake gratitude for love. Or, thought Rupert slyly, in the last moment before he fell asleep, one could persuade her that gratitude was love.

At breakfast-time he arrived at her hotel bearing freesias and a copy of Mitford's *The Pursuit of Love*. It was a foggy morning and they went to the zoo where wild calls echoed through the gloom and shaggy forms loomed and receded like science fiction beasts. After a lobster at Wheeler's they went to the Tower and in the evening there was *La Traviata*.

In the days that followed he courted her assiduously, lulling her suspicions of something other than honest sex. This was, she thought, seduction in the grand manner and she revelled in it. For someone who loathed logistics, who desired instant gratification but who recognized glumly that nothing came free, there was magic in the sudden appearance of tickets and taxis, of the best tables in restaurants, of surprises like a trip to Greenwich on a river boat, or attendance at a murder trial in the Central Criminal Court. She found everything fascinating, a factor which she attributed to his acute perception, although she had to admit that he was good company too. He made no emotional demands on her and seemed to be content to please her.

On the Sunday night, sitting in the empty lounge of her hotel, he raised the question of crime novels again, seriously this time, and she responded with glib excuses but he was prepared for that. He told her that she was scared of changing careers but that now was the right time: she had experience, she had energy and passion, and crime was a new country. He played on the delights of exploration – and he pointed out that she had little choice. It was unnecessary to remind her of Alder. It was her first love.

She capitulated, but unhappily. 'I don't know where to start,' she moaned. 'And Flora's just a hausfrau; you need a criminal mind for murder. She's going to panic and I can't handle that on top of producing something totally alien, something I have to learn to do. Expedition books are just reporting; all you do is put a gloss on your notes – but fiction! You have to create!'

'That's the fun of it.'

'If you know what to do why the hell don't you do it yourself? You're all talk.'

'I can't write.'

'We could collaborate.'

'Oh no. You're the author.' He smiled. 'It would be one in the eye for Daisy: you making a success of crime fiction, me in attendance as your agent: an unholy alliance.' Her eyes were sparkling now. 'You'd have free will again,' he reminded her, adding thoughtfully, 'I could come back with you, stay a week or so and get you started.'

She gasped. 'You'd do that?' Her face fell. 'But don't you have to find a new job?'

'I don't need the money. And working on a crime novel is going to be far more fun than some dull old job in London. We'll go to my place tomorrow, pick up some books and we'll take the night train to Inverness.'

Flora heard the car arrive and hurried along the passage, aware of the impression a traditional welcome should make on the Londoner: secretary and dogs at the door of the Highland lodge. She noted with approval that Danny was alone in the front of the Volvo, like a chauffeur. The dogs mobbed Vivien and the stranger advanced to shake Flora's hand: brown eyes, a wide mouth, sensible warm coat, thinning hair: a townie, attractive but old. It must be business, she thought, and relaxed; she had been anticipating a love affair and dreading the prospect of domestic upheavals.

They unloaded the car. There were two heavy boxes for the study: 'Books,' Vivien said. 'I've got a lot to tell you—' and went upstairs to show Rupert to the guest room. Flora made fresh coffee.

Vivien came down first. She was wearing a new dress in peach wool and she'd had her hair cut to frame her face. It took ten years off her age. London had plainly been good for her.

'We're going over to crime,' she announced.

Flora blinked. 'We?'

'You and me. Crime novels. No more bumming around, no more expeditions; we're going to start earning real money.'

'You're giving up the expeditions?' Flora was horrified.

Vivien's expression hardened. 'It's over, Flora.' She was firm. 'I came to the end of the line: books, lectures, TV, the lot. Now we're starting a new project. It takes a bit of getting used to but you will.'

'Fiction,' Flora said weakly.

'I know what it's about,' Vivien insisted. 'Modern crime novels are psychological and I've been there. I'm thinking in terms of a mountain background of course. Emotions are on the surface when people are climbing, even when nothing goes wrong; after all, the danger's always there: one slip – and it's oblivion. At the very least a slip means pain and everyone's terrified of pain. And when things go badly wrong they're petrified. In mountains everything's intensified: heroism, panic' – she grinned engagingly

– 'murderous inclinations. I'm a good mountain writer, Flo.'

The diminutive was endearing. 'The best,' Flora said stoutly, and glanced towards the stairs.

'It was Rupert's idea,' Vivien admitted. 'He's going to start me off. We need him.' Suddenly she was confiding. 'It was ghastly in London – at first. Australia was cancelled and they say expedition books don't sell any longer, only trash. Can you believe it: Daisy offered me a job editing a book by some bimbo who can't write and can't climb – oh, forget it, it's history. And then Rupert came up with this suggestion. Mind you, he's taken all this time to wear me down, but if he can see a way of implementing it, I'm not arguing.'

'You'll be the one doing the implementing.'

'And you. Look, let's be realistic about this. I'm thirty-five, I'd soon be too old for expeditions anyway; already I'm too cautious. By the law of averages I'd have to make a mistake some time, a fatal one. I'd peaked in that department, Flo. But crime-writing's open-ended and if I do as well at that as I did at climbing' – she looked round the kitchen – 'we can have a housekeeper!'

Flora's eyes went to the door. Rupert advanced with two bottles. 'Claret,' he said diffidently. 'I've been keeping it for a special occasion but it occurred to me you might have some venison?'

'I have some marinading,' Flora said stiffly. It would be a while before she could forgive him for changing Vivien's life so suddenly and dramatically. The fact that she recognized the necessity of dropping an unprofitable career for a lucrative one didn't help; she hadn't been consulted. Of course she was only the secretary, but then what was he? A week ago he didn't exist.

'Venison and claret.' Vivien was studying the labels on the wine. 'We must have a party: introduce the neighbours to Rupert' – she caught his eye, hesitated, then added – 'some time.' She gestured towards the study. 'How soon do we get stuck in?'

He considered the question. Flora poured coffee. He said warmly, as if indulging a child, 'Let's unpack the books.'

They went out, carrying their mugs. Even the dogs went with them leaving Flora alone and glowering.

Later, when she went to the study on the excuse of asking about the pudding for dinner, she found them sitting on the floor like a couple of kids, surrounded by books.

'This is the new section of the library,' Vivien told her. 'Listen to this: *Medical Jurisprudence and Toxicology*! Isn't that great?'

She riffled through the pages, stopped and snapped the book shut as if she'd been caught looking at hard porn.

'The illustrations are an acquired taste,' Rupert said easily. 'After a few weeks you'll be able to look at the worst of them without turning a hair.' They stared at him. 'Otherwise,' he went on, 'it's an excellent reference book: essential for signs and symptoms of poisons. And it shows you what bodies look like.'

'I've seen bodies,' Vivien said. 'They didn't look like that.'

The two of them spent the rest of the day together, only emerging from the study to walk the dogs. When they'd gone down the drive, Vivien in boots, Rupert in his beautifully polished brogues, the dogs rollicking round them, Flora went straight to the study, to the shelf with the new books – which weren't all new, she saw, most were secondhand. The first she took down had his name inside: Rupert Lasco. Did borrowing his books indicate some special relationship?

There were twenty-three of them. This one was *Trial of Madeleine Smith* and it was the actual trial, verbatim. And there was the one Rupert said you could get used to in a few weeks. She opened it warily. A tiny photograph in black-and-white, you couldn't really see ... the caption said it was 'decapitation due to firing an explosive charge'.

'You busy?' came Danny's voice from the doorway, making her jump. 'What vegetables d'you want for tonight?'

'Baking potatoes and celery. Danny, what did they talk about on the way home?'

'Murder. She's going to write murder stories. Hasn't she said anything to you?'

'Of course she has. Did he say when he was going back to London?'

Danny gave her his wide stare. 'He's staying a while. Does it make a difference?'

'A big difference,' she snapped. 'For one thing now we've got a guest we shall be eating in the dining room, at least in the evening – and you see you keep that tape player turned down.' There I go again, she thought, accepting that my role is running the household, and I'm supposed to be the secretary. She wondered how soon her services would be in demand for the new venture. Surely Rupert wasn't going to usurp—

'He's all right,' Danny said, watching her. 'We need a man here.'

'We manage very well.' She was furious. 'And you're employed to do the work we don't have time for so why on earth should we need another man?'

'Oh my!' He giggled, then sobered. 'Rupert's a dominant type,' he assured her. 'She could do a lot worse.'

In the face of his ingenuous stare she missed the possibility that she was being needled. 'Typical,' she grated. 'She's collaborating with a colleague and all you can see is sex. Typical of a man.'

'I was thinking more of marriage.'

'What would she want to get married for? Grow up, Danny, this isn't the nineteenth century. The trouble with you is you can't accept that a woman who gives you orders and pays your wages—' She checked, horrified that she might be antagonizing him, and he was indispensable to Vivien. She went on wildly, 'I take as much pride in my job as you do but I don't begrudge working for a woman. We all have our own niche; can't you appreciate that and get rid of this chip on your shoulder?'

He looked amazed. 'I only said she could do a lot worse than him. He's educated and polite, and he's good company – must be, they spent last week together.'

She wouldn't rise to that. She said coldly, 'You're right, we could have done a lot worse. Most editors these days are young and brash but Rupert's spent all his life in publishing; he has experience.'

'That's what I said. So what are you arguing about?'

'You mentioned marriage.'

He grinned at her. 'I'll be getting the vegetables then.'

It was dark when Rupert and Vivien returned, the dogs arriving first, barking at the back door, the others talking animatedly as they came in the front. Flora felt sure they'd talked all the time they were out: three hours of non-stop discussion. She persuaded herself that this was reassuring. Vivien needed professional assistance, not 'a man' as Danny put it.

Over the next two days the study became a workshop and there was less talk. Flora was aware of the silences because the door was left open and the house was like the grave. When she took them coffee or sandwiches Vivien would be hunched over her desk writing in longhand, scarcely acknowledging the appearance of a mug at her elbow. Rupert favoured the window seat with its view of the loch and he would be reading, more books beside him, bristling with markers.

It was on the third evening over dinner that he announced that he was going out the following day, only for a drive, but the proposal was significant: he was leaving Vivien to work alone. Flora waited for some word of his return to London but there was an unexpected snag.

'By tomorrow evening I'll have finished the chapter,' Vivien told him. 'Then you can read it. Flora will type it, won't you, love?'

Flora beamed. 'You've written the first chapter?'

'No! Three chapters. What d'you think I've been doing, incarcerated in there? It's only ten thousand words. I used to do that in a night.'

'Not often. And this is fiction.'

'Ah, but I had help.' She grinned at Rupert.

He made a gesture of protest. 'I only made a few suggestions.'

Flora longed to ask if Vivien was on her own now, if his contribution was finished, when – but Vivien was talking.

'It's got to be worked out,' she said earnestly. 'I can see what's going to happen but I'm bothered about motivation, how much I should explain – and the worst thing is the end.' She turned to Flora, perhaps realizing that her secretary had been left out in the cold. 'There are so many threads in a novel,' she pointed out. 'You have to draw them in at the end, and the last thing you want is that old-fashioned ending where all the characters come together and the protagonist explains everything.'

'We can talk on the phone,' Rupert put in.

'It's not the same.' Vivien's jaw set stubbornly. 'I want you here. It's your baby, you can't dump it in my lap and run. You look like thunder, Flo. What's up?'

She swallowed, searching for words. 'I'm typing it tomorrow and I haven't got a clue what it's about.'

'Oh, sorry!' She was laughing, reaching across the table. 'It's murder on an expedition, of course. In the Andes. Where else? It's what I know about.'

'So you see' – Rupert was expansive – 'all my assistance was on the human side; everything that mattered: plot, characterization, location, was yours. I just did the psychology bit – which is your weak point, my dear.'

Flora's eyes jumped. Danny stared at his plate. Vivien said gaily,

'Rupert's the expert on how people's minds work.' She saw that Flora was blushing and rushed on: 'You've been spending all your time in the kitchen, Flo; you can't do everything – but I'm depending on you to clean up this novel. We must find a housekeeper. Could we muddle through a few more weeks until this book's finished and we – er – know where we are?' Flora knew that meant when she could afford a third wage packet.

'It's only a matter of the evening meal,' she pointed out. 'I can do that and the secretarial work.'

'I'll cook tomorrow,' Rupert put in.

Danny and Flora stared. Vivien said, 'He's a man of parts. In that case I'm going to ask the Semples along for a meal.'

'I didn't say I'd do a dinner party,' Rupert protested. 'I'm taking the day off, I'll do something simple when I get back, just for us.'

'We'll have the Semples on Saturday then.'

Flora was amazed as much at Vivien's compliance as the revelation that Rupert could cook. She felt buffeted, as if she no longer had any say in life at Alder, even in her own life. Washing up, gruffly refusing all offers of help, she reminded herself that she was a paid hand, but she couldn't forget that merely a week ago she had looked on herself, and even Danny to a lesser degree, as partners in what Vivien referred to as a cottage industry. Still, accepting that she was only an employee subject to the whims of a boss who was careless about other people's feelings, the disadvantages were temporary. Time was on her side. She'd sit tight and wait for him to go. After all, she thought, glancing out at the dark garden, the snow had to come soon and townies couldn't tolerate being cut off by drifts. The Semples had a plough but Vivien never bothered to clear her own drive. They put a big tin box at the road-end for the postie to leave the mail and when the blizzards blew they battened down the hatches and sat it out. She couldn't see Rupert doing that.

Chapter 4

In the sixties a road further north had been upgraded and this became the route to the west coast, leaving the Alder area on a spur that ended at a group of abandoned crofts on a sea loch. Next day Rupert, anticipating a road empty of traffic, drove west until the tarmac ended above a stretch of water like a fiord. It looked as weird as the hinterland. The drive had amazed him, the road running under precipitous slopes with here and there a glimpse up a V-shaped cleft to dazzling white peaks as alien as the Arctic. There was no way he could relate to that wilderness, could imagine how it felt to be up there looking down. Vivien could. He sat at the wheel of the stationary Volvo and gloomed at the dark water on the fringe of which a heron stalked the weed and struck with a bill like a dagger.

He was preoccupied, thinking that he must come to a decision: to stay at Alder or return to London. Once launched on the new project, Vivien had applied herself wholeheartedly, treating him as a repository of facts, a gold mine – but inanimate. One way to make her aware of him as a person might be to leave. He shivered, thinking of the bleakness of London compared with the rich life at Alder – which he couldn't contemplate on this abandoned shore without a warm gut-feeling. She might not acknowledge him as a man but while he was at Alder he could watch her. The intensity of his passion astonished him: that he was content merely to be in her presence. He suspected that this was a temporary phase, that shortly physical needs must obtrude; it occurred to him that a hot and steamy summer would have produced a different situation but for the moment he revelled in the romantic poets, and fantasies in which he went away, and she telephoned to say she couldn't manage without him, he must return and make his home at Alder.

He tried to sink deeper inside his overcoat. It was bitter when the heater wasn't running. The heron struck again. What could it be catching in that frozen weed? She'd know. He pictured her hunched over her desk, writing furiously, pausing to look up and stare through him: unfocused eyes seeing something a world away from the loch and these Highland hills, away from him.

She was, he thought, putting too much into this book. He should be reading what she was writing but he'd suggested that, the suggestion had been dismissed and he hadn't tried again. Now he had to face the fact that if he couldn't sell the book she'd lose Alder and he'd lose all chance of winning her. And suppose he did manage to sell it? He knew her better now and knew better than to count on gratitude. Animals don't feel gratitude and outside her own close circle she had the morals of a cat. He wasn't part of that circle, might never be. He smiled ruefully; Flora couldn't hide her jealousy. That was to be expected: the quasi-lesbian as resentful of being excluded from the study as she would have been had she seen him as a rival for Vivien's affections. Money would make a difference there too: engage a housekeeper, bring Flora back to her word processor, let her feel part of the writing business again – he shook his head; he didn't think Vivien would be earning that kind of money... And now he had to go back and read three chapters. And he had said he'd cook supper.

Vivien stopped on the threshold of the drawing room and stared at him. 'Well?' she demanded.

He was sprawled in a chair, feeling that the stuffing had leaked out of him. 'It's incredible,' he said. He saw sudden eagerness give way to suspicion and rushed on: 'I thought people were your weak spot – emotions: describing them – you've never done it in the expedition books, I thought you couldn't, thought you didn't care about people. Why didn't you do this before?'

Flora came in, a triumphant gleam in her eye. He'd expected that; he'd discerned her hand in more than just the printing. Now she was sharing in the credit.

Flora hadn't taken him at his word. He'd returned to find her preparing supper herself. She'd bring a tray to the drawing room, she told him, adding smugly that he would find the script on the Benares table. Vivien was working. That was a clear warning not to disturb her and he heeded it, wanting to be alone when he read the first three chapters.

He went upstairs and washed, lingering in his room that looked out on the loch, seeing a few snowflakes drift past the window, going down to the drawing room where a loaded tea tray awaited him and a slim stack of paper that was almost innocent of corrections and gave no hint of what was in store for him.

She started with drama, with two skiers descending a slope. She started from the angle of the second man, the one who survived, and Rupert, who had never been on skis, felt the smooth glide of them, heard their silken swish, glimpsed the figure below crossing the fall-line and turning in a shower of powder. And he heard the crack, the deep muffled rent and, changing his viewpoint as in a dream, he saw an enormous geometric figure appear over most of the slope, widening from the top, parting from the sides, sliding in slow motion, crumbling at the base that rolled and spread while white dust rose and the skiers appeared, still upright, the one below trying to ride the avalanche, the other, in seconds that seemed a lifetime, skimming out to the side. And the rumble died and the last blocks tumbled to rest, and the survivor leaned on his poles and stared down at the tons of mounded debris, and Rupert – not the reader, but the onlooker – was filled with despair, knowing that there was a person inside that lot, not dead perhaps, but slowly suffocating.

'I thought,' he told Vivien, still sprawled in his chair, 'that you'd never be able to keep it up. Juggling with time can be awkward. Flashbacks are one thing but the avalanche is a flash forward. Well' – he gestured helplessly – 'you go on being good. The rest maintains the pace. I don't know what to say. You're wonderful.'

She looked like a woman who has just made love. 'I did the fourth chapter while you were out but you can't read it until it's printed.' She glanced at Flora. 'She corrects the spelling and she's the only person who can read my writing.'

He nodded. Flora didn't have an extensive vocabulary and sometimes she 'corrected' words she didn't recognize. It was a small point and not one to pursue at this juncture. But reading each chapter as it came could be counter-productive; Vivien might become dependent on his approval.

'Why don't we compromise and you write, say, five or six more chapters and then I'll read them?'

'Because if I went off on the wrong tack there'd be that much time wasted.'

'You're not going to do that. Have you got the plot straight now?'

'Of course.'

'You know who the killer is, how he did it, why?'

'Like we agreed: it's Gary' – the survivor of the avalanche – 'you suggested the motive: jealousy, a place on the World Cup ski team – that last was my contribution. How he did it was by means of the avalanche.'

'But that was an accident.'

She grinned. 'You don't know mountains. It's simple. He knew the slope would go once the first man got on it. He was listening for the crack and he could skim out to the side. If it didn't work there are plenty more ways to kill people above the snowline – below it too for that matter.'

He had to laugh at the sheer cheek of it.

Flora glanced at the windows. 'Speaking of snow, we're going to have a blizzard. The wind's getting up; can't you feel a draught? Must be a window open somewhere.' And she bustled out to find it.

They sat in a window seat and watched the forerunners of the storm drift across the loch. It was almost dark and the southern hills were hidden by what he thought was cloud but she said was snow. 'We're going to be cut off,' she said with relish.

She fetched a bottle of Tio Pepe and glasses and they drank to the book. He returned to his theme, he couldn't get over it. 'That opening, it's all thrill: involvement, physical, there's no indication of what's going on in their heads except as it relates to the danger then, after the avalanche, you get inside people's heads. And I thought you were – well – '

'Thick?'

'Thoughtless? Careless, it doesn't matter. Nothing matters. You're going to make a fortune.'

'I think you're prejudiced, but you'll stay and see it through? Please, Rupert' – as he hesitated and glanced at the snow which was heavier now – 'I only have to ask Alastair and he'll clear a track with his little plough. But I need you here, I'm terrified of going wrong—'

'You're not. You're on a high; you're over-reacting. Tomorrow morning you'll be rational and you'll know you can do it without help. Of course I'll read it but I don't think I should do it chapter by chapter. You're on your own now, kid.'

'Yes, you are something like an older Bogart. Right, I'll let you know how I feel in the morning.'

He was right. In the morning she was more reasonable but she proposed her own compromise based on a wild premise: that the book would be finished in a fortnight. He should go away, she said, and come back for a weekend. There was light snow cover down to their level but not enough to stop them reaching Inverness in the Land Rover. About to protest that a fortnight would exhaust her and probably kill the book he hesitated; perhaps working at white heat might be the only way she could do fiction – and then, he thought slyly, absence would show her how much she needed him. So he agreed and said he would go to London on Monday's sleeper.

'Tell me about the Semples,' he demanded of Flora as they lingered over their breakfast coffee in the kitchen. She had been disarmed by his reception of the early chapters and she was blooming. It was Vivien who was now excluded; the neighbours were coming this evening and they had been discussing food, a subject on which he was surprisingly well-informed. Asked about the Semples she told him how Alastair had sold Alder to Vivien, that he used the money from the sale to start a pony-trekking business which he ran with his father-in-law – but Rupert knew that much. 'What are they *like*?' he urged. 'They're your next-door neighbours, how do you get on?'

Flora pursed her lips. 'We don't have much to do with them. Aileen's very old-fashioned; Vivien dresses down when she goes there, at New Year and so on; she doesn't want to upstage Aileen. She looks as if she buys her clothes at Oxfam. As for Alastair' – she shrugged – 'he looks good in the kilt. He was educated at Eton – that would be before death duties cleaned out the family. He's fond of a dram but what Scotsman isn't? They're kind to their animals; they buy rundown horses and build them up as if they were fattening them for market. We ride there sometimes, Vivien and me. Mac helps with the ponies: Ian MacDonnell. He was a gillie.' Her tone was suddenly flat.

'The laird's father-in-law was a gillie?'

'*Step*-father-in-law.' Flora shifted in her chair. 'Jeannie MacDonnell was the housekeeper at the big house and she wasn't married when she had Aileen. And don't ask me who the father was because I've no idea, but I could make a good guess: someone up for the stalking; the woman's got good bones. The country people round here are stocky, you'll see. Jeannie hasn't long been married in fact; she probably wouldn't have married at all but Mac suddenly appeared on the scene. Alastair engaged him to help with the ponies. At first he lived over the stables and Jeannie fed him and I suppose they sort of gravitated.'

'And Aileen and Alastair gravitated too?' Flora didn't respond. 'You haven't told me what they're like.' Rupert leaned on the table and said earnestly, 'Vivien's perceptive without appearing to be. How about you?'

She sat back, eyeing him warily. 'They're just neighbours. I mean, Jeannie was only the housekeeper, Rupert.' She was reproving him. His lips twitched and she tried to justify herself. 'She still works in the house – well, she has to; the trekkers stay there and they can't get women from the village to help. It's an awful old place: damp and dark and crawling with vermin—'

'Oh, come on!'

'It's true! They don't allow cats in the house so they have mice. And rats. You've never heard a rat in this place, have you? That's because our cats go everywhere – and my Robbie of course. He's murder on rats.'

Rupert gave up. Vivien hadn't been forthcoming either, merely indicating the trees at the end of the loch and saying that was Lair, where the Semples lived. It was in London that she'd told him about Alastair's debts and the pony-trekking. In close proximity to her neighbours she was taciturn. He wondered if there'd been something between them. But she'd asked them to dinner. He awaited their arrival with interest.

Alastair Semple wasn't a sandy Scot but a dark, grey-eyed fellow in tweeds and cheap loafers. He appeared to be in his thirties and wearing badly. The body was still powerful but he had the watery eyes of the habitual drinker. He spoke well, greeting his hostess with boyish charm that seemed a trifle exaggerated. However, when he transferred his attention to Rupert he was coldly polite.

In the drawing room Rupert sat a little apart and considered the man. He wasn't all that attractive in his view: the nose was too large, the mouth too thin, and the forehead, that might have been high, was obscured by hair which he had an irritating habit of tossing back, a theatrical gesture that was curiously feminine.

His wife was languid and fine-boned as a whippet. Once seated, her eyes rested on Vivien, then moved to her husband and, with no marked expression, nothing you could identify, she gave off a charge which might have been no more than possessiveness. Her eyes were magnificent, fit for a tragedy queen, and accentuated by eye-shadow like charcoal. She wore flared pink trousers and what looked like her husband's Icelandic jersey, but then it was a bitter night. They had arrived in a Land Rover with a small plough hitched to the front, and they both wore gumboots and carried their shoes. Rupert thought that an amusing and domestic touch.

'He's going back on Monday's sleeper,' Vivien was saying in response to a question from Aileen. She smiled warmly at Rupert but addressed the Semples. 'He has to find a job; I'm not his sole concern.'

'You are for the moment,' Rupert said.

'I hope for longer than the moment.' There was no mistaking the affection in her voice and even Rupert was startled.

They were all looking at him, Aileen with the kind of coy recognition that implied she had divined their true relationship, her husband asking bluntly, 'What do you actually do?'

The devil was in Rupert. 'You mean as a rule, or specifically, with Vivien?'

Alastair hesitated. There was a crash and a cry in the kitchen. Vivien excused herself and dashed out.

'Both,' Alastair said, his eyes following her.

'Ah.' Rupert leaned back and laced his fingers like an elderly gent about to pontificate. 'A good question. What *do* editors do? Guide? Inspire? Nurture? All I can say is we're considered a necessity, like sausage machines – if you need sausages. We package the raw material and produce it processed and wrapped and ready for the consumer. Not, of course, in Vivien's case; her material is highly sophisticated, honed before it leaves her. She doesn't need me professionally.'

'Nothing sophisticated about mountaineering,' Alastair said. 'It's hard and dangerous, that's the point of it. We climb to get away from all that stuff: the rat-race, townies.'

'I was talking about getting inside people's minds.' Rupert was tart. 'She's a natural at that' – she was back, raising her eyebrows at him. 'Are you going to explain my presence here?' he asked.

'I'd have got around to it. How would you put it?'

'Oh no, my dear. It's your baby.'

Alastair gasped and glowered. His wife smiled wickedly. Vivien spluttered. 'Murder,' she told them. 'I'm into crime now. It was his idea – and I love it. I thought I'd hate it: such a grind, writing fiction, but he worked on me, and would you believe it, it's going like a bomb!'

'That's splendid, Vivien.' Aileen sparkled with enthusiasm. 'Isn't that great, Alastair? She's found a new career.'

'Great. It'll give you something to do.' The contempt was heavy. 'What about the climbing books? That's what you're good at.'

'How can you judge?' Vivien was indignant. 'That's all you read, apart from the *Scottish Field*.'

'That's all he can read,' Aileen murmured.

He ignored her. 'It's only a one-off, isn't it?' He was pleading. 'You'll write books after future expeditions?'

'I've had expeditions. This is something I can get my teeth into. It's wild and exciting and—'

'More exciting than climbing! You're off your head! You've been listening' – he gestured at Rupert – 'he's worked on you—'

'Come off it, Alastair!' The tone cut like a knife. 'I'm doing it for the money, but I happen to like doing it. What about the ponytrekking?'

'Whoever said I liked it? Leading a string of deadbeats who can't sit on a horse, who panic as soon as we're out of sight of the house? D'you know what one old bag asked me last summer?' He turned to Rupert, hostility swamped by outrage: 'Were there wolves in Corrie Ba?' He swallowed his Scotch at a gulp and looked round wildly. Vivien got up and replenished his glass.

'The road's icy,' Aileen said, the words like a cold douche.

'He can drive that road with his eyes shut.' Vivien was dry. 'Right, Alastair?'

'You shouldn't encourage him,' Aileen said.

'If I'm not fit, she can drive.' Alastair bared his teeth at his wife.

'If I'm driving I could put you in the loch.'
'I'd like to see you try.'

'Why didn't you warn me? No wonder you like to keep your distance from the neighbours.'

Rupert had gone to the kitchen to take over from Flora and to send her in for a drink.

She sighed dramatically. 'What's he done now? Usually he behaves himself until after the meal. Poor Rupert.' She was indulgent. 'You've stolen his partner. He'll be after your blood.'

For a moment he was speechless. 'In front of his wife! How can she come here? How can Vivien— You're kidding.'

'Not a bit of it. She's been too wrapped up in the book to tell you, or maybe she thought it wouldn't interest you. But for my money, after a few more whiskies he'd have warned you off, and no wonder. It isn't just that she's the only person around to partner him, it's that she's so good: miles better than him. They'd have been on the Ben every day this week but you were monopolizing her. At least, that's how he'll see it. You'll never convince him that writing's more important than climbing. He must hate your guts.'

'Climbing,' Rupert breathed. 'He's a climber.'

'Of course. What did you think? That's how they are; mountains come before family, home, work, everything – and you arrive from London, and she won't even speak to him, can't be bothered. It was me who had to tell him she wouldn't go out.' She grinned. She was enjoying this. 'But he must have seen you walking the dogs together.'

'It sounds like kids: "She can't come out to play".'

She shrugged. 'Big kids with one-track minds – except that *she's* grown up. Since she met you,' she added quietly. 'He'll resent that too.'

'Balls.'

'Oh, he has got under your skin, hasn't he? Seems to be mutual.'

'Not at all. He's a boor. Still, thanks for telling me. I know where I am now.'

She went out and he lifted pan lids, sniffing abstractedly. He was thinking of Aileen; obviously she didn't climb or she'd have gone with them, but it was still a triangle: wife, husband, other *person*: not sexual, or not directly sexual. But if Alastair considered climbing more important than family, a wife might feel just as abandoned when the husband climbed with another woman as if he were jumping into bed with her. And now, with this new book, Vivien had abandoned Alastair, and Rupert had unwittingly abetted her. He was puzzled; hadn't she realized how fraught her dinner party would be?

The showdown came after dinner. Rupert suspected that Vivien had emphasized his professional assistance when he was out of the room, could even have demanded that Alastair behave himself in her house, at all events he was so charming throughout the meal that Rupert was suspicious. Vivien and Aileen appeared to be pandering to the man, goading him to increasingly bizarre accounts of his trekking experiences. Flora said nothing, all her attention on the table, on plates and the contents of people's glasses, or some personal plan which she must adhere to in order to keep things running smoothly. Rupert thought she was trying to distance herself. And Danny? He had distanced himself completely, not even appearing. Vivien had said that Danny was uncomfortable at formal gatherings but Rupert wondered if it wasn't so much formality that bothered the lad as the presence of Alastair Semple.

They moved back to the drawing room for coffee. Aileen asked about the spiced mussels that had preceded the venison and was referred to Rupert. He enthused happily and Alastair, silent and disregarded, settled to what looked like the preferred business of the evening, the whisky bottle at his elbow. Had he placed it there himself or was Vivien responsible?

Rupert progressed to the venison. 'The left-overs can be used like beef in Indian dishes, or Chinese,' he burbled, staring as Alastair filled his glass as if the whisky were water. He was aware of Aileen's gaze, of her eyes turning to her husband, coming back to him, smiling – reading his thoughts?

'We'll have to buy an Indian recipe book,' Vivien said. 'How about it, Flora? Oh, there I go again: assuming you'll do the cooking.' She turned to Aileen. 'If this book's a success we're going to engage a housekeeper. Flora does everything; it's far too much for one person. I need her to help me.'

'It's difficult to keep servants out here,' Alastair said pleasantly, not sounding in the least drunk. 'My mother-in-law stayed only because she was attached to the family.'

Vivien's eyes widened, Flora looked blank as if her mind were elsewhere. Aileen said clearly, 'She wasn't that close. Ours wasn't an incestuous marriage, sweetie.'

Alastair inhaled deeply and stared at her. Flora stood up. 'Back to the grindstone,' she announced brightly.

'Leave it, love.' Vivien made frantic movements of protest. 'We'll do it in the morning.'

'No problem. I like doing it.'

'Then I'll—' Vivien threw a glance at her guests.

'We'll all pig in.' Aileen stood up, graceful and controlled. 'The men can entertain each other.'

'So that's us dismissed,' Rupert said inanely when they were alone.

Alastair stared at a bookcase, his mouth drooping. Now, with the charm switched off, the flesh of his face seemed to sag, pulled down by heavy jowls. Putting on weight, Rupert thought smugly: fighting but losing the battle. Not fighting the Scotch though.

'She's a better climber than a writer,' Alastair said, not turning his head.

'Your opinion.'

'I know.' Now he did turn. 'You don't know the first thing about her.' It was as if for the past hour he had been displaying the bright side of his personality and now a coin had been flipped and, with the main audience gone, he reverted to type. This was the dark side.

'Should we be discussing our hostess?' Rupert asked.

'What's in it for you?'

So etiquette was suspended. 'She has to realize her potential,' Rupert said.

'You mean you have to. Worth a lot now, is she?'

'I don't benefit financially.' Why was he taking this? He grimaced; he was – they were both guests in the house. He had to try to sustain a conversation, not allow it to degenerate into a slanging match. 'I'd like to have a part in establishing her as a novelist,' he pointed out. 'But so far I've done little more than make suggestions.'

'And you're leaving Monday.'

'That's the arrangement.'

'Do you intend coming back?'

'If she needs me.'

'Is there any reason why she should?'

Rupert thought about this, considering whether the question held an ulterior meaning, how drunk the man was, cursing the situation he found himself in. 'Yes,' he said. 'There are a number of technical reasons.'

'Such as?'

'Do you really want a lecture on editing? This is a party and I don't care to talk shop when I'm off duty; I don't have the kind of amusing anecdotes about my work that you—'

'Are you sleeping with her?'

'That's not your business.'

'It is.'

'Perhaps you'll explain that.' Rupert was amazed at his own appearance of calm when he was sure the fellow was about to beat him up there in the drawing room. He couldn't believe what was happening.

'She climbs with *me*,' Alastair said, as if Rupert were a rival mountaineer.

'What's that got to do with it?'

'The snow's been in perfect condition for a fortnight.' The fellow slumped in his chair like a big sulky child. 'Now there's all this new stuff on top and we shan't be able to do a thing till it consolidates. We lost two weeks!' He sounded as if he'd lost a fortune.

'Why can't you climb in fresh snow?'

'It avalanches.' He reverted to staring at the bookcase. 'It's just balanced there on top of the old hard surface and it slides off as soon as you step on it. Not every time but there's always the risk. And the cornices come down because they're top-heavy. Treacherous stuff, new snow; I hate it.'

'There are avalanches in this country?' Rupert winced at his own shrill tone but evidently Alastair was well past the point of acute perception, although still capable of enjoying the sound of his own voice. Once he started to talk about his experiences on unstable snow there was no stopping him.

At the end of the evening, when the Semples had left and Flora had gone to bed Vivien was eager to know how he'd coped with Alastair on his own. 'I got him to talk about himself – again,' he said drily. 'Are they going to get home all right?' Alastair had insisted on driving.

'He'll manage. The water's a long way below the road but in most places the trees are so close that if he does go over the edge the Land Rover can't slide between the trunks, particularly with the plough attached.'

'You've considered the possibility.'

'Not specifically but people have gone off the road there. However, drunks never hurt themselves, do they? Well, fishermen walk off docks on their way back to their boats, and crofters get stuck in drifts – but Alastair's got nine lives.'

'Have you any idea how possessive he is about you?'

'He reckons he's my climbing partner.'

'Reckons?'

She shrugged. 'He's a bit of a pest. I prefer to climb with people who are better than me. You learn more that way.'

'Men or women?'

'Oh, men. I don't know any women who are better than me.' It was said neutrally, it was a fact.

'There are women who are better?'

'I'm sure there are. It's just that I haven't met them. I'm talking about snow,' she added quickly. 'Rock climbing's a different matter; I'm merely competent on rock, in a different league from women at the top.' She sighed. 'Time for bed. Did you enjoy the evening? The meal was delicious. I never suspected you could cook like that.'

'Flora's very cooperative. The hard work was hers. I provided the flair.' He smiled. It was a joke. 'I found the evening fascinating. Tell me, what's Aileen's attitude to Alastair's climbing with you?'

'I never thought about it. She doesn't climb. There's nothing between us, Rupert, no sex if that's what you're getting at. Climbers are asexual – on the hill, I mean.'

He couldn't control his expression. 'Honestly,' she assured him. 'There's no time, no opportunity; you don't *need* it. The rock – or the snow – demands total commitment; after all, it's a life or death situation. Sex is just an itch to a climber.' She spread her hands helplessly. 'You wouldn't understand.'

'Itches have to be scratched. D'you think Aileen understands?'

'It's immaterial. We just climb together – and I've been thinking of ditching him anyway. Now I've got the perfect excuse: I'm far too busy.'

'He's not going to take that lying down.'

'That's his problem. If he wants to climb all that much he has to learn to do it solo. I do it all the time.'

'Solo?'

'Without a rope, on his own.'

'Isn't that dangerous?'

'Not if you know what you're doing, keep within your limits. I do. Alastair – well, yes, he could be a bit shaky on limits.'

'He's a bloody wimp!' Alastair blundered into his kitchen and made a familiar bee-line for the bottle on the dresser. 'What's his angle? He's a townie; what's she see in him?'

Aileen knew better than to walk out and go to bed when he was like this; they weren't rhetorical questions. 'She needs the money,' she said. 'The man's helping her with a book.'

But although he'd demanded some response he didn't listen to the sense of it. 'A fortnight!' he protested. 'She gave up climbing for a fortnight! And what am I expected to do? Hang around till she's finished with him – finished the book?'

Aileen turned away to hide her smile. 'I don't think it's sexual,' she murmured, but quite sure that it was.

'What was that?' It was odd how drunks missed so much but could catch the crucial remarks.

She turned back, straight-faced, inquiring. 'You're suggesting they're lovers?'

'Never! That—' He checked, staring at her. His lip curled. 'Hardly her style,' he said coldly. 'She wouldn't look at anyone who wasn't a climber.'

'Perhaps she'll take *him* climbing.'

She caught her breath but he missed the barbed emphasis. 'She's wasting herself,' he protested. 'She's good!' He paused, glowering at her; sensing that something had passed him by? He licked his lips. 'Really good,' he insisted, and now he was sly. 'She can follow me up anything; I've never known a woman like her.' He paused again, letting the words sink in. He grinned. 'Climbing, of course,' he added.

'You're quite right.' She nodded gravely. 'She knows what she's about; you've only got to watch her on telly. She treats cheeky interviewers like dirt. She's got no time for wimps.'

'So what's she doing with Lasco?'

'Perhaps she prefers a good brain to brute strength?'

'Are we being personal here?'

'It was an observation. You're taking it personally?' She backtracked carefully. 'She'll come back when she's got this book out of her system – and Lasco's leaving anyway. This is just a nine-day wonder. And after all, you manage to live without her when she's away on expeditions.'

He studied her face, suspecting innuendo, but she returned the scrutiny calmly. 'Basically she's a climber,' she insisted, knowing she couldn't go wrong there.

He grunted. He poured himself another drink and pulled out a chair. She was dismissed and she left the room quietly, not risking further disturbance by saying goodnight. He would drink until he was incapable of getting up the stairs and then he'd sleep on a sofa. Once again she'd got away with playing this alarming game: just managing to guard her tongue or to slip sideways when he sensed malice, but the game couldn't go on like this; she knew that restraint slipped a little more with every confrontation. Living with Alastair was like living on the rim of a volcano.

Chapter 5

Vivien called the book *Thin Ice*. Rupert went back to London with copies of the first four chapters and on the morning after his return he started a carefully planned programme to build up her new career. With a background of thirty years in the business he was in a privileged position; he knew everyone, he could be agent, editor, publicist, and he would do anything for his author, even fight dirty if necessary.

Rupert was happy, he blossomed in the knowledge that she was already well beyond the line that separated gratitude from affection. She'd snatched an afternoon from the book and had driven him to the station where she'd kissed him goodbye – on the cheek but she'd hugged him too. She told him that he had to come back within two weeks, that she was utterly dependent on him.

He left his house the following morning sparking with confidence. There was a New York publisher in town, and an American film company (with an English director) were throwing a party tomorrow in the Fishmongers' Hall. Today he'd invited the son of an old school friend to lunch. He was reasonably certain that by the time he went to bed tonight he would have passed the first hurdle.

For the British hardback edition he'd deliberately chosen a publisher who was new to the field, clever and ambitious: Joss Clark, a plump young man who was trendy in his dress and sported an East End accent. Rupert had been at Stowe with his father. After the casually dropped snippet that he was no longer with Chedwin, not with anyone, Rupert produced the script. They were in the Gay Hussar and had not yet ordered lunch but books came before food; delicious protracted lunches were how you courted women, not publishers.

Joss raised an eyebrow at the title page. Cunningly Rupert hadn't put the package in a file, not even an envelope. 'Vivien Reid,' Joss said flatly. 'Travel books – no, mountaineering.'

'Crime. That's the working title.'

'*Thin Ice*. It sounds like a come-on. Crime.' He was muttering, lifting a corner of the title page without removing the paper clip. 'Give you a bell this evening?'

'Have some more sherry. Read the first page.'

Joss was expressionless behind his Ray-bans but he was too wily to waste words. Rupert wasn't giving him lunch because he'd been to school with his father. Besides, it took less than a minute to skim down a page.

Rupert sat and forced himself to observe the other customers. He was aware of Joss turning a page, of the waiter approaching. He shook his head. The waiter faded. Joss turned the second page. Rupert relaxed his facial muscles and focused on an exquisite redhead with long pearl earrings, trying to guess the relationship with her flashy young escort. Another page turned. Rupert lifted his glass.

Joss flicked to the last page. 'Where's the rest?'

'She's working on it at home, in Scotland.'

'Are you her agent?'

'She doesn't have one.'

'But you're acting for her.'

'We–ll' – Rupert spread his hands – 'you know how it is: living up there in the sticks, doesn't come to town, got no business sense . . .'

'Right.' A sharp glance, accepting he was probably the woman's lover, dismissing that but still watchful. 'I'll offer three thousand.'

'But did he say he *liked* it?' Vivien shrilled on the phone.

'He wouldn't say that, not this chap. He adopts the persona of a barrow boy and he wouldn't give anything away. Of course he liked it, he couldn't put it down. You've taken off, love.'

'Three thousand, Rupert? I know it's a fair sum for a first novel in these days but—'

'It's peanuts – but it's the way in, the "open sesame". Now we can build on it; subsidiary rights, that's where the money is. How are things up there in the wilderness?'

'I'm on chapter seven and we're snowed in. I only just got home from Inverness last night. So we have nothing to do but work. By the time you come back I'll be finished.' He hesitated. 'Why are you so quiet? Oh, you wanted to read it at the halfway stage.' Her voice rose. 'You think I'm going to make a mistake, that I can't keep it up!'

'Of course not, but don't do anything until I get there.'

'Such as?'

'Well, send it to anyone. You must have met people when you were writing non-fiction.'

'But you're my contact now!' She was astonished. 'More than a contact: it's as much your book as mine. Of course I wouldn't do anything without you.'

Northern Scotland was cut off for the best part of a week; at one point fresh falls of snow brought down the telephone lines. In London Rupert worked like a demon: in his element with his one cherished client, sounding out prospective markets, leaking gossip that a new and exciting property was on the scene and awaiting bidders. Joss Clark became anxious, demanding the remaining chapters, pleading for a finishing date, his intensity measured by his reversion to the accents of his upbringing. Glottal stops were for yuppies.

In Scotland the telephone line was reconnected and Rupert learned that Vivien was approaching the end of *Thin Ice*. He should come back within the week, she said, the ploughs had cleared the roads. Then one night at eleven thirty, there came a cry of panic: she had been trying to reach him for *ages*, where had he been? Flora had discovered a mistake; one of the main characters was in two places at the same time. There was no way round the error, all the action after chapter ten was wrong, wasted, impossible.

'You have to go back,' he said comfortably. 'You're working too fast. Go back to where you went wrong, scrap everything after that – don't try to re-write it, burn it – and start again, writing one thousand words a day. In the afternoon take the dogs for a long walk. Clear your head.'

'Jesus! Go back? I can't.'

'Everyone else does when they go wrong. What makes you different?'

'You—' She was shaken. 'You bastard! You don't think I'm any good, you've been stringing me along—'

'While you've been beavering away' – he overrode her – 'I've sold the German rights – and the Brazilian, forgot to tell you – the one will buy you a Roller, the other its number plates. Then there's a studio in Burbank – that's Hollywood to you – is showing more than a casual interest, and this evening I had a drink with the producer of *A Book at Bedtime* who wants to see a copy as soon as you finish. There's an elite circle up here where they're all talking about a new star rising in the Highlands, but don't let it go to your head. Just listen to Flora, she's obviously a careful reader. Trust her.'

When he replaced the phone he felt as if he'd run a marathon. The situation was fragile, it rested on the first four chapters, on her potential, on his confidence and a lot of hard-won professional interest which meant nothing if she were to fall down on the job now. Apart from Joss there were no sales, neither German nor Brazilian; that had been for her benefit. Plenty of interest but no contracts – yet. He slumped in his chair. If those four chapters were no more than a flash in the pan the spark could have been extinguished by this first setback. Was there anything he could do other than try to talk her into renewed enthusiasm? Call her back? Not now, it was too late. Tomorrow morning? He jerked upright. His brain had changed gear. Tomorrow she'd be herself again: vital and brilliant. She was volatile, authors were like that: up one moment, down the next, oscillating, euphoric or crawling round the pit: manic-depressives. Fortunately she had him on hand, at least at the end of a telephone line, and there was Flora: sensible, involved, a tower of strength. As for himself, he must forget his love and concentrate on the book; art was passion disciplined. He would discipline and divert his passion and create a best-seller. Next time they met there'd be more than a hug and a peck on the cheek.

The following day he saw a Danish publisher and a television producer but he was distracted; he was waiting for the evening and a telephone call. It didn't come and he dared not phone in case he should interrupt work. The call came the next evening and it was from Flora. On hearing her voice he felt himself relax and expand; it was like emerging from shade into sunshine on a frosty morning. He welcomed her as an old friend, and waited for Vivien to come on the line.

'Everything's under control,' Flora assured him. 'She doesn't want to come out of it, is how she put it, but I thought someone should phone you.'

'She's working hard then.' He was deflated and knew he sounded stupid.

'Fourteen hours a day. She's nearly—'

'Flora! I told her to slow down, to walk the dogs—'

'Hold on, Rupert.' She was amused. 'She walks the dogs, I see she eats properly – and she's fit, but she's totally involved. She says you're to come back next week and collect the script.'

He was silent, every response he could think of liable to precipitate a quarrel – and she was his only contact with Vivien. 'So she wants me there next week,' he repeated flatly.

'You've worked so hard, Rupert: selling the British rights was a tremendous boost for us. Congratulations. When can we expect you?'

He gave them two days ('them' as if they were a team and he was the outsider) then he went north. Danny picked him up in Inverness: a bright and amusing Danny whose chatter fell on deaf ears. Rupert had chosen to sit in the front of the Volvo but propinquity meant nothing. Having satisfied himself that Vivien was well he responded in monosyllables to Danny's observations on the scenery, on Alder, on 'his' garden. After a while they both stared through the windscreen, Rupert wondering how she would greet him, Danny mulling over the cruelty of men – and this one had seemed so thoughtful and kind, so perceptive.

Emotionally the visit to Alder was a dead loss, professionally it was a milestone, but they would know that only with hindsight. There had been another small error which had set them back and when Rupert arrived Vivien was still on the penultimate chapter. Flora was working on the one before that, and Rupert felt like an intruder. As he closed the front door Vivien came out to the hall, kissed his cheek, said languidly, 'Lovely to see you, my dear. Make yourself at home, you know where everything is,' and went back to the study where he could hear Flora at her keyboard. He trudged upstairs, trying not to feel rejected, trying to be amused at such dedication.

The women remained preoccupied. At dinner Vivien stared at her food or into space, speaking in spurts, continuing a line of thought. At one point she stated firmly: 'He's too drunk. That degree of drunkenness would have been apparent in the writing on the note.'

Flora stopped eating. 'No problem,' she said after a pause. 'He spends the same amount of time in the bar but he drinks less. You strike out all references to his drunken condition. I'll see to it.'

'Right.' Vivien turned back to her mutton stew.

The women finished eating and excused themselves. Danny went to his room. Rupert was still eating cheese. He decided that his job, until the script was ready for him, was that of houseman and chef. Mutton stew!

The next morning he occupied himself with cookbooks, pondering the contents of the larder, marking time until the afternoon. He took them coffee at eleven and sandwiches at midday. Vivien thanked him but scarcely looked up from her work.

At three o'clock the dogs, dozing in their baskets, snapped alert and rushed out to the hall. He followed. She was taking her anorak from the coat-stand.

'Hang on,' he said, hurrying to the stairs. 'Let me get a coat.'

'No, I'm going alone.' She saw his expression. 'Oh, my dear – please! I love you, Rupert, but bear with me.'

He stood on the bottom stair, gaping at the closed door. He stepped down and walked into the study.

'Good God, what happened?' Flora asked, seeing his face.

'Does she – always go alone?'

'Usually; it only needs one person to walk the dogs. Ah, you wanted to go with her. No way. She can't tolerate interruption, you see. Even I don't talk to her – about anything other than the book, I mean. I'm sorry it's like this; we meant to be finished by the time you arrived. Don't look so stricken, you must know what authors are like.'

He returned to the kitchen. He would prepare a magnificent meal – and she wouldn't even notice. No matter, she'd said she loved him.

'Where d'you want these peats, Miss Gunn?'

The shout came from outside the back door. It was two days after Rupert's arrival. He rubbed the window clear of steam and saw a stocky fellow in a deer-stalker and breeches walking to a decrepit Land Rover in the yard. He dried his hands and went to the door. The man pulled a loaded sack from the back of the truck and stared at him.

'And who might you be?' He was as aggressive as a pit bull,

and looked something like one: short, powerfully built with a large head under the drab hat, an intense shadowed stare.

'You must be Mac,' Rupert said. 'What was it – peats? Put them in the stable, will you?' He was getting into the rhythm of the place.

Mac came clumping to the back door. Rupert had the kettle boiling. 'I'm Rupert Lasco,' he said brightly. 'Coffee or tea?'

'I usually take a dram,' Mac said. It was four o'clock. 'So you're the one from London,' he went on as Rupert went to the cupboard for the Scotch.

'That's right' – he hesitated – 'I'm in publishing.'

Mac said nothing but he grinned slyly.

'And you must be Mrs Semple's step-father,' Rupert said carelessly, turning to the stove where a pan of bones was simmering.

'You tend to the cooking?' Mac asked in astonishment.

'Naturally. Don't you?'

'I never touched a pan in me life.'

'You eat your food raw?'

'Me wimmen look after me.'

'That's sad.' Rupert shook his head. 'Unable to look after yourself.'

Mac glowered. He was no good at this. 'What do they call you? Kitchen maid?'

'Oh no! I'm the chef.'

'You said publishing.'

'I can turn my hand to anything.'

'Hi there.' Vivien stood in the doorway. Her voice was strained and slightly slurred. She looked exhausted and her eyes in their deep sockets were feverish. 'Give me a Scotch, love. A big one. It's over.' She ignored Mac completely.

Rupert handed her a stiff whisky. She drank, not taking her eyes off him. She smiled slowly and he grinned. They could have been alone.

'Congratulations, my dear.' He lifted an eyebrow at the sound of tapping from the study. 'Still working?'

'She'll soon be finished. She works like a horse.' She turned to Mac. 'What are you doing here?'

'I brought the peats.'

'Ah, the peats.' She pulled out a chair, raised her arms and stretched luxuriously. 'I should go on the hill.' She looked at the steamy window. 'There will be primroses in the gorges soon. I finished in the spring! Perfect timing.'

At Lair Alastair came in from the stables smiling. 'I'm climbing tomorrow!'

'That will be a relief.' Aileen was wary. She added quickly, 'You'll be glad to get on the hill again.'

He nodded at her with a kind of triumph. 'Viv's finished her book. She's free at last. She sent Mac home with the message.'

'I don't like it. You said the climbing's dangerous towards the end of the season.'

'So?'

'Tell her to find someone else. She'll be feeling like a hard route after so long.'

She turned to the dresser and he studied her back; she knew him too well for him to protest that he led the routes. 'There's more to climbing than doing hard stuff.' He tried to keep his voice even but she could detect the shake in it. 'The company's just as important. And she's great fun, for a woman.' He showed his teeth like a dog. 'But then a man couldn't be the same kind of fun, could he?'

'Not unless he was gay.'

For a moment his face was blank with incomprehension, then: 'No one can say I'm gay. That is, no woman could.'

'Has someone been throwing accusations around then?'

'You know something? You remind me of a snake: one of those mambas: long and thin and cold and dripping with venom.'

'Good God, Alastair! What have I said?'

'And slimy too. That's why *she's* such a relief to go to, not just for the climbing neither – and you're no match there: you couldn't get off the ground. She's strong as a horse and she's a real woman with it: never bothers to hide it. Ultra-feminine, that's Viv: knows what she wants and makes no bones about it. She takes the initiative.'

'Possibly, but I think she and Rupert are very well suited.'

He gaped, pulled up short. 'He's a one-off,' he snapped. 'She's out with me tomorrow. She said so. She wants me. Lasco's a deadbeat; what Viv needs is a *man*.' The silence stretched. 'Well, say something! Run out of poison? Recognize the truth when it's staring you in the face?'

'There's nothing to say. Vivien needs a proper man. You hit the nail square on the head.'

Rupert returned to London with the completed book and sold the German rights immediately for thirty thousand pounds. More sales followed. He had prepared the ground well. At first Vivien accepted the news listlessly but he wasn't deceived; for weeks all her vitality had been absorbed by that other world: of plotting and suspense and violent death. She had been difficult to work with after she'd finished, wanting nothing more than to escape to the mountains, but he insisted on some re-writing, although little was needed; she'd got it right and she'd done it well. His queries were easily resolved: matters of syntax or repetition, the need for a map. She drew it in an hour, neat and without an obvious mistake.

'Are you sure you got the distances right?' he asked.

'Of course. I lived there for weeks.' She meant in imagination; the book was more real to her than Alder – an Alder where Rupert now seemed to be accepted as another member of the household, on a par with Danny and the dogs. He finished work on the script with Flora, packed his bag and left. Flora took him to the station. Vivien was on the hill.

Now all the preliminary work paid off and he was on a rising tide. He enjoyed the action for its own sake but kept a wary eye open for pitfalls, reading the small print with great care, not only looking for the best deal for the book but scouting ahead, aware that there was a future after *Thin Ice*. By the time contracts arrived for signature at Alder Lodge he could tell her to sign them without trying to understand the jargon. He'd done that part.

The tenor of his life had changed again. Now it was he who telephoned Scotland, and almost every time he had news. At Alder Vivien was recovering quickly; the first weekend after he left she was on Ben Nevis: a great gully, she said, probably the last time it would be climbed before the thaw set in, four ice pitches and a tunnel through the cornice. Who with? Oh, Alastair, no one else was around. He'd coped very well, she said brightly, considering. She didn't elaborate but his delight in an image of Alastair trying to cope with steep ice was marred by the sudden horror of what would happen to her if he fell. 'He's heavy,' he said harshly. 'Could you hold him if he slipped?'

'He won't.' She was dismissive. 'He's all right with a rope from above. It's more likely he'd have to hold me if I came off—'

'Have you ever—'

'Pack it in, love! I haven't and anyway, it's over; the thaw's come. Everything's awash. We can't climb now until the rock dries out.'

Next time he called she had turned her attention, not to writing – she'd told him that *Thin Ice* was a one-off, she wouldn't do another novel – but to the delights of spending money. She decided on not one, but two new bathrooms, and she was going to convert the hay-loft above the stables into a flat for Danny. She'd had planning permission for ages but had never had the money to avail herself of it. And would Rupert advertise in the *Lady* for a housekeeper?

In June she came to London. Joss had put a bomb behind his printers and publication was scheduled for July. She arrived at Euston thin and tanned in faded Levis and a torn shirt, and for Rupert there was no one else on the station concourse when he caught sight of her and saw her face light up with something that was deeper than mere affection.

Joss was captivated; so were all the men who met her, but not the women, not all of them. Rupert came to the conclusion that the kind of confidence that Vivien possessed is easily interpreted as arrogance. She inspired adoration or a resentment which could deepen quickly to dislike; there was nothing neutral about her. Joss saw it too. 'We'll have to screen her interviewers,' he said. 'She can put people's backs up.'

'That's no problem,' Rupert countered. 'She'll shoot them down.'

Joss sighed. It was obvious that Lasco was head over heels in love – and the lady seemed fond of him too; he hoped that the affair would last, at least until she was established as a crime writer.

Publication was three weeks ahead. Vivien was photographed. She hated it and said she photographed best when climbing. She had Flora send some pictures of herself on long snow slopes: a fly at the end of the rope. Joss and Rupert looked at them, then at her, and both had the same thought.

'Is there any way,' Rupert ventured, 'that we can get a close-up of you climbing, rather less bundled up perhaps, without losing the sense of danger, the feeling of being on your own, out there, in space?'

She suggested Cornwall. They went to Land's End with three other climbers, one a professional photographer, and they returned with a collection of pictures – colour and black-and-white – of Vivien in a white bikini and little white boots on rock: on vertical walls, in cracks, arched out on overhangs like eaves, the rope a thread of gossamer and the sea sparkling an immense distance below. It was the epitome of summer, of grace, of danger.

'They're stunning,' Joss breathed, sifting through the collection. 'How's it done?'

'I'm not with you,' Rupert said.

'Why, it's faked of course?' Joss's voice rose.

'No fake.' Rupert was smug. 'I was there. I watched her doing that.' He shivered. He'd been on a rope just to look over the edge.

Joss stared and went back to the proofs. 'My God!' He giggled. 'She's even better than her book.'

Rupert preened himself and waited.

'Paperback,' Joss murmured. 'I'm glad we held on before selling paperback rights. These increase her value out of all proportion. You're going to have to do something about the money, you know, or she'll lose it all in tax and decide it's not worth the candle and go back to those ghastly dull expedition books. You'll need to become her agent, or marry her or something. Have you thought about it?' The tone was deceptively casual.

'I'm working on it,' Rupert said.

Vivien was staying in his house in Notting Hill. She had no hotel expenses and she had never mentioned money (except as it related to improvements at Alder) so he was taken by surprise, having told her of Joss's reactions to the Cornish proofs, when she said, 'Prints are going to cost an arm and a leg and, by the way, can you take money from me? You're not my agent. What's the tax position?'

'What are you on about?' He was embarrassed and he sounded petulant.

'Agents take fifteen per cent, probably more if they're good. If I give you twenty per cent as starters ... How much have you spent to date? Why, there were all those people we took to Cornwall!'

'I've no idea. It doesn't matter.'

'Don't be cross. You're not earning so all those expenses have come out of your savings. How much? Come on, I insist. We're in this together, you idiot.'

'I don't know.' He was literally squirming. 'How can I tell until I've had a bank statement?'

'You've had lots since we met. Right: I don't know what I've got, it seems to grow by the day, but I'll write you a cheque, and in future I'll pay the expenses.'

'I don't want the money,' he blurted. 'I want to marry you.' He stopped, appalled. 'Forget it.' He gestured wildly. 'This is your fault, you have this dire effect on me: away from you I'm a rational human being; with you I act like an adolescent. And I'm fifteen years your senior,' he added forlornly. 'You'll still be climbing mountains when I'm drawing my old age pension.'

'I've been thinking about that,' she said seriously. 'Joss mentioned that there would be financial advantages to marriage. Of course,' she added quickly, 'he assumes we're living together – which we are, in a manner of speaking: sharing each other's houses. Close your mouth, love, you'll catch a fly.'

'I'm not marrying for financial advantage.' He looked hurt.

'*My* advantage. This way you would be helping me claw back a bit from the taxman.' He recognized an echo of Joss's words. 'But that's a side-issue,' she went on impatiently. 'I need you.' She grinned at his expression. 'Look, we're fond of each other, we work well together, and as for the business side – I must have an agent. That has to be you; look what you've done for *Thin Ice!*'

'You're trying to persuade me to be your agent? Using your body as a bribe? How could you!'

'Be serious. I'm proposing a partnership based on good sense. Not forgetting the extra lolly. You can be agent, secretary – lots of people have two secretaries – you can be my manager: anything we can use to advantage where the Inland Revenue's concerned.'

'You left out "husband".'

'That's taken as read. That's for me; the rest is for the taxman.'

'I'm fifteen years older than you.'

'So you never meant it, you were kidding me along—'

'No! I said: I shall be—'

'—a pensioner fifteen years before me. Balls. Men father kids at ninety. Are we going to get married or not? I want you back at Alder so make up your mind.'

'You've bullied me into it; I hope you'll remember that.

Coercion's the word. And I insist on an outrageously romantic location for the honeymoon – we're going to have a honeymoon – to make up for this blatant materialism.'

'Think of it as an arranged marriage and count your blessings. You might not have liked me. It could have been all business.'

An arranged marriage was exactly what he was thinking: happy as a lark, convinced that the affection that she acknowledged so carelessly would ripen to love, had already ripened in her subconscious mind. Why else would she remind him that a man's age made no difference to his ability to father children?

The next three weeks were frantically busy. While Rupert attended to business and the logistics of the honeymoon Vivien divided her time between dress shops and interviews. At least there were no more photography sessions. The Cornish prints had been distributed to people who had review copies of *Thin Ice* and new posters had been produced.

The book came out in a blaze of publicity and there was only one dissenting voice: Vivien's. On the Sunday morning after publication they were in Rupert's minuscule patio garden drinking coffee and surrounded by newspapers when he remarked with feigned boredom that all this praise was monotonous, didn't one reviewer have it in for her?

'That's the point,' she said gravely. 'They love me because of the pictures' – every national paper had printed one of the Cornish photographs – 'but they're not all that keen on the book.'

'Rubbish! Where's that one' – he plunged into the pile – 'who said you're "a new star in the cosmos"?'

'It sounds like the *Express*.'

'And "an astonishing sea change" and something about "this long-legged golden beauty".'

'There you are: proves what I said.'

The media did love her but they liked the book too. Joss started to pester her for a date for the next novel. Vivien, startled and scared, feeling shackles about to snap shut, took refuge behind Rupert, holing up in his house until the day they were married and flew out from Heathrow.

They had compromised on the honeymoon. He knew she would want to climb and the only outdoor activity that he might enjoy was some quiet riding. So, by means of tourist information services and a lot of expensive telephone calls, he had tracked down a guide who would take them into the Montana Rockies on horseback.

The trip was a success. They travelled from lake to lake, camping in high corries and, while the men idled the days away fishing for trout, Vivien climbed. In the evening their guide told stories and Rupert, watching her face by the light of their fire, saw that she was spellbound. The stories were full of violence and mystery; they were bizarre, alien, wild: they were the richest of raw material. Ostensibly Rupert accepted them at face value and left them to work their own magic on the crime writer.

When they came back from the States it was to learn from Flora that the builders had run into a problem with the plumbing for the new bathrooms so Vivien returned to Scotland leaving Rupert to pack his personal possessions and to interview candidates for the position of housekeeper. They had decided that he should see people who applied from England, she would deal with the Scottish applicants. There had been dozens of replies to the advertisement but no one had got as far as a personal interview. As yet they'd found no one who could face working in a Highland lodge sixty miles from town.

Rupert was keeping the Notting Hill house for the time being, because of the depressed state of the market, he said, but privately he was thinking that, with a series of novels to follow *Thin Ice*, a London base would not only be convenient but necessary.

Vivien had still said nothing about a second mystery, had refused to discuss it even with Rupert, in fact the return to Scotland was also a flight from the increasingly anguished pleas from Joss. 'Give her time,' Rupert urged. 'Let her enjoy the summer, she'll get down to work as soon as the bad weather sets in, I promise you. There's nothing else to do up there when it rains. She can write a book in six weeks. You'll have the next before Christmas.'

At Alder Vivien settled the builders' problems – revelling in the new financial freedom where almost any difficulty could be overcome with money – and then, assuring Flora she'd cope with the job applicants in a day or two, she took to the hills, lively as a colt and just a little careless. Because he was available she climbed with Alastair and he, delighted with the chance to get on steep rock again, was on his best behaviour – at first, even laying off the whisky, at least when he was with Vivien.

The summer had been warm and dry and everyone knew the

heat wave couldn't last much longer. The climbers were out every day and, because the big cliffs were some distance from Alder, they often stayed away all night. Back at Lair Mac led the pony-trekkers and Jeannie catered for them with the help of Aileen. At Alder Flora worried over the mounting pile of mail. The climbers gave no thought to anyone or anything but themselves and the rock, and the rock was perfect. Vivien couldn't remember such a prolonged drought when she was free to enjoy it – with a reasonably competent second, when the sense of achievement at the top of a thousand feet of walls and slabs was surpassed only by the thought of tomorrow morning and the thrill of arrival at the foot of the next great climb.

She was superbly on form and even Alastair was going well. Unfortunately his delight in the climbing and his unaccustomed sense of wellbeing goaded him to exploit the situation. One afternoon, when they were sprawled on a ledge halfway up a cliff, wondering which delectable route to take to the top, she said dreamily, 'It's as if it's gone on for ever, and yet it has to end some time.'

'It needn't.' She said nothing. 'We can go away together,' he went on, not looking at her, staring at the sky. 'Spend all our time climbing: the Alps, Nepal, you name it.'

'You *are* an idiot; I meant the weather: the weather has to break eventually. Besides, I'm married.'

'What's that got to do with it?'

There was a pause, then she said thoughtfully, 'He's solid.'

'Meaning I'm not?'

A mountain ringlet flitted through a sunbeam. 'You're volatile as a butterfly,' she said.

'A what!' He was grinning.

'Volatile *and* solid: a disastrous combination.' But her eyes were teasing. 'So get off your arse and sort this rope out.'

She stood up and moved to the foot of the next climb, back to the rock, shutting him out. He came up behind her.

'I'm serious, Viv.'

She turned. 'For God's sake! You're treading on the rope!'

'Fuck the rope.'

She stared at him and said coldly, 'I could solo from here on.' He swallowed and closed his eyes; it was a body-blow and she didn't have to follow it up, didn't need to ask how he would get off the cliff without her. She was untangling the rope slowly and deliberately, giving the air time to clear.

'Right.' She straightened her back. 'There's a reasonable belay.' She pointed.

She climbed in silence and he followed awkwardly, the first clumsy movement initiating more. 'Take in the slack!' It was a frantic shout as he became aware of the loop in the rope which should be tight to her.

'It's caught,' she said evenly. 'You'll have to free it yourself.'

The rest of the climb went no better and as he lost his equanimity she became brusque. The old sense of comradeship, of shared pleasure, was gone.

'That's a rubbishy route,' he protested when it was over and he collapsed on the summit. 'That's the last time I do it.'

'Have a day off tomorrow,' she said, coiling the rope.

'Good.' He brightened. 'What shall we do?'

'I shall climb.'

'Who with?' She looked at him. 'Well,' he blustered, 'it's a reasonable question, isn't it?'

She shrugged and turned back to the rope. At that moment he hated her.

In London Rupert was keeping in touch with Flora and was utterly bewildered by the situation in Scotland. Joss was incredulous when he heard, urging him to go up there, sort it out: 'It's time she started work again, she's going to lose her touch – and what about the emotional angle? I thought she was settled with you.'

Next time he phoned Flora told him that the climbers were on the Isle of Skye and no, she didn't know when they'd be back.

'What's Aileen's attitude to all this?' he asked roughly.

'She's probably glad he's out of the way for a bit; she was sporting a black eye last week.'

'He did that?'

'Who else? Unless she's got a lover on the side too.'

'Too?'

'People take lovers. That could be why he hit her. But you're an intelligent guy, Rupert. You knew Vivien was a climber when you married her, surely you never thought she was going to give it up?'

'No, but...' He trailed off. He couldn't tell her secretary that he didn't expect his wife to spend nights with her climbing companion. He wanted to ask where they stayed, and castigated himself for wanting to know.

'It's always the same when climbers marry non-climbers,' came that infuriating voice. 'They think they know what they're getting into but when it happens: the fellow goes off and leaves the wife at home – there's trouble. People should discuss it before they marry.'

'Is there anything else I should know?' he asked coldly.

'Not that I can think of at the moment.'

When he put down the phone he was trembling with anger. Vivien paid the woman's wages but who put the money in the bank, who made *Thin Ice* a success? Cheeky, jealous – that was it: Flora had been jealous of his professional assistance, now it was the marriage she resented: sex. So why wasn't she jealous of Semple? Because she didn't know whether Vivien was sleeping with – Christ, where was he going on this? She was only climbing with the fellow. But the nights? He felt sick, prurient, vicious. And it wasn't just the sexual side, he rationalized, there were the books, her livelihood, not to speak of all those dependent on her.

He forced himself to breathe deeply. He poured a small Scotch. The anger wasn't baseless. Here he was weeding out prospective housekeepers while at Alder Flora said there were now twenty-three applications waiting for a response – and at this very moment his wife was frolicking on the Cuillins with someone else's husband, and a neighbour at that. Tomorrow he would cancel the advertisement in the *Lady* and go north to the place which he'd been starting to think of as home. But he wasn't sure now that it would ever *be* home.

On Skye Vivien knew that the glorious season was over. Alastair had been prickly since that ridiculous suggestion that they should go away together. True, he'd not referred to the subject again and, after he'd fallen on a tricky slab and she'd had to give him a pull, she'd lowered the standard so that he might recover his confidence on easier routes. He was climbing quite well again by the time they reached Skye which, as always in good weather, was magical. Sun and rock conspired and they romped happily on the massive walls and along the knife-edge ridges until this last afternoon when she looked west and saw the Outer Isles etched on a glassy sea, and the air turned sticky.

'That's it,' she announced as he came up the final pitch. 'I'm going home tomorrow.'

'Why? What happened?'

'The weather's breaking. It'll rain shortly.'

'No! You can't go! What's a spot of rain?'

He continued to protest. She was amused, then curt, finally angry. They arrived at the camp site scarcely on speaking terms and when she refused to drive him to the inn (they were using her Volvo), he hitched a lift with another party.

That evening the weather forecast confirmed her own observations and she started to pack her gear. She didn't see Alastair until the following morning when he came over as she was checking her tyres. He told her he was staying on Skye. 'I'm not bothered about greasy rock,' he said.

She sighed. He was obviously hung over and looked as if even dry rock would be too much for him. 'Have you found a partner?' she asked, feeling responsible, aware of the bond forged between people who have been intimately engaged in a dangerous activity.

He stared at her from bloodshot eyes. She frowned, what the hell, she wasn't his keeper – but they had been partners. 'Come back with me,' she urged. 'Once it starts it'll rain for days.' She looked around. 'Everyone else is leaving.'

'So what? I'll climb solo.'

'The way you look after last night, you'd fall off a ladder if you weren't tied on.'

'Look who's talking.'

'I know your limits better than you do. You're no good in the wet.'

He took a step towards her. 'Now you listen to me: I've had all I can take of your insults, and no one's telling me what to do, least of all you—' He wasn't so angry that he didn't hesitate on the brink of saying something disastrous.

'Go on.' Her tone was loaded; he had no monopoly on menace.

'You're in for a very nasty surprise,' he grated.

'It's you who's in for a shock: soloing in bad weather.'

'I'm not talking about climbing—'

'And that's what's wrong! You've got your feelings mixed up with the climbing and that's not just stupid, it's bloody dangerous

– and I'm having nothing to do with it. I'm going home.' She pushed past him to the back of the car.

'You're scared.' She ignored him. 'Not of the wet: you're scared of me!'

She giggled. 'With that hangover you couldn't put the wind up a rabbit.'

As she went to close the boot he grabbed her wrist. She stood still, regarding him coolly, waiting for his next move. Around them other campers were packing up, studiously ignoring them. After a moment he released her arm and walked away.

She shrugged and got into the car thinking that she'd had Alastair; in future she'd climb with other people or go solo, and then she forgot him as she drove up the glen and the familiar mountains stood up to be counted, clear and shadowless, waiting for the rain.

Chapter 6

By the time Rupert arrived at Inverness the heat wave had broken and as his train ran down Speyside he could see the cloud low on the Cairngorms. Flora was beaming when she met him at the station. 'Welcome back!' she cried, trying to relieve him of his luggage. 'Vivien rang this morning; she's on her way home. If you ask me she's had enough. I have to shop. Do you mind?'

She was driving the Land Rover: a dusty old farm vehicle. 'Vivien took the Volvo,' she explained. 'She can sleep in that.' It was an estate.

Rupert did a mental double-take but he made no comment. He wondered if Flora were trying to tell him something.

The Volvo wasn't visible as they approached the lodge but the dogs came rushing out of the open front door. 'It could be Danny inside,' Flora said, but then Vivien emerged, not in a hurry like the dogs but looking beautiful and – innocent, hugging him, kissing him briefly, releasing him so that she could help carry the shopping to the kitchen, chattering. She had weeded out the applicants, she told them, now she would start telephoning, compiling a short list. There was one likely-sounding woman in Edinburgh, a widow, but that could wait. She made tea and they sat at the kitchen table, a kind of recognition between them of something – a project, a phase – being finished. Now they could start afresh.

'How was the climbing?' Rupert asked.

'Terrific. I put up a new route on Skye; it would have been two but Alastair chickened out of the second and I had to abseil off. Still, it was hard.' She checked and looked thoughtful. The others sipped their tea and Flora's eyes jumped as someone passed the window. 'Danny,' she murmured, and got up to fetch another mug.

'I haven't seen him yet,' Vivien said. 'He wasn't around when I arrived home.'

He came in with a trug full of greens, not smiling but easy, nodding at Rupert. 'Nice to see you,' he said, and Rupert thought he meant it, as Flora had done. 'Good climbing?' he asked Vivien, and she grinned at him. 'Did Alastair fall off again?'

Rupert couldn't read her expression. 'Why don't you come out with me, Danny?' she asked, as if she had asked many times before. 'You're a natural.'

The lad reached for his tea, ignoring the question. 'Saved a few lettuces from the deer,' he said. 'They jumped the gate last night. I've been putting wire across to make it higher. Just finished before the rain.'

They looked up, startled. It had indeed started to rain. 'It followed me home,' Vivien said. 'You could see it coming in across the Minch.' She looked meaningly at Rupert. 'Now we can get down to work.'

'What did you have in mind?' he asked cautiously.

'You remember the tent and the dirty towel? Chuck – our guide in Montana' – she explained to the others – 'he said they came on this tent at some place called Death Canyon Shelf in the Wyoming Rockies and there was nothing inside, just the old towel tied to a guy rope, and no one ever discovered why the tent had been left, or if anyone intended to come back and was somehow prevented, and he could still be out there, in a gully or a hole. You remember, Rupert?'

He did. He allowed himself to look dubious. Devil's advocate.

Danny said, 'Perhaps it was just abandoned. Was it a good tent?'

'That doesn't matter,' Flora put in eagerly. 'It would be a good tent in the story. Could be an insurance fraud.' She turned to Vivien. 'If there was foul play though, wouldn't the killer take the tent down?'

'Not if he didn't know where it was – he or she. You would locate it in a hidden place, where it couldn't be seen from a trail – or from a peak; you'd put it in trees.'

'So how would it be found?'

'Is he a hiker?' Danny asked.

'Which one?' Vivien's eyes were glazed, she was leaving them behind.

'Excuse me.' Rupert hid his excitement under embarrassment. 'Are the bathrooms finished?'

'Two of them,' Flora told him proudly. 'You've got one of your own now. It stinks of paint, which is why the window has to stay open. Close it a bit if the rain's coming in – and the other one, please.' She turned back to the table. 'The killer could have followed him: a chase or a hunt, now that would be exciting.'

'And an avalanche,' Danny said.

'Don't be daft! She had an avalanche in *Thin Ice*.'

Rupert went upstairs exulting. The climbing was over. Alastair had fallen off (a pity the rope hadn't broken), she was into murder again. Automatically he turned into the guest room and then remembered that he was married to the owner of the house now. He approached the master bedroom. The door was open and inside there were two beds, not singles but not a double either. They both liked to sleep alone.

What had been a dressing room was now a bathroom, shining white and redolent of new paint, with a sparse collection of toiletries on a shelf. Outside at the end of the drive the loch was pewter under a leaden sky. He closed the window a couple of notches against the lovely rain.

Now Vivien went into purdah, but before she could escape to the study Rupert insisted on a discussion. This had a very different character from the miserable quarrel he'd anticipated before he left London. With rain lashing the Highlands climbing was forgotten and it was obvious from Vivien's impatience to start work that Alastair meant nothing more to her than a person on the other end of a rope. Outside the world of imagination Rupert was the most important person in her life. He was to guard her privacy.

In return for that he told her that he must have a workroom with his own telephone line, and since she would be needing Flora as soon as she'd finished plotting, the question of a housekeeper was urgent. He would see to that and he would also take the builders in hand. They'd left when the rains came, and the new flat was essential. With one bedroom about to be converted to an office, and the housekeeper needing her own bedsitter, they were running short of space.

'For God's sake!' Vivien cried. 'I can't cope with all this!'

'That's what I'm saying,' Rupert soothed. 'I'll do it. That's my department.'

'So why ask me first?'

'Viv! It's your money. I'm not earning—'

'We had this out in London – I thought. You must pay yourself a salary as my agent. You're a sight more than that. If it wasn't for you I'd be re-writing Staubach's trash now; worse, this place would be up for sale. So you work it out, but take care of everything else for me, won't you, love? Keep the callers off my back, handle the builders – you've got a free hand.'

The immediate problem was the housekeeper. Vivien had weeded out the impossibles, and by means of telephone interviews he reduced the remainder to a short list of seven. These he arranged to see in Edinburgh.

When he left to drive south Vivien withdrew to the study and Flora pottered about the kitchen, torn between delight that she would soon be back in the world of vicarious thrills and resentment that she must give up one of her duties to a stranger. How would another woman fit into this household? She wasn't sure where she stood with Rupert now he'd married her employer; he was making significant changes: his own office and telephone line – there was a phone in the kitchen, an extension in Vivien's study, why did he need his own line? And he was interviewing women for the new job when she, Flora, knew exactly what was needed. She should have gone to Edinburgh. But the builders would defeat him. A fat chance he'd have of getting them back. She'd tried herself without success.

In the study Vivien set up her projector, drew the curtains and lost herself in the Rockies. She had used her camera only on the climbs but Rupert had photographed everything: flowers, trees, all the trivia of camp life from knots on a pack saddle to trout in the pan. Sensations came flooding back with shots of herself, mounted on that muscular chestnut, descending a steep draw, splashing through a creek, traversing a meadow where wild flowers dusted her boots with pollen. There were little lakes and grand symmetrical firs – and there were the views from her summits. She smelled sun-warmed rock and felt the breeze. She could see for a hundred miles.

Flora came in with coffee, was told to sit down, and Vivien talked, sharing the bliss. She didn't mention murder and Flora was careful not to suggest any motive behind the play of these exotic images but she recognized involvement. Vivien was working herself back into the other world.

*

After two days Rupert returned. He had engaged the Edinburgh woman, he told them. She was in her fifties, a widow with no children, and she had been brought up on a farm on Deeside and knew what it was like to be cut off for weeks at a time in winter. She would arrive after the weekend for a month's trial. She would have the guest room until Danny's flat was ready. 'I'm going to call the builders now,' Rupert told Vivien.

'They won't come,' Flora warned. 'They'll use the rain as an excuse.'

'They're working indoors.'

'They'll come,' Vivien said, knowing Rupert's ability to charm, and sure enough, when he put down the receiver, it had been agreed that the men would resume work on Monday.

The rain stopped late Sunday evening and Monday dawned sparkling fresh with belts of cloud along the slopes and steam rising from the road. A robin sang outside the open kitchen window and a woodpecker drummed at the top of the garden.

'What kind of woodpeckers do they have in Montana?' Vivien asked as she rose from the breakfast table.

'We saw flickers,' Rupert reminded her. 'Red-breasted?'

'Or red-shafted? We should have some field guides: birds, flora, mammals. Can we get them in this country?'

'I'll see to it.'

She went to the study. She made no mention of the lovely day and Flora didn't ask if she wanted to walk the dogs this afternoon. No one, not even Rupert, asked her about her movements; they treated her like a heavily pregnant monarch: fragile and immensely valuable.

The builders arrived at nine o'clock. Flora was putting a load in the washing machine when the van rattled into the yard. Rupert came downstairs and went across to the loft to supervise proceedings. Danny had left early to pick up the new housekeeper in Inverness.

By nine thirty Alder was humming like a small factory. From the far side of the yard came the sound of sawing and hammering, punctuated by a drill and underscored with the faint strains of the builders' radio. Amazingly Rupert had prevailed on them to keep the volume low. In the kitchen, her own radio a murmur, Flora selected raspberries for a bombe. If tonight was to be the last time she produced a dinner it was going to be a memorable one. She was straining the fruit when she heard a car. The dogs rushed barking out of the front door and she glanced at the clock. Too early for the mail, and Danny wasn't due back for ages.

There were steps on the gravel and they didn't stop at the open door. By now she was in the passage and Alastair Semple was advancing across the hall, passing the closed door of the study.

'Morning, Flora,' he said loudly. 'Is—'

'Ssh!' She gestured frantically. 'Come in the kitchen.'

'What the hell! Something wrong?'

She drew him inside and shut the kitchen door. Immediately Robbie yelped to be admitted. She opened the door and saw Rupert on the stairs. 'I'll handle this,' she said quietly, but not quietly enough.

'Handle what?' Alastair demanded as she closed the door again.

'Vivien's working,' she said softly. 'We're not—'

'Oh no, she's not.' He was jovial. 'She's coming out. It's a superb day, look at it! Can't waste it working. What's she doing?'

'She's started her new book.' The tone was intended to put him in his place. He might be the laird but Vivien was a famous author.

He stared at her, then, 'She'll come,' he said shortly. 'Soon as she knows I'm here. Where is she?'

'She knows you're here.'

'You're trying to put me off, Flora. What is it with you?' He gave her a nasty grin that didn't reach his eyes. 'You don't like her climbing, do you? Or is it that you don't like her climbing with me? But she's the one who chooses, you know – and she didn't hear me arrive or she'd be here. So where is she?'

He moved to the door and Flora took a step forward. 'You'd stop me?' he asked in amazement. 'My God, Flora, you're jealous!' His eyes narrowed but before he could say anything else, the door opened and Rupert came in, closing it behind him.

'Good morning, Alastair.' He was the courteous host. 'Are we having coffee, Flora?'

She nodded quickly and turned to the stove.

'I've come to take Vivien climbing,' Alastair said roughly.

'She won't be coming today.' Rupert was casual but not unfriendly. 'She's working on her new mystery.'

'I'd like to hear it from her' – he saw Flora glance at Rupert – 'does she know I'm here?' His voice was rising, the tension starting to reveal itself.

'I'm sure she does,' Rupert said.

'Then why doesn't she show herself? Did you tell her not to go out?'

Flora giggled. Rupert smiled. 'We don't have that kind of relationship,' he said gently.

Alastair was seething but by now he'd got himself in so deeply that he didn't know how to extricate himself. He must have realized that, because the study and the principal bedrooms were at the front, Vivien had indeed heard him arrive, would know that he was still in the house, and since no one did give her orders – as he was well aware – she was choosing not to appear. If he were to insist on seeing her...

Flora made the coffee, Rupert watched her idly, but they were both waiting for Alastair to make that demand and praying that he wouldn't.

He moved to the door. 'You can't stop her,' he flung at Rupert. 'No way are you going to keep a climber imprisoned in a house. You'll see!'

They listened to his footsteps receding, passing the study. Feet scrunched the gravel, a door slammed, an engine came to life. He put his foot down too hard and the tyres spun before they gripped and he roared away.

For Alastair the thought of going on the hill now was anathema. It was too early for the bars to be open so he went home. Aileen would be there.

At Lair the doors were closed and the kitchen was full of cigarette smoke. Aileen sat at the table drinking coffee and wearing an old plaid dressing gown with a cardigan over the top. She looked ghastly, she would have looked ghastly even without the fading bruise round one eye. The sink and the draining board were cluttered with used pans and crockery and there was a scatter of ash in front of the Aga.

Alastair wedged the door with a piece of wood and opened the window wide. He'd left the back door ajar and the smoke started to dissipate. He poured himself a large Scotch and Aileen's mouth twitched.

'You're thinking something,' he said. 'Go on: out with it!'

'I can't be bothered.' And she did sound listless. 'The ball's in your court. You left to go climbing.'

'So?' She sketched a shrug. 'You look like death,' he said in disgust. 'If that's what tranquillizers do you'd better get the doctor to give you a stimulant – like strychnine. Look at this place! It's a slum. Where's Jeannie?'

'She'll be over shortly.' Aileen got up and moved to a cupboard. She took down a bottle and a glass. Alastair gaped.

'You're drinking too? *Brandy?* How can we afford— Drugs and cigarettes and alcohol: no wonder you're trailing round like an old slag.'

Aileen drank and closed her eyes. She smiled dreamily.

'Jesus! You'll be injecting heroin next!'

'You're out of touch. You haven't been home for weeks, just on short visits.' Her fingers traced the bruise but there was no malice in her expression.

He exhaled breathily and his eyes gleamed. 'We're both happy then. You've got your crutch and I've got the climbing.'

'Until today?'

The clear tone surprised him – and the implication; he'd thought her full of drugs. His eyelids lowered fractionally. 'It might be as well to finish it,' he said. 'He's put his foot down. We had a talk, him and me. She's promiscuous of course, she made a hell of an exhibition of herself on Skye.'

'Climbing or screwing?'

His nostrils flared – but two could play this dirty game. 'She was chasing all the fellows,' he said flatly. 'It's not funny! I saw you grin! How does that make me look, eh: camping with me, in and out of other guys' tents like a bloody bitch on heat?'

'Her private life is her own business.'

'You're not listening! She's a whore!'

'But an elegant climber.'

'What's that got to do with— Who says so?'

'I've watched her on television.'

He had a sudden vision of her alone with the image of Vivien climbing. He was furiously jealous.

'That's not genuine climbing. It's faked.' She said nothing. He took a pull at the whisky and sat down, staring at her: the uncombed hair, the pallor, the fading bruise... 'She wants to go away,' he said.

'You've only just come back.'

'For good, I mean. She's all set to leave him. He married her for her money of course. She's fed up already. Naturally: he doesn't climb. Well?' he barked. 'What have you got to say to that?'

'It's fresh. I don't remember you suggesting this before today.'

'It was her idea.'

'Oh yes. How did she put it?'

'I'm not with you.'

'How did she word the proposition?'

'We've been having an affair for months,' he said heavily, but with a satisfaction that made her blink and return his stare. Before it his eyes softened deceptively. 'She's genuinely in love with me,' he assured her. Aileen looked away. 'I'm sorry for her,' he went on wildly, desperate to hold her attention, 'she can't help her behaviour, it's a condition. She's just too passionate.' He grinned, shaking his head in awe of his own fantasy.

'I've met her.' Such a gentle reminder.

'And what do *you* know about her? What the hell d'you know about sex? I tell you, that woman's insatiable!' He tipped back his chair, laughing again, feeling that he'd dealt a blow to two sluts at the same time.

'Why insatiable?' she asked curiously. 'Couldn't you get it up with her either?'

The chair came down with a crash and he started to rise. Aileen let her breath go, concentrating on her new-found ability to faint at will, the theory being that no one, not even a madman, can surely take pleasure in beating a woman once she's unconscious.

Danny came back from Inverness with Una Fraser, a big bosomy person in a grey felt hat and a grey coat. She spent the afternoon with Flora, learning about the running of the house, and it was after six when Rupert found her alone in the guest room and insisted she come downstairs for a drink.

They stood at one of the drawing-room windows. The sky had a soft sheen of eau de Nil and rose, and below the house the loch reflected colours like the inside of an abalone shell.

'Do you fish, Mr Lasco?'

'I might go on the loch some time. We have a boat. I tried my hand at it in the Rockies on our honeymoon. We hired horses and a guide and went exploring: crossing passes, camping by the lakes. The new book's about it' – he gestured towards the study – 'that is, it's located there – I believe. No one would dare to ask about it.' The tone was light but a warning was being conveyed. 'Everything revolves round the book,' he went on. 'My wife isn't rude in not joining us, she's merely forgotten it's drinks time. And in a moment Flora will sound a gong. That's my innovation. Vivien can respond or not, according to how preoccupied she is.'

'I wouldn't expect an author to keep normal hours,' she said comfortably.

'But the rest of us have our regular hours and days off,' he assured her. 'And the working conditions are reasonable, I hope. It's just the queen bee who doesn't observe the conventions, but then it's the queen bee who lays the golden eggs. Oh dear, such mixed metaphors.'

'It will make a pleasant change from Edinburgh.'

He looked at her sharply, suspecting irony, but she smiled at him and at that moment the gong sounded softly, just loud enough to carry past the study door.

'Ten minutes to go,' he murmured. 'Time for a mad dash upstairs and a shower. Flora holds things back until she comes down again.' He was smiling fondly. Una thought that he was very much in love with his wife.

She had met Mrs Lasco – Vivien Reid, the author – on arrival. She had emerged from the study to shake hands limply, like a woman in a dream and saying, 'I do hope you'll like us, Mrs Fraser; we need help so badly and no one else will live out here – no one responsible, that is, but it's a lovely place, even when we're cut off, if you can stand solitude.' She must have seen something in her husband's eyes, something anguished. 'We have good television reception,' she added doubtfully. 'There's a set in your room. I think we bought the best model.'

She was the same at dinner, at first. She appeared, smelling of talcum powder, her hair wet where it had escaped the shower cap. She didn't say much and when she did speak she was obviously making an effort to present herself as a normal hostess. At this she failed but Una, forewarned, addressed herself to the husband and secretary. She was surprised to find that Danny ate with them but she reflected that if this group worked as a team, to exclude one member from the dining room would have been outrageous. She noted that Danny was too shy to contribute much to the conversation; Rupert referred to him occasionally but she had the feeling that Rupert was still feeling his way with Danny. On the other hand, Flora treated the lad like a young brother.

A watchful woman, Flora, although the watchfulness seemed to concentrate on people's reaction to the food.

It was a good meal. Una thought that Flora might have done better had she stuck to flaky pastry instead of attempting *pâte brisée* for the steak and kidney pie but the raspberry bombe was a delight and she saw that this was a household after her own heart. Clearly no one at Alder was bothered about cholesterol. She was helping herself to Stilton when the phone rang.

Flora leapt up to answer it. In her absence Una suggested that they would be sorry to lose Flora's services as chef and Vivien, anxious that she shouldn't be intimidated by the high standard, assured her that this meal was special; Flora had been determined to impress. Rupert's shoulders slumped visibly; it was obvious that, at least while she was in the throes of the current mystery, his wife would say exactly what passed across the top layer of her mind.

Flora returned and whispered to Rupert.

'Who is it?' Vivien asked.

'Alastair,' Rupert said, and started to rise. 'If you'll excuse me—'

'What does he want?'

Flora hesitated. 'Wants her to go climbing?' Rupert asked tentatively, and she nodded, her eyes wide.

'I'll speak to him,' Vivien said firmly, and left the room by the door that connected with the kitchen, closing it behind her.

Flora took her seat again and pressed them to take more cheese. Danny accepted happily and in the lull while Flora fussed and Rupert sat preoccupied, Vivien's voice could be heard raised angrily.

'What is the routine?' Una asked quickly, addressing Flora. 'What time does the first person get up in the morning?'

'I get up at seven,' Flora said, 'and make a big pot of coffee. I'll show you how it's done. Sheep-herder's coffee, she calls it.' She looked doubtfully at the closed door and rushed on: 'Breakfast's not formal. People eat in the kitchen as they come down, but usually they're out from under your feet by eight, eight thirty, and you can get on with your work—'

The door opened and Vivien came back, glaring at them. 'If that bastard rings again, I'm not in,' she said. There was a stunned silence. She laughed angrily. 'Sorry!' She gestured at the kitchen. 'Chap wants me to climb,' she told Una. 'Wouldn't take no for an answer. He *argued* with me! Doesn't have the faintest notion what work is – the kind of person who says, "Why don't you get a proper job?" Name's Semple if you answer the phone. You'll have to fend him off.' She walked out by the door that led to the drawing room, muttering under her breath.

Rupert came to life. 'Back to work,' he announced cheerfully. 'Oh no, my dears, not us! Shall we have coffee in the drawing room?'

Chapter 7

Vivien settled to the book and within a few days Flora was summoned to the study to print the first chapter. The working title was *Cutthroat*: a play on words; it was the cutthroat trout that was found in the high lakes of the Rockies. 'I think it's going to be all right,' she confided to Rupert, alone in their bedroom the night she finished the second chapter. 'I've got the design clear in my mind – but I'm not ready to talk about it' – quickly, sensing his curiosity.

He was sitting on the side of his bed, *The UK Tax Guide for Authors* open on his knees. 'Poor love,' she murmured, dropping down beside him. 'You get all the dirty work. What's happening in the outside world?' She yawned luxuriously, not really interested in the answer although she was less distrait than she had been for days.

'Nothing that need concern you,' he said. 'Joss is putting out feelers for a television contract but, since it would involve a series character, you won't be interested. There are some fan letters, and a woman in Fort Worth is producing a feature on "Alpha Women in Communal Sports" and sent a questionnaire nine sides long. I mailed a polite refusal saying climbing wasn't communal.'

She heaved a sigh. 'Alastair called several times,' he went on. 'I've told Una to let me deal with him. He's a persistent fellow, isn't he?' His tone was light.

'Climbers. They think they're on another plane.'
'You mix well enough with lesser mortals.'
'I was referring to men: male climbers.'
'He certainly thinks he has a prior right to you.'
'You don't mean that.'
'He virtually said so.'
'I don't believe it.' She was laughing. 'You misread him. He's

just mad to climb and I'm the only climber around; as far as he's concerned I'm still available but since I won't go out he reckons I'm playing hard to get – either that or you've put your foot down. He thinks if he nags enough he can wear you out – or me. It's the Chinese water torture.'

'He's been sober when he's telephoned: always in the morning on the nice days.'

'Meaning?'

'He could be different when he's drunk.'

'He is.'

'I mean, if he wants something – or someone – when he's drunk.'

'Then he couldn't climb.'

'I think there's more to his persistence than wanting to climb with you.'

She shook her head, and stopped, frowning.

'He seems to think he has a hold over you,' Rupert said, not looking at her.

'It's an odd set-up,' she mused, not really listening. 'His machismo forces him to do routes above his standard but he can't lead them. That must play hell with his self-esteem – and where's his machismo when he yells at me to give him a pull?'

'I hate to think, but he must be a very confused man.'

September flowed into October and a glorious Indian summer with the rowans exploding in bursts of fire among the rocks and the air sparkling clear. The book monopolized Vivien and Flora like a tyrant. By evening they were both exhausted but each morning, after a night's sleep, they were raring to go. In his office Rupert dealt with requests for interviews, channelling them into a period ahead when *Cutthroat* would be finished. Meanwhile he played with ideas for future books: studying newspapers, watching selected programmes on television, always with a notebook at his elbow. Danny had lined the office with shelves to hold more books from the Notting Hill house, and catalogues began to arrive from specialists in criminology. Rupert didn't discuss any of this with Vivien who was now 'she who must not be distracted' as he observed facetiously to Una, but Una needed no hints. She knew her place: to keep this household running on oiled wheels.

Her trial month passed with only Rupert remarking it, pronouncing himself delighted that she should elect to stay. She was industrious and although her cooking wasn't flamboyant (she didn't want to upstage Flora) it was good. She was accepted by everyone and adored by the dogs and cats. Now it was Una who removed thorns from pads, who cleaned cuts, who, with one deft movement, had the most slippery young cat rolled in a towel and the worm tablet popped down its throat.

She had Danny building a hen house; she said it was ridiculous that they must drive forty miles for free range eggs. They would have their own hens and roasting capons and she would look after them, and why not geese? She even suggested a couple of cows but they hadn't the grazing, and Rupert said that they weren't going to rent pasture from Alastair. Una didn't mention cows again.

Occasionally she walked the dogs along the path they called 'the back road' that connected Alder with Lair. She'd met Mac and she didn't like the fellow. He asked impertinent questions about her employers and he leered – there was no other way to describe it. However, she turned his questions neatly with her own. How often were the ponies shod, did they get discounts for bulk shoeing, who kept the books and coped with Value Added Tax? Mac told her nastily that she wanted to know a lot and she agreed. Didn't everyone? One day he was more forthcoming. 'He was grumbling because he's on his own,' she told Rupert on her return. 'Although there can't be much to do because the trekking season's over. I met him on the back road looking for some bullocks. His son-in-law's gone climbing apparently. He left today for a week.'

'Who left?' Vivien asked, entering the kitchen.

'Alastair,' Rupert told her. 'He's away for a week.'

She was silent, absorbing this, then she came to a decision. 'Right, I'm riding tomorrow. I've been dying to get on a horse, to have the feel of it again. I need it. *Cutthroat*'s all horse travel.'

'We could have gone any time,' Rupert pointed out. 'There must be heaps of stables round the Beauly Firth.'

'No good. It has to be wild country. We'll do the Corrie Ba loop: all of us. Make a day of it.'

Una declined but Flora was eager to go and an appointment was fixed with Mac by telephone. Three of them, Vivien, Rupert and Flora, left next morning, taking a packed lunch.

Rupert was curious to see the big house although he disliked

Alastair so much he knew the antipathy would extend to his home, and he was right. Lair appeared as they came up the drive, overpowered by trees and half-obscured by huge shrubs. It was larger and taller than Alder, with an angled tower at the corner above the drive and a row of dormer windows. It should have been impressive but there was an ominous sag to the slates and layers of whitewash were flaking off like bark. The lower windows might be well-proportioned but only a few panes were visible above the rhododendrons. There was a glimpse of a portico in front but the cats crouched at a side door indicated that this was the only entrance in use. There was no sign of Aileen.

The MacDonnells' house was almost a hundred yards distant, beyond a stable yard. It was a simple croft cottage: two up and two down, with a small fenced garden in which Michaelmas daisies were on their last legs. Like the big house it was overshadowed by trees, many of them conifers. Both places must be miserably dark inside.

Three ponies were waiting for them. Mac appeared, and saw to it that their girths were tight when they were mounted, his eyebrows raised suggestively as he observed each person's seat.

Vivien led off, following a route used by the trekkers, stopping for a blow at the top of the first steep rise above Lair. She was euphoric. 'What we should do next spring,' she said, 'is take a pack-pony and a tent and some food and ride north until we come to Cape Wrath.'

'Nights in the heather in Scotland?' Flora jeered. 'It can rain for days.'

'We could go back to Montana,' Rupert suggested. 'Or we could try Wyoming.'

'Now you're talking.' Vivien turned approving eyes on him.

They continued in single file, the ponies plodding along a route they knew well. They were tough little beasts, sure-footed and well-muscled, accustomed to bringing deer down off the hill; there was nothing for the rider to do but enjoy the scenery.

They were riding up a bare glen where the only trees were hardwoods on the banks of a burn. Ahead of them was a pass with mountains on either side. There was a sprinkling of snow on the tops but down here in the glen the sunshine was balmy and they rode without coats.

The pass was approached by zigzags which the ponies climbed

without a halt. The crest was sudden and sharp: a small-scale col a world away from the wide stony saddles of the Rockies. On the other side was a high basin with a large loch and a few scattered lochans still and black among the rocks. This was Corrie Ba and it was enclosed by lateral ridges like long arms. Beyond, in the north, mountains were heaped on mountains in receding shades of grey. In the bowl of the corrie there were glimpses of a path that appeared as a dark line on turf, a pale streak on bedrock.

'There are two paths,' Vivien said. 'One continues north to another glen and on – to Cape Wrath' – her eyes danced; she was revelling in the country – 'we take the one that crosses the ridge, there, this side of Creag Dubh. That's the big black cliff.'

The lateral ridge on their left was broken by a buttress that didn't look all that big. This side of it, and rather lower than its summit, the ridge was rounded and grassy and the line of a path could be made out rising in a long diagonal.

'We cross there,' Vivien said: 'descend into the next corrie, turn at an angle and come back over this main ridge on the far side of Garsven. That's this peak above us. We shall have ridden right round it, crossing three passes. Next summer we'll go to the top.'

The ponies minced downwards and, reaching the comparatively level corrie floor, stepped out gaily, only to be checked on the shore of a lochan. The riders dismounted to eat lunch. Rupert noticed Vivien looking at the sky but it was Flora who said casually, 'Rain's not forecast till this evening.'

'The front's moving quickly,' Vivien said. 'And rain will be snow on the tops.'

'Not at our level surely.'

'Where did Una say Alastair had gone?'

'You're never bothered about him!' Flora was astounded. 'I don't know where he went. Who cares?'

Vivien's eyes were on the black cliff. From this point Rupert could see that its base wasn't in the corrie but out of sight, on a lower level. This was a hanging corrie with a long drop below its lip.

'There are some routes on that,' Vivien said, seeing that the cliff had claimed his attention. 'They're quite hard. He wouldn't be there.'

'You don't think he's had an accident!' Flora was incredulous.

'Of course not. He hasn't been gone long enough. What I meant was he'd never go there. He's gone to Glen Coe or Skye where he might be able to pick up someone to climb with.'

They packed the saddle bags and continued, rising to the grassy ridge, the whole of Creag Dubh now visible below on their right: about five hundred feet high, Vivien said. It was impressively steep but somewhat vegetated, with a field of jumbled boulders at its foot.

They crossed the ridge, descended to another corrie, bearing left under the mighty buttresses that formed the north face of Garsven – 'Great ice climbing there in a good season,' Vivien observed – and they came to the last pass.

They halted on top. Several hundred feet below them a little green pool was set in a saucer of bumpy rock, its outlet flowing down a glen to trees, a glimpse of white walls and a smear of smoke rising in the still air from Alder's chimneys. As they moved off again an eagle flew out from the headwall and circled lazily, coming so close on its first pass that they could see its head turned to survey them. Vivien said it nested in this corrie.

Mac met them on the return. They were tired after the ride and their thighs were sore. Vivien dismounted, threw her halter over the hitching rail and started across the yard, feeling in her pocket. 'I'll see Aileen,' she called to the others. 'I'll only be a minute.'

'Ye can give me the cheque,' Mac shouted.

She stopped, frowning. Flora, pushing up a stirrup iron, paused and stared.

'I'll take the cheque across,' Mac persisted.

'Alastair runs the business,' Vivien said coldly and moved off again.

'No—' Mac dropped a saddle and hurried after her. She turned. 'Ye don't want to see her,' he said, then he grinned and shrugged. 'Have it your way,' he grunted, and went back to the saddle.

Vivien's lips tightened but she continued across the yard. Mac avoided the others' eyes and went to the tack-room. Flora and Rupert busied themselves with their bridles.

Vivien opened the side door of the big house and shouted. There was a rattle of china but no one replied.

'Aileen?' She advanced along the dark passage to the open door of the kitchen. Jeannie MacDonnell, in a pink overall, was standing on the far side of the scrubbed table, two cups and saucers in front of her and the kettle spouting steam on the Aga.

Jeannie was a stout woman with permed grey hair and a dumpling face. Normally she had the capable air of a woman who had run a big Highland house for decades; she didn't look incompetent now but Vivien knew from the lack of greeting and the intense stare that something was wrong.

'Good afternoon, Jeannie.' She was cheerful. 'Where's Aileen?'

'She's sick.' Jeannie's lips hardly moved.

Vivien looked meaningly at the table. No tray. If Aileen were in bed Jeannie would use a tray. 'I want to pay her for the ride. What's wrong with her? Mac's mighty protective all of a sudden.'

'Who would he be protecting?'

'Aileen?'

Jeannie's eyes wandered: to the window that looked towards the stable yard, back to the table. Behind her the lid of the kettle chattered. She turned and filled the teapot that stood on the side of the stove. She looked at Vivien. 'Ye'll take a cup of tea,' she said resignedly, as if she were announcing a death.

'What's wrong with Aileen?' Vivien was impatient.

'Alastair's away to Glen Coe, or somewhere. She thought he'd gone with you.'

Vivien snorted in amazement. 'But we arranged to ride last night! She knows I didn't go climbing – that he isn't with me.'

'You were.' The tone was soft but it was an accusation. 'She's highly strung,' Jeannie went on. 'And him – you know what he's like: he lives for the mountains. She makes a fuss. He's away a lot.'

Vivien stifled a sigh. She had no time for martyrdom. She looked round the kitchen: neat, clean and warm, and kept that way by Jeannie, not by Aileen. Doormats, both of them.

'You do too much,' she observed. 'Running two houses and catering for the pony-trekkers. You'll be glad the season's over and you can have a rest.'

Jeannie poured tea and handed the milk jug across the table. 'She's having a bad time,' she said. 'Doctor put her on tranquillizers and sleeping pills – for all the good it does.'

Vivien stared. 'What on earth's wrong?'

Jeannie looked away. She said uncertainly, 'I try to bring her out of it but she's got this idea into her head, you see, and he encourages it; but I been telling her, he's teasing, isn't he, being spiteful, it's the way he is. There's nothing in it, I tell her; it's all your imagination, I say.'

'What's her imagination, for Heaven's sake?'

'You're having an affair with my husband.'

Vivien swung round, spilling tea. Aileen stood in the doorway, in cords and a black jersey, sickly pale and with a yellow bruise on her jaw.

'Wrong,' Vivien said. 'It's your mother who's right. Alastair said I was having an affair with him?' Aileen said nothing and she looked strangely calm. She wasn't a calm person. Tranquillizers, Vivien thought; she's drugged. 'Did he do that?' she asked. 'To your jaw?'

'Of course.' Aileen's lips tried to stretch and she winced.

'Flora said she'd seen you with a black eye. So it was true. Why's he suddenly started doing this? It is sudden, isn't it – or has he been doing it for a long time?' She turned to Jeannie, amazed and horrified.

'It's nothing to do with you,' Jeannie said weakly but Vivien ignored her as Aileen spoke.

'You don't get it, do you? He beats me because I ask questions about you. I'm curious. Who isn't? But he's touchy about the more – intimate side of your love-making. Did I say love?' she asked calmly, clear as a bell.

'What are you going to do about this?' Vivien asked Jeannie.

'What can I do?'

'You're her mother. You let him—'

'Leave her out of it,' Aileen said. 'Haven't you caused enough trouble already: screwing my husband, now blaming my mother? Look at me.' She pushed up the sleeves of her jersey to expose fresh bruises on her thin arms. 'They X-rayed my skull in hospital,' she went on in a monotone. 'But that was just a bump, not a fracture. It hurt as much though. He beat my head on the tiles.' She pointed at the floor.

Vivien's mouth hung open. 'It's criminal,' she breathed. 'Leave him. Send him packing, good God—'

'You're making it worse,' Jeannie said quietly. 'I think you should go.'

'But Jeannie! If he continues like this – for her sake you should— Isn't Mac any help?'

'I don't know which of them is worse,' Aileen said. 'Is it too much to hope you'll leave my husband alone when he comes back?' Vivien could only stare at her. 'No, I thought not,' Aileen went on. 'He says you're insatiable.'

Vivien exhaled heavily. 'I'll kill him when he comes back,' she said. She stepped forward and Aileen moved aside. 'Unless you do it first,' she added.

The others were waiting by the Volvo. Mac was nowhere in sight.

'You drive,' she told Rupert, handing him the keys. She got in the back with Flora.

'Trouble?' Rupert asked as he started away.

'Aileen's covered with bruises and drugged out of her senses. He beat her head on the stone floor! Can you believe that?'

'I knew he was knocking her about,' Flora said. 'I told you.'

'You didn't tell me *that*! A black eye, you said. It didn't have to be him, she could have fallen downstairs, that place is a deathtrap, it's so dark. I suppose I didn't want to believe – Rupert!' She had caught his eye in the mirror. 'What's funny?'

'A naughty thought, my dear. Perhaps they've done away with him.'

She slumped in her seat, the remark raising no reaction. Flora was expressionless, staring at the familiar view while Rupert concentrated on driving the tricky stretch – which wasn't difficult in itself, but on the left the ground dropped steeply for about fifty feet to the loch.

Alder appeared as they rounded a corner and they looked straight up the glen to the pass where they had been earlier this afternoon. Rupert had a sweet feeling of triumph; here was one skyline that was no longer alien.

'It was a good day,' he said.

'It certainly was,' Flora agreed, a shade too quickly.

Vivien said nothing.

'There's something you haven't told me,' he said after dinner. They were alone in the drawing room. Danny was putting up shelves in his flat and the others were watching television.

'He's gone mad,' Vivien said, as if coming to a conclusion.

'Any man who batters his wife has to be unhinged. Why is he doing it?'

'I don't know. Jealousy?'

'She's got a lover then?'

'Has she? Who said so?'

'We're at cross purposes. I thought you meant Alastair was jealous because Aileen has a lover.'

'I can't imagine it. I was wondering if he was jealous of me.'

'In what respect?'

'I'm the better climber.'

'He's jealous of your climbing expertise so he knocks his wife about? Come on, Viv; you're an intelligent woman' – with a blind spot, he added privately – 'if it does have anything to do with you, it's because you won't go out with him, and he's blaming me. He's lost face so he's taking it out on her.'

'It's a drag,' she mused, not really listening: 'living close to a family like that. Jeannie's all right – well, so is Aileen usually, but if she behaves like that when she's drugged, how's she going to act when she comes off the tranquillizers?'

'How does she behave?'

'Why, she's repeating what he says. He's told her a load of lies: that we're having an affair, and that I'm the prime mover in it; "insatiable" was her word – his word, rather.' She was wryly amused. 'Me! Insatiable!' She gave an angry laugh.

'You're right.' He took a deep breath, making an effort to appear objective. 'He's trying to discredit you; he's probably spreading the story abroad. He's vicious.' He changed tack. 'You've driven him mad. Women can do that. I know how he feels, but I can afford to be magnanimous, I'm the one who married you.' He paused. 'Did you sleep with him?' he asked quietly.

'You believe him? An affair with Alastair! Now your thinking's gone haywire.'

'I didn't say an affair. I meant did you make love on Skye? I assume it was Skye.'

'If you stopped employing euphemisms we might be able to communicate. That's our job, isn't it? What we're supposed to be expert at? You mean, did we screw? Yes, once.'

'Ah.' He was devastated but he was fifteen years her senior: the sophisticated old man of the world. 'That's the problem,' he said. 'Just one night and he thinks he has sole rights over you. Hence all the pestering: rationalizing, maintaining he wants to climb when he really wants to take you to bed. The lies he told Aileen are wish-fulfilment.'

'He did not take me to bed. I took the initiative.'

'Why, for Heaven's sake?' His poise collapsed. 'Aren't I— Don't we—'

'You weren't there. And I don't like your choice of words.'

'I see.' A long pause. 'You were climbing?' – politely.

'Not literally. It was the top of a good route and I was climbing well. It was hot, no one was around – and it was over in a few minutes, like dogs coupling.'

'Jesus, Viv! Is that how you see it?'

'That's how I saw it. You're being obtuse, Rupert. I'm fond of you, I live with you; outside these bloody books I share my life with you, and intend to go on sharing it. Alastair satisfied a momentary lust, that's all.'

'It's not how he sees it.'

'Too bad.'

'Nor how the rest of his family see it – and they are our neighbours.'

'Since when did we start bothering about what the neighbours think?'

'You were more than bothered about Aileen. You were livid when you joined us.'

Vivien said nothing.

'You feel responsible,' he said shrewdly.

'No.' She was thinking it through. 'And I wasn't furious because he was telling lies about me; most men exaggerate their sexual exploits. And even the awful battering he'd given her didn't make me nearly as mad as the sadism: that ploy of using *me* to torment *her*. It was like – driving a wedge between us. And yet,' she added in surprise, 'there isn't much affection between Aileen and me. Probably it was because we're women; he has a compulsion to make us hate each other.'

Chapter 8

Rupert was amazed at his own reaction to Vivien's disclosure. He had convinced himself that the indignation he'd known in London was neurotic and possessive. As Flora had pointed out at the time, he had forgotten that he'd married a climber. Now, the discovery that Vivien could treat sex so casually shocked him profoundly.

After the scene in the drawing room she went back to work. He felt they should talk it out like civilized people but when she came to bed she wanted to discuss some trivial problem that had arisen in the book. He was dismissive and she was surprised. He wouldn't look at her.

'Forget it,' she chided. 'It didn't mean anything.'

'It does to me,' he blurted, and then, grabbing at his sense of balance: 'We should discuss it.'

'There's nothing to discuss.'

'How can I trust you? How do I know it won't happen again?'

She saw that he was really upset. 'It won't happen again,' she assured him. 'How could it, after what Aileen told me – and showed me? And you know you can trust me in important matters.'

'This isn't important?' But he knew her answer.

She sighed. 'Sex isn't that important. And what happened between Alastair and me isn't in the same league as our climbing together. Now I could understand your being jealous of that – but then, perhaps you are?'

'I'm not jealous!' He was furious.

'You're not retaining your cool very well.'

'I feel as if I've been betrayed.'

He flung into the bathroom, cursing himself for behaving like a slighted girl while she was so reasonable. I could kill that bastard, he thought.

*

But even Rupert was dominated by the book. Vivien now came up with a date for completion: the middle of November, and he gave his mind to consideration of subsidiary rights and logistics. A holiday would be in order too and he started to think about locations that would be congenial at this time of year, that would furnish material for the next book and be exciting enough that Vivien would forget that she might be climbing on snow and ice in Scotland.

They saw nothing of the folk at the big house. Now, with work intensifying, Vivien took to walking alone, driving to the west end of the loch (in the opposite direction to Lair), leaving the car and walking in unfamiliar country. The others walked singly or together but no one was out for long; there was too much to do at Alder. Una didn't meet Mac now that he'd taken the bullocks closer to home.

Alastair had returned. They wouldn't have known but that Danny reported passing him on the road. Flora had told Una about the man's treatment of his wife, and after he came back they waited for his telephone calls to start: Flora ready to flare into defiance, Una, who hadn't been on the receiving end of Alastair's abuse, merely curious. As for Rupert, he was watchful. Vivien seemed unaffected; she was sunk in the book. There was no sign of Alastair.

November came with a three-day storm followed by a mild spell when all the new snow melted and only old drifts showed below the skirts of the cloud. The book was finished a few days ahead of schedule, Una gave them crab jambalaya to celebrate, they drank champagne and Vivien announced that in the New Year she and Rupert were going to Texas for several weeks. The others could go away or stay at Alder – 'We can discuss details later,' Rupert murmured, and the staff appreciated that he was referring to wages and the responsibility of running the house in the absence of its mistress.

Danny was unconcerned; his work didn't change whether or not the family was home. Flora thought about a winter break, and Una was the only one to feel disorientated. In two months she'd become so accustomed to looking after them that the absence of several, perhaps most of her charges, loomed like a void. Of course there would still be Danny to feed; even if Flora went on holiday Danny would never leave his precious garden. Who'd mend the fence if the deer broke it down again? She was grateful that Vivien didn't follow the custom of earlier days and close the house when she went abroad, dismissing the servants to their own homes. For these employees Alder was home. Vivien knew that. Una felt a flood of affection; the woman possessed more understanding than she'd credited her with.

Rupert and Vivien went to London with the script of *Cutthroat*. Flora and Danny drove them to Inverness, Danny to bring back a new car which was awaiting collection at the dealer's. At Alder Una was left in charge. At four o'clock Flora telephoned to say that Rupert didn't like the stereo in the new car but it couldn't be changed until tomorrow so Danny must stay the night in Inverness. She was staying to keep him company and they were going to the cinema.

'That's fine,' Una said. 'Enjoy yourselves.'

'You don't mind being on your own?'

'Of course not!' Una stared at the phone, flummoxed.

'We thought perhaps – it's just that Alder's a bit remote.'

'I've been here over two months, Flora.'

'I know, but not *alone*.'

Why the emphasis? she thought, replacing the phone.

After she'd eaten her supper – at the kitchen table, the thought of eating alone in the dining room was ridiculous – and after she'd washed up and put the dishes and the silver away, she didn't go to her room. It seemed isolated, as did the drawing room; the kitchen was her domain, it was central, the heart of the house. She sat in the armchair by the Aga, the young tortoiseshell on her lap, reading a biography of Bernard Spilsbury (she'd read all Vivien's books). Thomas, the collie, and Flora's Robbie were asleep in their baskets, two cats were on the window sill.

It was the ginger tom who warned her. He growled deep in his throat and the dogs were alert immediately. Deer, she thought, and stood up as the dogs burst into a cacophony of barking.

The back door opened. 'Anyone home?' a man shouted.

The dogs rushed into the passage. Una, with a flashback to childhood, saw her father's shotgun on its rack in the family kitchen. She thought of the carving knife – but she called out calmly, 'Yes, who is it?'

The dogs had stopped barking and they weren't attacking anyone so by the time the man showed in the doorway she knew he wasn't a stranger to Alder. He was dark and looked unkempt because locks of hair fell over his forehead. He was flushed and sweating but he had an arrogant air and before he spoke again she guessed that this was Alastair Semple.

'You must be the housekeeper,' he said.

'I'm Una Fraser.'

'Where's Miss Reid?'

'Miss Reid. You mean Mrs Lasco? They're away.'

'I know that. Where did they go?'

There was a strong smell of whisky in the warm kitchen. She was faced with a dilemma. If she didn't humour him and he did any damage it was she who was responsible. Cunning was called for; he was past the stage where he could be taken to task tactfully.

'I'm only the housekeeper,' she said. 'Mrs Lasco doesn't discuss her business with me. Can I take a message, Mr – ?'

'Semple.' He grinned unpleasantly. 'I own the land.' He said it as if Alder were still part of his estate.

She took a pad and pen from the dresser. 'What shall I say? Or would you prefer to write it?' She pushed the pad across the table.

'When's she coming back?'

'She didn't say.'

'Flora will know.'

'That's so. As her secretary Flora would know her arrangements.'

'So when's Flora coming back?'

She drew in her breath sharply but said nothing, waiting for more. He watched her and he grinned again. 'Danny too,' he said softly. 'The queer bugger.'

Her expression hardened. 'Danny is a colleague of mine, and a friend. I'll ask you to mind your manners in this house, Mr Semple, and next time you come calling I'll have you remember that you don't own Alder Lodge any longer, and you'll knock before entering.' Her eyes were very bright.

His grin had faded. 'Tell your mistress I called,' he said. 'Tell her I'm back, and we're going out soon as she returns, and I'm not taking no for an answer this time. That goes for her old man too.' He hesitated. 'I don't suppose you're aware of the situation here' – he shook his head – 'no, you're just a paid hand. You don't know what you've walked into. *Mrs* Lasco' – he snorted in contempt – 'she's my mistress just as much as yours. Come to think of it she's anyone's mistress: freely available is Mrs Lasco.' And he giggled. That was when she was frightened, when he giggled.

She bolted the door behind him and hurried to throw the bolt at the front. She heard no sound of a car's engine and when she looked out of a darkened bedroom she saw no sign of lights on the drive.

She came downstairs and put the kettle on for tea. Resolutely she wouldn't look at the window – which had no curtain and no blind. She thought of the police but dismissed the impulse. She considered phoning Mac to tell him that his son-in-law had come visiting and she was worried about his ability to find his way home, particularly with that nasty drop to the loch... No, she couldn't ask for Mac's help.

How long had he been watching her before the cat became aware of his presence on the other side of the glass? He'd known before he entered that Danny and Flora were absent; he must have gone round the house looking for lights. He'd known she was alone and he'd come for information, or something else. How many nights had he been out there, in the yard, in the garden, watching through the drawing-room windows, watching them at table? We're going to have to buy a shotgun, she thought grimly, the fellow's not normal.

'Of course we'll get a gun,' Vivien said. 'A load of shot up his arse will teach him to spy on us. Bloody peeping tom! A Rottweiler would be a better idea except that I'd be worried about it taking off after sheep.'

'He wasn't violent.' Una was surprised at this reaction. She'd thought Vivien would be dismissive. 'I wasn't frightened,' she pointed out, omitting mention of that final giggle.

'I'm not frightened,' Vivien protested. 'I want to teach him a lesson.'

Alastair hadn't come to Alder again. The following morning Una hung a curtain at the kitchen window and when Flora and Danny came home it was the first thing Flora noticed. Danny listened to the story with a kind of sullen fury but his anger was on behalf of Vivien. Privately he suspected that there was more to Alastair's bizarre behaviour than the loss of his climbing partner, but it was obvious Vivien wanted rid of the chap so his sympathies were all with her. They would have been even if she was in the wrong. Danny had his own code of ethics; people he loved were right, those who offered them harm were wrong.

Flora was angry and vociferous on Una's account, maintaining that it was her fault, she shouldn't have stayed in Inverness.

'You guessed something like this might happen?' Una asked, remembering that ambiguous telephone call.

Flora was brought up short, aware that her fantasies had been overtaken by reality. The fantasy had been wild (the handsome chieftain turning to the servant girl when the lady spurned him) but now, faced with the uncomfortable fact that real life could be more dramatic than fantasy, she was confused. And the knowledge that Alastair could have been watching them at night through uncurtained windows was disturbing.

'He's the laird!' she exclaimed, childlike. 'What's he up to: spying on us?'

For the rest of the week that the Lascos were in London their staff drew the curtains at night and locked the doors. When Vivien and Rupert returned Una waited until she could get Vivien on her own before giving her the gist of the confrontation. Then she asked bluntly for a shotgun.

'You don't have to shoot at the man,' she said. 'One shot in the air should be enough to deter him. He'd never come here again.'

'Have you told me everything?' Vivien was puzzled. 'Did he threaten you?'

Una had gone over the scene several times in her mind and she didn't have to think. 'He said I was to tell you that you and he were "going out": "tell her we're going out" were his words, and "I'm not taking no for an answer this time". It sounded threatening but the threat wasn't explicit. Unlike the abuse. That was quite out of order.'

Vivien's lips twitched. 'Abuse of me?'

'He's unbalanced.'

'He attacked my morals? Called me a whore? That's par for the course.'

'Actually, not so much abusive as slanderous.' Una was grave. 'He said you were his mistress.'

'He's been spreading that around. He told his wife, can you imagine! He really is the pits. We'll go to town tomorrow and buy a shotgun: two of 'em. I'll teach you to shoot.'

'I was a fair shot as a girl.' Una was bland.
'That's two of us!' Vivien was delighted. 'We'll settle his hash.'

'Why did he come?' Rupert asked.
'I hadn't thought about it.' Vivien was surprised at the question. 'Una told me everything he said, which wasn't much really. I assumed he wanted to know our business.'
'From what you say he knew it already.' Rupert was dry. 'He knew we were away, and Flora and Danny; he came because Una was alone. Why?'
'Well, she didn't tell him anything. On the other hand he told her: he repeated that lie that I was his mistress. Perhaps that was the object: to turn her against me. You know, Rupert, I think this guy hates me.'
'He's confused. It's the classic situation: he's infatuated with you, you reject him, and then you turn to me, which exacerbates matters. He's in a mess; hatred is just one of his reactions.'
'But you're not bothered?'
'Why should I be? It's not my guts he wants for garters. Oh, I'm sorry, love' – as she glared and licked her lips – 'that was unpardonable. Tomorrow we'll go to town and see about firearms.'
'Guns. Firearms are the lethal ones: rifles and pistols and such.'
'Shotguns can be lethal too. That's why we're buying them.'
She looked at him. 'It's gone beyond a joke, hasn't it?'
'It never was a joke, my dear.'
Vivien was exasperated and it didn't help that Rupert should be so cool. She realized now that Alastair was unbalanced, had always been teetering on the brink, but it was her own behaviour that had pushed him over the edge. She didn't blame herself for one moment of carelessness so much as her lack of judgement but then, who can predict the moves of a madman?

They bought shotguns and she went out with Una, shooting crows in the woods, knowing the sound of gunfire would carry to the big house – but suppose Alastair started shooting in his turn? The thought of Alastair armed with a rifle, approaching one of the others, was appalling. Vivien gave little thought to the danger to herself; when Rupert remarked that she would feel more secure now that they had guns she smiled.

'Personally I'd welcome a confrontation with him,' she said. 'It would bring matters to a head. What enrages me is this *haunting* of my home, and not being able to do anything about it. I know what hag-ridden means. And what makes it worse is his trying to get at me through the rest of you. Maybe he's trying to drive you all away. That bothers me. I'd never get such a good team together again.'

'They won't leave you; they're loyal to the core.'

'In ordinary circumstances. These are exceptional.'

December came, and gales, then the wind dropped suddenly and heavy air pooled like blood in the glen, stirred by vagrant currents. The sun shone intermittently and even then it was milky, ringed by a spectral halo. People took to watching the sky more than usual and, without being told, Danny filled the outhouses with logs and peats. Shovels were brought indoors each night against the morning when they would have to dig their way out through the drifts.

One evening, thrilled at the risk she was taking, Flora drove alone to Inch, their nearest village, to hear a lecture on the Pyrenees. She took a sleeping bag, survival clothing and skis. The lecture was dull and she couldn't give it her full attention because, once seated, she started to worry about the snow. She'd had a clear run to the village but everyone knew winter must come some time and it would be just her luck to have chosen the wrong evening to be absent from Alder.

She fidgeted through the vote of thanks and leapt up as people started to move towards the exit. Delayed by acquaintances (everyone knew she was Vivien Reid's secretary) she finally reached the open air and was relieved to find the night still clear and dry.

In the glow of a street light she saw that someone was leaning against the Volvo: a man. For a moment she assumed it was a member of the audience but then she realized that it was Alastair. She was unhappy but her pace didn't falter. She raised her chin and said coldly, 'Good evening, Mr Semple,' and waited for him to move away from the driver's door.

He didn't move. 'D'you mind giving me a lift?' he asked. 'My Land Rover won't start.'

He spoke clearly. Village people were passing, recognizing him, saying goodnight. Flora felt awkward.

'There's a taxi—' she suggested.

'Now you know I don't run to taxis.' He said it loudly enough to be heard by the passers-by. 'And I'll never get a lift this time of night, even partway. You think I'm going to assault you, Flora?' She saw his teeth flash. She heard a giggle behind her. She reasoned that since he'd said that in someone else's hearing she was safe – and this was the Highlands in December, the snow could arrive at any moment; to leave a man to walk twenty miles on such a night was tantamount to murder... She could tell him to phone Mac but to suggest a neighbour drive forty miles on a winter's night when she was going that way with room to spare was ridiculous.

'All right,' she said ungraciously. 'Get in.'

She regretted it almost immediately for the smell of Scotch was nauseating as the car warmed up. She opened her window a crack. He moved and out of the corner of her eye she saw that he was drinking from a bottle. They had left the village now. She tried to concentrate on her driving.

There was a flare of light. He had lit a cigarette.

'I didn't know you smoked,' she said, recalling that this was what you should do: talk to people who might prove dangerous.

'But then you don't know me,' he pointed out. 'Where's the ashtray?'

A good sign: he wanted to keep the car clean. She flicked on the interior light so that he could see the ashtray.

'Leave it on,' he ordered as she turned the light out. She put it on again, schooling her expression.

'Can you get to her on the quiet?' he asked, out of the blue. 'So that he doesn't know?' There was no trace of drunkenness in his speech.

'What do you want me to do?' Her voice gave no hint of her fears.

'Give her a message. Tell her I know what's happening. I don't want to do anything to hurt her. She must be able to get away on her own. Tell her to go on the hill; he can't follow her there. I'll be waiting.'

Flora felt like a hypnotized rabbit: immobile in her seat, staring at the road lit by her headlights.

'Well?' he demanded.

'Yes. Yes, I'll tell her. To meet you on the hill.'

'Tomorrow. On the pass...' He trailed off.

She daren't look at him. The silence was full of menace.

'Pull in here,' he ordered.

A passing place showed in the lights. She braked and skidded. She gasped, thinking that she could have killed him had he gone through the windscreen. He wasn't wearing his seat-belt.

'Bloody women drivers,' he said, but without heat. 'What did you stop for?'

'You told me to. You wanted to think, to decide what time Vivien should meet you on the pass.' This was ghastly; he didn't sound drunk and yet he couldn't remember from one moment to the next what was in his own mind.

'That's right,' he said clearly, and there was another long silence. She wondered why he could get no further with the details of this assignation. Thoughts must be jostling in his head and when he spoke again he was in the middle of some process: '... all the time – never sure; it's the uncertainty of it, like torture. How could he mean anything to her, all she cares about is climbing. You know that, she lives for it. He has to have some hold over her, it can't be physical, he's not strong enough. So it's money; it takes a fortune to run that place; I should know: the wages bill, the new car... Danny brought a new car back from Inverness. Money doesn't mean anything to her. What is it, Flora? Tell me.'

'She needs a friend,' she ventured, trembling. The light was still on; anyone passing – from either Lair or Alder – would stop, but no one would pass; she had to get out of this on her own. He wasn't aggressive – yet, but she felt as if she were sitting beside a coiled cobra.

'He's helping her with her work,' she said.

He didn't seem to hear. She wondered if she might dare to drive on. Did she ask permission or just start? The engine was still running. She risked a sideways peep and saw something which shocked her. The man was crying without a sound: tear trails gleaming in the dim light.

'I'm sorry,' she whispered, but what she was sorry for was seeing the man who had been her fantasy chieftain behaving like a child.

'You don't know what it's like,' he said, and she heard him gulp. She daren't look at him directly. 'We've climbed together for years,' he went on. 'I can't believe it's happened, that she'd throw me away like an old boot. What was she doing? Playing with me? We were so happy in the summer, I've never been so happy. I've waited for years, I've *courted* her, d'you realize that? Don't laugh' – it was the last thing she'd do – 'and she finally gave in. She said he meant nothing to her, she'd leave him and we'd go away together. We were going to go—'

'Go where?'

'Anywhere. Nepal, the Alps... She said we'd buy a chalet above Zermatt...' He trailed off, sounding desolate. There was a sudden movement and she cringed against her door. He struck the dashboard with his fist. 'What's wrong with her?' he shouted. 'What did I do wrong?'

'Nothing,' she gasped, frantically trying to think of a ruse to get him out of the car or failing that, escape herself. 'Are you feeling sick?' she asked.

He thought about it and to her astonishment it worked. 'Not too good,' he admitted in a neutral tone. 'Better get home.'

She drove on. He didn't speak until they reached his road-end. 'I'll get out here,' he muttered.

He opened the door and got out clumsily. She waited to see if he would lurch in front of the Volvo and when he didn't, she drove home.

She left the car in the yard and went in the back way, bolting the door, then she went to the front and bolted that too. Una was coming down the stairs to make her cocoa. 'Have you enjoyed yourself?' she asked brightly.

Flora burst into tears.

'But he didn't hurt her,' Rupert pointed out. 'He wasn't hostile. He merely let his hair down – and that's what worried her: a man in tears. In Flora's book men should keep a stiff upper lip.'

'She was terrified,' Vivien said. 'You didn't hear her. She was in shock.'

The Lascos had retreated to their bedroom, the one place in the house where they were assured of privacy. Alerted by the commotion in the hall, Vivien had taken Flora to the study and kept her supplied with tea and brandy as she poured out the story.

'It was his manner,' Vivien told Rupert. 'He wasn't making sense. Not only that: he's living in a fantasy world; he told her I'd agreed to live with him in an alpine chalet!'

Rupert brushed that aside. 'How did he know Flora would be at the lecture? I'll bet it wasn't coincidence that they met. Of course, he'd guess someone from here might go down – that's it! He'd have a few drinks in a bar and then go along to the hall on spec – and he saw the Volvo. His Land Rover hasn't broken down; that was a ploy. But why did he approach Flora?'

'It's a kind of subversion: getting at me where it hurts, through my staff. I said that when he walked in here and confronted Una.'

'It happens.' Rupert was following his own thoughts. 'They know it's the most infuriating behaviour: to annoy and frighten people close to you, while at the same time there's nothing you can get hold of. If you did try to obtain an injunction it wouldn't be granted unless he uttered threats – and then you'd need proof.' He was morose.

'He's a threat on his own: not to our physical well-being but to our peace of mind.' Vivien smiled wickedly. 'Now if he were some creep like Mac with a big dominant wife I'd visit the wife and suggest discreetly that she take him in hand—'

'No!'

'I said if—'

'Aileen's as neurotic as him. That would make real trouble. Just leave it, my dear, ignore him, he'll get bored with it. After all, he's never approached you personally.'

'Of course I wouldn't dream of approaching Aileen; she's a victim herself. It was wishful thinking. What Alastair needs is a violent shock. It would have to be a very special woman to administer it,' she mused. 'Or man.' Rupert blinked. The imp danced in her eyes again. 'And don't think I'm trying to do a Henry the Second: "Will no one free me of this turbulent priest?" That's plain irresponsible: asking someone else to do your dirty work.'

'Perhaps you should go away for a while.'

'We're going in the New Year.'

'Yes.' He looked at her and then away. They were both thinking that there was over a month to go before they left for Texas.

Chapter 9

When three days went by without any sign of Alastair, Vivien wondered if he could have been so embarrassed by his own behaviour that he was deliberately steering clear of everyone at Alder. Then, on the Friday afternoon following the lecture, Flora and Una went to Inverness and in Safeway Una ran straight into him. He was empty-handed and wild-eyed and obviously drunk.

'Where's Flora?' he asked, and her eyes flicked to the next aisle even as she said doubtfully, 'I'm not sure – ' but he had followed her gaze and was stumbling away.

Flora was turning to her trolley, two packets of cereal in her hands. He came up to her and stood so close that she had to step back until a shelf dug into her shoulders. She clutched the packets protectively to her breast. He leaned over her, one hand on a shelf, his face close to hers. He reeked of drink.

He said clearly, 'Don't you ever breathe a word about that night, d'you hear?'

She gave a tight nod, not daring to look away, to find Una.

'Because if you do I'll throttle you.'

'What's happening here?' It was Una, but Flora had never heard her use that tone before; it took her back to primary school. 'Can I help you, Mr Semple?' She was booming now. She stood at a distance, throwing her voice, giving him space, leaving an escape route free. Like a snake, Flora thought: you never back a wild animal into a corner. 'You remember that,' he said grimly, holding her eyes.

She slipped sideways, dropped the cereals in her trolley and blundered away. She was shaking when Una caught up with her.

'He's gone,' she said. 'Are you all right?'

'Did you hear him?'

'I did. Come along, we'll find ourselves a cup of tea and go home.'

'Suppose we run into him on the way?'

'He's not fit to drive – but if he tried and it came to a shoving match, the Volvo's a heavy car and I'm a better driver than a drunk.'

'That's it,' Vivien announced, when she heard. 'Now we tell the police.'

'Hang on a minute.' Rupert was thoughtful. 'Dead drunk, you said, Una?'

'He couldn't stand up. He had to lean against the shelving. He bumped into people on the way out.'

They were assembled in the kitchen. 'I'd rather you didn't bring the police into it,' Flora said miserably.

Vivien started to speak but Rupert was there first. 'Flora is involved,' he said meaningly. 'It was her he threatened.'

'But as her employer—'

The telephone started to ring. He turned to it abstractedly. 'Yes?' He listened; his eyes widened, then he frowned. 'She's with me,' he said coldly. 'No, I'm not going to—'

'Who is it?' Vivien mouthed. He shook his head and raised a hand, refusing to relinquish the receiver, listening intently.

'I can tell you where he *was*,' he said neutrally. 'He was in Inverness this afternoon, drunk, and making a nuisance of himself in Safeway. According to my information he wasn't capable of driving out of the car park—'

Vivien turned her back in disgust and started to unpack the shopping. Behind her Rupert laughed angrily. 'You can't make demands like this, Aileen; we're your neighbours, you used to—' He replaced the receiver. 'Slammed the phone down,' he said, and sighed heavily. 'She thought Alastair was here,' he told them, and walked out of the kitchen. Vivien ran after him as he went upstairs and followed him to his office.

'What was behind that last statement?' she asked.

'It was for the others' benefit. It's not true. The fact is he rang Aileen and told her he was with you, but in Inverness, not here.'

'You should have let me speak to her.'

'Why should we descend to their level? She's neurotic, Viv.'

'So if she thinks I've gone off with Alastair why did she ring you?'

'Mischief-making. With her kind of mind she'd think you lied to me about where you were going for the weekend, so she was informing me where you really were – where she thinks you are: shacked up with her husband.'

'Well, no harm done. Except his behaviour to Flora. He's winding things up. Why are you so thoughtful?'

'When I said he wasn't fit to drive she said you'd be doing the driving. It occurs to me that he could have been with Mac, in which case they might be back at Lair now.'

'We'd better load the shotguns.'

To their knowledge no one approached Alder that night or on successive nights, and they saw no Land Rovers on the road. Perhaps Alastair and Mac were helping other people get their sheep down but that was unlikely; most flocks were already in the glen, safe against the snow that everyone felt must come before December was over.

For a week the days were still and cold and when Vivien came in from her walk one afternoon she said there was a great bank of murk in the north that was surely snow, and yet it didn't advance, only the occasional flurry drifted down the glen and over Alder's roof, and it was so quiet you felt you should hear the snowflakes fall. The atmosphere was pregnant, as if the North were about to spawn blizzards unprecedented.

Vivien was excited and uneasy, like an animal uncertain whether to retreat to its den or, like an eccentric human being, to go out there, on the tops, where the danger was, to be there when the first storm came. There was an air of tension at Alder; no one could settle, and it wasn't helped by Vivien's being at a loose end. Flora had nothing to do so she hung around the kitchen getting under Una's feet, while Danny, unusually for him, seemed affected by the unease and he became listless: pale and off his food. Prudently, Rupert made no mention of his ideas for the next book, least of all the project that he had in mind for Texas.

On the Thursday Danny didn't come in for dinner and Flora went across to the flat to see what was keeping him. She returned to say that he had toothache; she thought it might be an impacted wisdom tooth. Despite the hour Vivien telephoned her dentist and made an appointment for the following day. Flora said she would take Danny to Inverness and Una decided to go with them to complete the shopping that had been cut short by Alastair the previous Friday.

'I'm ashamed of myself,' Vivien confessed to Rupert. 'I should have realized Danny was in pain. I'm a thoughtless sod. Why didn't you notice?'

'I keep my distance from Danny. We have enough raw emotion around without inviting more. He has a tendency to unburden himself when we're alone.'

'So you keep him at arm's length because he may be gay and you think he's attracted to you.' Her tone was teasing but there was a bite in it. 'Don't you realize he regards you as a father figure? For God's sake, you could be his grandfather!'

'Not quite – '

'And he needs someone to talk to; he doesn't open up to women. The kid's lonely, Rupert, be kind to him. If he did make a pass at you, you've enough experience to handle it. Why are you staring at me?'

'I'm surprised at your perceptiveness.'

'No, you're not; you remarked on it when you read the first chapters of *Thin Ice*.'

'That's fiction. Where real people are concerned you have blind spots—' He stopped in mid-flight.

She dropped her eyes. 'I can be objective with Danny – oh, I'm fond of him but – he's like one of the animals, you know?'

'Yes, I know.' He suppressed a sigh.

On the Friday morning, as if compensating for her self-styled neglect of Danny, Vivien announced that she was not to be interrupted, she was going to do a travel feature on the Hebrides. So Rupert retired to his office and Una and Flora loaded Danny in the back of the new Subaru and left for town. The day was clear and, in the concern about Danny, no one noticed that to the north, at the back of the pass, the sky was leaden.

At midday Rupert came downstairs, glanced at the closed study door and continued on his way to the kitchen. He made himself a sandwich and, when Vivien failed to appear, made one for her, brewed coffee and took a tray to the study.

She was writing. On the desk beside her was Simpson's *Forty Years of Murder*. 'I got side-tracked,' she admitted, indicating the book. 'Then I decided to do a short story instead of an article. It's not bad.' She smiled smugly.

'I'm sorry, I interrupted you.'

'Not at this stage. Momentum's carrying me along. But I must keep at it. Walk the dogs for me, love.'

'Of course. I have some telephoning to do but I'll see to things, don't worry.'

'You're sweet. Anything interesting?' But her eyes had strayed to her writing and she hadn't put down her pen.

'Nothing that can't wait.' He retreated, closing the door softly.

He was expecting a call from a woman in Texas who had been doing some research for him. She came through after three o'clock and talked hard facts while he took notes. He was pleased with the information and wished he could share it with Vivien but he had to break this project to her gently. He'd got carried away and the work he'd done so far smacked a little of going behind her back. She had no idea that he was interesting himself in crime in Texas, let alone that he was employing a researcher. He put his notes away and went downstairs to find the dogs.

He sniffed suspiciously as he started down the drive, catching a faint odour that was indefinable; not a farm smell, not animal, and it was too cold for the earth to smell. Maybe it was the scent of cold itself – or snow. The cloud was just low enough for him to fancy he saw a wisp round the summit of Garsven.

It had been gloomy all day and now the sky was almost totally overcast but beyond the head of the loch there was a window in the cloud through which the sun streamed like a searchlight to gild bracken on the slopes of Garsven. A bog shone green, there was a flash of quartz – and at the head of the glen, above the stark headwall, the sky was unshadowed: a looming presence. Rupert was awed. This was his home and he was deliciously afraid. Yet his wife adored the place. Alone here he would go mad with terror. With Vivien, who knew how to cope with the country, he was safe. What a curious situation he had married into: like espousing an alien world – but thrilling; he would never be bored.

He looked back fondly at the house which was suddenly dazzling white against the leafless woods. Something moved on the back road. He squinted, the light shifted and revealed the forms of deer scattering up the slope. They had come down ahead of the snow. He hoped the others would get back in time from Inverness.

The study door opened.

'You walk the dogs, darling,' Vivien said, not looking up, forgetting the arrangement. 'I have to finish this story.'

'Viv.' It was soft but urgent.

'What—' She raised her head, disorientated. She could see nothing beyond the circle of her desk light.

Alastair approached and they stared at each other. She blinked. Her first thought was that it was a good thing she was alone, her second that now this problem could be settled once and for all.

'Sit down,' she said sternly. 'I can't say I'm glad to see you. Why have you been telling all these lies about me? What's the motive?' Unconsciously she'd dropped into the idiom of crime.

He took an armchair by the fire. She didn't think he was drunk, not to show anyway, but he was undecided how to proceed. She had taken the initiative.

'And how dare you threaten Flora,' she flung at him, her anger rising. 'How dare you!'

He frowned and she recalled exactly why he had threatened Flora. Without a change of tone she went on, 'What has she ever done to harm you, to upset you? What have any of us done, come to that? You're trying to damage me by way of my staff. Why's that, Alastair?' She had a grip on herself now; reminding him of his humiliation had been dangerous. With relief she saw that she'd diverted him, he was trying to follow her thread. 'I respected you before you started this – campaign against me,' she said, allowing a hint of bewilderment to show. 'We got on well together, climbing. What's made you change? Did I do something?'

Was that over the top? She had no experience of dealing with disturbed people; in accepting blame for not climbing with him she was trying to imply that she was in the wrong, and therefore no threat. It didn't really matter what she said, she could talk nonsense so long as it didn't rile him, so long as he listened; it was like talking to a large animal that can't make up its mind what to do, but while it listens it doesn't do anything else, such as attack. And how was she going to get him out of the house before Rupert returned? Because Rupert, given time, would go for a shotgun. A gun wouldn't be a deterrent. Alastair didn't look violent but too much had happened, even the fact of his walking into her house, her study, without so much as a knock – and he'd known she was alone. He'd been watching. Alastair was past caring about guns.

'Have you got any whisky?' he asked.

Right. Get him drunk. Of course. She made to rise.

'You stay there. I'll get it.' He smiled and was suddenly, haggardly, handsome. He'd lost weight – and he was already fining down on Skye. But she was still no match for him; she had no knowledge of unarmed combat, and the guns were in the kitchen. It would have to be the whisky: a lot, quickly; get him incapable before Rupert returned.

He had left the room. She thought of rushing to the kitchen – but the guns weren't loaded. She thought of wrenching open the front door and running down the drive but he'd reach her before she had the door open, and her action would surely trigger violence. She glanced at the windows; did she have time – but he was back.

He was carrying two bottles – *two* – and two glasses. He filled each glass and brought one to her. He stood for a moment, not touching her, holding a bottle in his right hand: a heavy weapon if he should raise his arm...

'Thank you, Alastair,' she said. 'Now we can sort things out in comfort.'

He went back to the armchair and drank as if the Scotch were milk. He sighed. 'I'm drinking too much,' he said.

'It's all right as long as it doesn't affect your climbing. What did you do on the Ben?'

'When was that?'

A pause. 'Recently. Someone said you were on the Ben, or was it Glen Coe?'

'God knows. I drank all one weekend in Fort William.' He was morose. 'I haven't climbed since Skye.' The tone changed. 'You do still care for me, don't you, Viv?' He was intense, staring.

She forced herself to sip her whisky, eyeing him with speculation which she didn't trouble to conceal. 'We never talked like this before. After all, when you're climbing—'

'Sod the climbing!' He was savage. 'I'm talking about *us*: you and me. We were lovers.'

There were a dozen responses, mostly concerning semantics; she blocked them out, she had to think of one that would keep him in his chair, drinking whisky.

'Yes,' she mused. 'We were. Did it mean so much to you?'

'Everything. I've loved you for years.'

'You never said so.'

He shook his head and smiled shyly. He was as slippery as mercury. 'You frightened me.' He drank and re-filled his glass.

She laughed. 'Come off it! I frightened you?'

'You did. You're a superb climber and you were always so – aloof. I worshipped you.'

She fidgeted with a pen. 'You never gave any indication of it.' Would he remember all the passes he'd attempted and all the times he'd been slapped down?

'And then you go and get married,' he said sullenly. 'Why? We got on so well, I thought I was the only man in your life. But of course, I don't have any money, and that's everything to you—'

'It's unimportant,' she said sharply.

'*I'm* talking!' This must be how he spoke to Aileen. He stopped there and in the silence she heard the clock ticking above the fire. A log settled. Had he confused her with Aileen? He was drinking as if drinking would help him. 'Where was I?' he asked.

'The – difficulties of carrying on a business?' she ventured. 'Leading a mob of pony-trekkers must be deadly dull when you want to be on the hill.' That was imprudent; talk about climbing was counter-productive, he could think only of climbing with her. 'You could try deer farming,' she said wildly. 'Or salmon.'

She reached for her glass with her left hand, allowing her sleeve to ride up and expose her watch. Past four o'clock. Rupert could come back early. The curtains weren't drawn. If he were to look in and see Alastair he'd be forewarned, he wouldn't come blundering in ... Yes, and then he'd come in with a gun. She must get Alastair away.

She stood up. 'I'll drive you home,' she said firmly.

'Sit down! I don't take orders from you or any other bloody woman. That's your problem: always giving orders, throwing your weight around. "You're treading on the rope!" "Belay on that spike!" Do this, do that: who do you think you are? You lost me when you married Lasco, you know that?' He stood up. 'I've had enough of this,' he said harshly. 'You got this house by a trick, it's worth three times what you paid me; in law it's still Semple property and you're no more than a squatter. I'm seeing my lawyers Monday. I want you off my land, you and all the rest of your mob: out of this glen ... and if you don't go quietly—' He stopped and gave her a ghastly grin. 'No witnesses,' he said, suddenly quiet: 'You're going to get shot in mistake for a stag.'

'We were moving out anyway,' she said comfortably, walking towards the door. The statement was correct procedure: designed to distract him; the movement was disastrous. She knew that even before she saw him stiffen. Her eyes flashed left and right: from the full whisky bottle beside him to her desk where there was nothing as heavy as a bottle.

She dodged as he launched himself at her. She saw his eyes shift and knew he'd changed direction in mid-stride, but he hadn't seen the ruck in the carpet and he went sprawling. He was scarcely winded and as he started to stagger to his feet she brought the bottle down with all her strength, smashing it and covering him with Scotch and broken glass.

The door opened and Rupert looked from her to Alastair, immobile at his feet. 'Was that a single malt?' he asked.

She was in no mood for joking. 'Bring the Land Rover round,' she snapped. 'I want him out of here before the others come home. He's scared them enough already; if she knows he attacked me, Flora will have hysterics. D'you know, he actually told me to get off his land? Said he'd shoot me if I didn't. We'll take him home, his family have to deal with him now.'

'Did he hurt you?'

'No. He tripped over the carpet and I clobbered him as he was getting up. I had to knock him out before you came in. I thought you'd burst through the door with guns blazing.'

'I'll get the 'Rover.'

He couldn't help giggling as he brought the truck round. She was magnificent – then his stomach lurched as he realized what could have happened if Alastair hadn't tripped. Rape, or murder, or both?

'This is a police matter,' he said grimly as he re-entered the study. She was on her knees, picking glass out of Alastair's hair.

'We can't report it.' She was firm. 'He could sue me for assault; it's my word against his.'

He stared at her. She was thinking more clearly than he. 'But—' he began.

'Don't stand there,' she chided. 'You have to get him to Lair before the others come back.'

'I still think we should—'

'Stop arguing, Rupert! Is the tail-board down?'

Despite his loss of weight Alastair was still heavy but eventually they manhandled him into the back of the Land Rover.

'If you meet the others don't say anything about this,' she said.

'They won't see him in the back. I'm going to clean up the mess in the study. Don't be long.'

He drove away. It was easier to take orders than to think. But it was only two miles to Lair. Mac must help get Alastair out of the truck but how much should Mac be told? The fellow stank of whisky. The obvious line was to say that he'd fallen. Fallen where? Downstairs? That meant he'd been upstairs at Alder, which involved bedrooms, and Vivien – and she had to be kept out of this: she was right when she said he could sue for assault. She'd certainly done some damage, he was still unconscious. A fall in the open would be much more probable, away from Alder too, like here, above the loch.

He was halfway to Lair and he hadn't got his tale straight. A white diamond gleamed, marking a passing-place on the left. He pulled in and stopped, dousing his lights because he didn't want the others to see him, forgetting that their headlights would pick him out.

There was no sound from the back. Alastair had been unconscious for – how long? Ten minutes? Rupert knew little about first aid but he had an idea that people came round pretty quickly after being knocked out. And there was something about choking: on their own tongue, was it? Why was the guy so quiet?

He got down, walked round the back and lowered the tail-board, cursing himself for not having brought a torch. He felt Alastair's neck as he'd seen it done in films. Then he felt the man's wrist. He could find no pulse.

He leant on the tail-board. With a supreme effort of will he forced himself to be rational. If the fellow were dead then this place was one where he could have fallen. Across the road the ground dropped straight into the loch. But if he were alive – and recovered – they would never feel safe again. He wasn't bothered about a court case; what worried him was Alastair's next visit to Alder, when he came gunning for Vivien.

The job could be done without risk. Suppose Alastair were to come round now: stagger out of the Land Rover and across the road, only half-conscious . . . Rupert turned and worked his hands under the shoulders.

He dragged him out of the truck, across the tarmac, and paused. He looked around. No lights, no sound. He pushed.

The trees were close enough to catch a sliding car but not a body. He was surprised how much noise it made but then his hearing seemed abnormally acute, and it was a still evening. There was a splash which he expected to be much louder but maybe the water was shallow at that point.

There was no sign of the others, and Lair was masked by its own woods; nevertheless, he returned without headlights, driving very carefully.

At Alder Vivien had all the downstairs windows and doors open in an effort to blow the smell of whisky out of the house. 'How did it go?' she asked, trying to dry the carpet with a towel.

Rupert had his story straight. 'He's dead. He started to vomit so I stopped and tried to turn him over to prevent him choking but he got out and pushed me away. Then he staggered across the road and fell over the edge. I heard him land in the water.'

She stood up slowly and carried a bucket to the kitchen. Rupert lifted her down jacket off the coat-stand and followed. 'We'll stand at the front and watch for the others,' he said. 'When we see their lights we'll close all the windows and we'll each be working in our respective rooms. Your story is that you spilled a glass of Scotch. We don't want any references to a bottle.'

'Why not? He can't talk if he's dead.' She sounded sullen but he knew she was in shock. He didn't feel shocked himself, only protective.

'There will be glass in his hair,' he said.

They stood on the front steps and watched for lights on the road.

'How do you know he's dead?' she asked. 'Did you go down after him?'

'No. I heard the splash.'

'That could have been a rock. He may have been caught and held by a tree. That drop's no more than fifty feet anywhere and often drunks don't hurt themselves. We have to go and look.'

'I know he's dead,' he said firmly.

There was a long silence. When she spoke she was quite calm. 'He was dead before you pushed him over. I killed him, didn't I?'

'No, he fell over the edge.'

'There's no time to argue. So what happens now?' But she was asking it of herself. 'We don't tell anyone he was here; I've washed his glass, there's nothing to show – in fact, he wasn't here. That takes care of our lot. And if he told Aileen he was coming to Alder, we all know he had these fantasies—'

'There has to be an explanation for where he was, for what he was doing there when he went over the edge. He could only have been coming here.'

'If the police do get to us, and they must do – we're the nearest neighbours – we'll tell them straight that he used to – spy? No, we can't say "spy". This is difficult; if we admit he kept watch on the house – and we have to admit it because the others know about it – that opens a whole can of worms.'

'There they are!' Rupert was galvanized. 'Quick, close the windows and doors. We'll discuss our story for the police when we go to bed. We've got till daylight at least, before he's found.'

Chapter 10

Una came downstairs at her usual hour of seven o'clock. The dogs crawled out of their baskets, stretching with abandon. She unbolted the back door and opened it. A small drift of snow collapsed inwards. The dogs hesitated. 'Out!' she commanded. She switched on the yard light to reveal a shifting world like the inside of a shaken paperweight.

Flora was next down, bubbling with excitement; she was a cross-country skier. She put on her boots and anorak and went to see how Danny had passed the night. His tooth had been extracted and when they'd brought him home she'd put him to bed with hot milk and Nurofen. She came back to say that he was feeling better than he had for days, that he was ravenous, and that there must be six inches of snow in the yard. They wondered when the snow had started; it had been clear when they went to bed. At eight o'clock Rupert and Vivien appeared. Flora thought they looked jaded, in need of a good holiday.

There was no sunrise and as the light strengthened they saw that the snow was still falling heavily, but with little wind there appeared to be no drifting. With difficulty Danny was dissuaded from making nest-boxes and ordered to take the weekend off. Flora said she would print the new story. Una settled in the kitchen with the latest cookbook; the Lascos retreated upstairs.

Vivien closed the office door and they stood at the window watching the falling snow. 'What's happening at Lair?' Vivien whispered, although only Rupert was in the room. 'What's Aileen doing? She must have called the police by now. Or d'you think he told her he was going away?'

'But he didn't drive here—' He stopped and they stared at each other, each visualizing the approach to Alder. 'No,' he went on, 'there's nowhere he could have concealed his 'Rover. So he walked

– along the back road of course! I saw the deer scatter when I was taking the dogs out. I looked back from the road and they were moving up the slope. I didn't think anything of it at the time but if they'd come down ahead of the snow someone had to be on the path to send them back again.'

She was thoughtful. 'She knows he hasn't taken transport. Then where could he be except here? She's going to call us.'

'He doesn't have to be here.' Rupert was impatient. 'He was wearing his anorak and boots; it was still daylight when he left Lair, he could have gone for a walk. The police would think first of the glen at the back of Lair, even of Garsven. If we say he wasn't here, that's where they'll look.'

'No one's going to do any searching in this.' She nodded at snow like a fall of lace on the other side of the glass.

'You'd better go downstairs,' he told her. 'You never do work with me in here. We don't want to do anything out of the ordinary today. Later I'll come down and we'll sit in the drawing room and talk openly about Texas. Before you go: have you had any second thoughts about the story we're going to give the police?'

They'd discussed it during the night and been forced to the conclusion that they had to tell the truth about Alastair's approaches to Una and Flora, even the encounter in the supermarket, but they would play it down. They were agreed that the others shouldn't be asked to lie on their employers' account, not only because it was unethical but because it was less risky to have two people involved in a conspiracy than five. Vivien would be quite open about her climbing with Alastair, but she would dismiss any suggestion of a sexual liaison as fantasy. The story went that no one at Alder had seen Alastair since yesterday week when he had accosted Flora in Safeway, and Vivien hadn't seen him since they returned from Skye. 'We got it straight last night,' she said now. 'It's simple: the truth, with omissions. That's it.'

Flora was coming along the hall. Seeing Vivien on the stairs she said wryly, 'Aileen just called. Asked to speak to Alastair.'

'Oh yes.' Vivien raised an eyebrow and walked into the study. The smell was still obvious.

'What a waste of good Scotch,' Flora said, wrinkling her nose.

'We'll open the windows once the snow stops.'

'Yes, we'll do that. He can't have told her he was spending the *night* here!'

'Who?' Vivien was leafing through *Forty Years of Murder*.
'Alastair, of course. Apparently he's been out all night.'
'He's sleeping off the booze somewhere.'
'She'll be anxious because of the snow. He didn't take his Land Rover.'
'Then someone picked him up. The police have probably given him a warning about being drunk in charge so one of his mates was driving him last night.'
'You think he has any?' Flora picked up the pages of foolscap on her desk. 'I'm looking forward to reading this.'
'I think we might try *Vogue*. We'll see how it reads when you've cleaned it up.'
Flora took the hint and pulled out her chair. Vivien went back upstairs. Rupert was still at the window, staring at the snow.
'Aileen called and asked to speak to Alastair,' she told him.
'Was that bluff, or had he told her he was coming here?'
'I didn't ask. I pretended not to be interested. But even if he did tell her he was coming here, *he* could have been bluffing. That's our theory, isn't it? Aileen told Flora he didn't take his 'Rover. I said someone must have picked him up.'

After telephoning Alder Aileen huddled by the stove, drinking coffee and considering what she should do next. A door banged upstairs, making her jump. She lifted her head and heard the wind moaning through the old house. She frowned, trying to remember if Alastair had told her he was going to Alder; probably he had, he never missed an opportunity to torment her. But did it matter whether he'd told her or not? Was it important? She knew she was terribly confused. She thought of the brandy but she drank more coffee.

A flurry of snow swept the window pane. She shivered and moaned, full of self-pity: alone in this crumbling mansion while Vivien – who'd been the cause of it all – was ensconced snugly in her warm house surrounded by people who adored her – were loyal anyway; no betrayal there, only tenderness. She laughed at the word. She tried to visualize Rupert Lasco being violent and shook her head at the very idea. In support of his wife perhaps, but against her? Never. There were men out there who were actually kind to women. Not for me, she thought, I attract violence; there's something wrong with me . . .

The back door opened and Mac came in. She laughed shrilly. She needed a good man, now more than ever, and she got her step-father.

'Where is he?' she asked.

'You and me's going to have a talk,' he said.

It was eleven o'clock when the police telephoned Alder. The Lascos were in the drawing room and Rupert was giving Vivien details of the Texas crime. He was talking about mule trains fording the Rio Grande loaded with marijuana when Una appeared to say that the police wanted to speak to Vivien.

'Now what?' she muttered, going to the kitchen.

Una hesitated in the doorway, uncertain whether this call was private. 'What do they want?' Rupert asked curiously.

'He didn't say. It's the sergeant from Inch.'

'Probably checking on the outlying houses, making sure everyone's all right.' It was still snowing. He got up and went to the kitchen, followed by Una.

'No,' Vivien was saying, glancing at them. 'We haven't seen him. His wife called earlier too. I'll ask the others – what? In the afternoon? Some of our people were in Inverness, they could have passed him on the road... *Walking?* In this weather? Oh, I see. In that case, hang on.' She turned. 'It's about Alastair, Rupert. Did you see him yesterday afternoon? He told Aileen he was coming here.' He shook his head. 'Una?' Vivien asked, not covering the mouthpiece completely. 'He was out walking; did you see him on the road when you came home?' She turned back to the phone. 'No, no one saw him on the road and he didn't come here. He must have changed his mind after he left Lair House... That's quite all right, anything we can do— What?' She listened for a long time, while Rupert looked on and Una moved to the stove as if to dissociate herself from the neighbours' problems.

'The obvious place,' Vivien resumed, 'is the glen at the back of Lair...' She glanced at the window. 'We've got well over six inches here and the wind's rising...' What had been a softly falling curtain outside was now whirling confusion, subject to the wind eddying round corners in the yard. In the open this would be a blizzard. 'Yes,' she went on, 'that's a point. We're fine, thanks: plenty of food and fuel, and we're all fit.' She replaced the receiver.

'Thank God you got Danny to the dentist before the snow came,' she told Una. 'At least this household's all right. But what can have happened to Alastair? The sergeant says they won't search until the snow stops; they couldn't see a thing now, and it's getting worse.'

'If he was lost...' Rupert trailed off. Mountains and mountain weather were alien to him. 'What do the police think happened?'

'If you give Aileen the benefit of the doubt,' Vivien said wryly: 'meaning she's not making mischief, then he probably went for a walk, even tried a quick dash up Garsven.'

'Who's that?' Flora asked, entering the kitchen. 'Not Alastair! Hasn't he come home yet?'

'Aileen's reported him missing to the police,' Vivien told her. 'Of course she repeated her story that he came here.'

'He could have told her he meant to do that,' Flora pointed out. 'Why don't they think someone picked him up, like you suggested?'

'I didn't ask. You don't tell the police how to do their job.'

'You do when it's about mountains. The fellow's mad. He could be anywhere.'

Vivien was staring at her, biting her lip. 'There's something in that,' she said thoughtfully. 'I was considering where a rational mountaineer might have gone late on a winter's afternoon. The police didn't say what time he left but it was late apparently. And Alastair's been very odd lately' – Flora gave a snort of derision – 'and with a few drinks inside him – if he'd been drinking – he could have gone anywhere, like you say.'

'Are they going to search?' Flora asked.

'They'll have to, when the snow stops. I wonder how long it's going to last.'

Rupert and Vivien drifted back to the drawing room, the same thought in both their minds: that the snow had covered the body and it wouldn't be found for days, and that the longer the interval the less likelihood of any clue remaining that could connect the death with Alder.

After lunch Vivien told Rupert privately that someone should phone Lair. 'We would do that in normal circumstances,' she pointed out. 'We'd ask for news.'

'Well – yes. But I'll do it.'

He used the phone in his office. Aileen answered on the third ring. He announced himself and asked if there was any news. He listened, raising his eyebrows at Vivien. 'I called,' he cut in sharply, 'to ask if there was anything we could do—' He held out the receiver. 'She cut me off.'

'What was her side of it?'

He indicated the door and she closed it gently. 'She asked me where we'd put him! She said she knew he was here yesterday so since he hadn't come home he must still be here.'

Vivien gasped. She walked over to him and stood close. 'Are you sure no one saw you?' she whispered.

'There were no lights anywhere. And if Mac was out and saw me he'd have told her where the body is. No one saw me, Viv, and – look – if anyone had been there, it was pitch-black. They couldn't say he *didn't* stagger across the road on his own feet, that I *didn't* try to stop him.'

'Then the police would want to know why you didn't climb down to him.'

'I was scared – it's too precipitous. I'll think of something, leave it to me. Aileen's bluffing; no one could have seen me. We stick to the original story, right? Now I'm going to call Jeannie.'

'Why on earth?'

'Because Aileen's obviously beside herself with worry and I want to speak to someone who's rational. These are our neighbours.' He looked meaningly at her and she saw the sense of it. She nodded, and waited tensely to see what this call would produce.

'Ah, Jeannie,' he said warmly as she came on the line. 'It's Rupert Lasco at Alder. Is there any news?' He listened, miming relief at Vivien. 'I've just spoken to her, she doesn't seem to be herself at all ... Yes, I understand ... of course ... I'm sure she is ... If there's anything we can do, Jeannie, we'll be only too glad to help ... Oh, forget it, she's in shock; this weather doesn't make things any easier ... No, no trouble at all, my dear. Goodbye.'

'Phew!' He dropped down on the sofa. 'She's full of apologies for Aileen. So she's told her mother Alastair's here. Jeannie's perfectly normal towards me: accounts for Aileen's behaviour by rabbiting on about booze and tranquillizers and a vivid imagination. She could be implying Aileen's having a breakdown.'

'And that could be a smokescreen.'

'Yes.' They considered Jeannie MacDonnell, or what they knew of her, which wasn't much. 'She had no news,' he added. 'Of course, there can't be any, can there?'

At four o'clock the snow stopped. Danny came in to say that

the wind had dropped and he could see the stars. Flora and Vivien skied down to the road to find, not only total snow cover, but deep drifts on either side of where they thought the drive must be. The loch was a dark gulf in a desert illumined by a lemon glow. Cloud was still low on the mountains but there was a patch of clear sky above the glen, and in the faint light, augmented by the afterglow, they saw that even the woods were white.

'There'll be a few trees down after this,' Vivien remarked. 'They can't stand the weight of so much snow.'

They looked east towards Lair, past the crags above the loch. They could hear water lapping against snow banks.

'It'll take ages for the ploughs to get through this lot,' Flora said, and shivered. Vivien stared at her. 'I just had a thought,' she went on. 'Here we are: all cosy and warm, with lashings of good food – and where's Alastair? Up there?' She nodded at the cloud obscuring Garsven.

Vivien hesitated. 'I can't say I'm much bothered, not after what he said to you.'

'No. But if he is – up there, it seems rather severe when you balance it against one threat, and that uttered by an alcoholic, don't you think?'

Vivien gripped her poles and started to move. 'If he is up there,' she said grimly, 'he brought it on himself.'

'Oh, wow!'

'What?'

'It's started to snow again.'

They looked up. The stars had vanished.

Snow fell for two more days and they were cut off for another day, but the telephone and power lines were still intact so they knew what was happening in the outside world. Alastair's disappearance had been mentioned on television and radio but he was only one of several people who had gone missing over the weekend. A walker was lost in Glen Coe, and two students on a survival course had disappeared in the Cairngorms. The blizzards were worse in the south and east and no searches could be mounted. Teams were standing by, waiting for conditions to improve.

A snow-plough reached Alder on the second clear day, its crew bringing the information that they had been followed up the glen by a police car which turned off at Lair, someone having cleared the drive as far as the road.

At four o'clock Sergeant Drummond with a driver arrived from Inch and they, like the plough's crew, were entertained in the kitchen, everyone gathering there as if Alder were in the Antarctic and had been cut off for months. Vivien asked when a search would be mounted for Alastair.

Drummond shook his head solemnly. He wasn't a local man but he was a Highlander and he knew what he was about. 'There's no chance now, Mrs Lasco, not after five days and the snow covering everything – no chance of finding him alive. Those others that are missing in Glen Coe and on Cairngorm: they could be holed up in a bothy or some isolated croft but Semple now, there's nowhere he could be, is there? You know the area. What do you think?'

Vivien considered the question. 'All the ruins are just that: ruins, without roofs. There are no caves.' She sighed. 'I'm no help, I'm afraid. What does MacDonnell think?'

'He reckons Semple's in the loch.' They stared at him, dumbfounded. Only Una didn't react.

'What's the thinking behind that?' Rupert asked.

Drummond was a big bluff fellow, overweight and ponderous in his speech. Now he turned his attention gravely to the master of the house. 'Because Mrs Semple insists her husband was coming here, sir, and since he never reached here, whatever happened to him happened between Lair and Alder. The only place he could have come to grief is where the road runs along the top of that wooded crag, where the ground falls away to the loch.'

'Then we must go and look,' Vivien exclaimed, and as quickly subsided. 'Of course it's no good now. You know,' she went on in amazement, addressing the company, 'I never thought of that... The point is, Sergeant, none of us took Mrs Semple seriously when she said he was here. She did that before and of course he wasn't here at all. I never thought of the loch—'

'Nobody did,' Flora put in. 'We didn't believe her.'

'What's this, miss?' Drummond turned to her with interest.

'The morning after he went missing,' she told him eagerly, 'his wife rang and asked to speak to him, as if he'd been here' – her eyes went to Vivien who was regarding her blandly. She faltered. 'She's mad,' she said flatly. 'That is, she's having a kind of breakdown?' Her voice rose doubtfully.

'We've met Mrs Semple,' Drummond said. 'She's in shock. So you took no notice.'

Rupert came in calmly, apologetically. 'Mrs Semple has a bee in her bonnet. Her husband climbs with my wife, and Mrs Semple thinks the worst.' He smiled ruefully, man to man.

'Ah, these climbers!' Drummond was waggish. He drained his dram and then his mug of tea. He glanced at his driver. Chairs scraped as everyone stood politely. Vivien and Rupert accompanied the police to the door.

'If we can help in any way,' Vivien said firmly, looking out at the white yard, 'you must let us know. We have a boat you can borrow.'

Back in the kitchen Flora said, 'But he'd never walk off the road in broad daylight! And him a climber—'

'Drunk,' Danny growled. 'He was always drunk lately.'

'They could be thinking of suicide,' Una said.

'Suicide?' Vivien was in the doorway. 'You weren't surprised when the loch was mentioned. You think he could have drowned himself? Why?'

'He's unbalanced, and then there's the drink. Is he a manic-depressive? You know him better than I do. I only met him twice. Something may have snapped in him. Why drowning? Because, after shooting, hanging and drowning's the favoured methods. Out here,' she added, looking towards the window – and everyone thought of the wilderness beyond the glass.

'He'd have shot himself,' Flora said. 'Hanging and drowning are working class.' Vivien giggled. 'Are you going to help?' Flora asked curiously.

Vivien shrugged and looked at Rupert. 'If they ask me to, but I can't see what use I'd be. I'm certainly not going to row them up and down the loch. Where I could be of assistance is on the hill – except that by now the body must be deep in a drift.'

'Let's hope it's in the water,' Danny said. 'Easy to see like that.'

Vivien looked an inquiry at Rupert and called the dogs.

The snow was lit by the brilliant stars. They set off down the drive, staring as if mesmerized at the loch.

'Mac knows,' she said harshly. 'He *was* out that afternoon. Perhaps he followed Alastair. He could have seen everything; the study curtains weren't closed.'

'We'll brazen it out. It's his word against ours. There's no proof.'

'We'll have detectives here next, and Forensics. There's the carpet; they'll find the broken glass. I vacuumed but there have to be tiny bits. I told the others I'd broken a glass, but Forensics will find the remains of a bottle. They'll ask why I lied. If Mac was watching through the window I've had it.'

'He's bluffing.'

They walked on, studiously not looking left at the wooded crags below the road. 'We've got to think of another story,' she said.

'A contingency story. We deny everything unless they come up with proof that Alastair came to Alder. If they do that's when I maintain that he was alive and he fell into the loch under his own steam.'

'That involves you.'

'It's manslaughter at the worst. Just leave it to me. He attacked you and you hit him with the only weapon available. I was taking him home – alive, Viv. And we hold even that story in reserve unless we're backed into a corner. Our attitude now is that Mac's supporting Aileen out of sheer bloody-mindedness.'

They tramped on, scrunching the snow, the dogs floundering in the drifts on either side.

'Mac isn't bloody-minded,' she said after a while. 'He's a sly bugger, always looking to the main chance. I wonder why he's backing her up.'

'It is logical, you know. If he thought that Alastair did come to Alder then, like the police say, that steep drop is the only place where he could have come to grief. By accident, that is. We could be the only people who know he came by the back road.'

She was sceptical. 'Aileen means to imply I killed him. Maybe she's actually accused me. I reckon Mac's got his own reasons for suggesting the body's in the loch.'

'Just go on as you are. You did fine with Drummond.'

'It's not me at risk if you play your contingency hand. I don't like that; I wish we could think of something that lets you out. Couldn't you say you did climb down, and he was dead, so you panicked and left the body?'

'I'll work on it. Let's wait and see what they discover. It was windy after it started to snow; the body could have been dashed against the rocks so all the glass will have washed out of his hair, and the smell will be gone. There'll be the bruise on his head but he must have hit several tree trunks as he went down. There'll be nothing to show he was at Alder.'

*

Next day the postman came through with a load of accumulated mail: Christmas cards, fan letters for Vivien, and parcels containing presents ordered from catalogues. People carried their packages away to their rooms to gloat in secret and only Rupert and Vivien weren't excited by the Christmas mail. The postie had told them that there were police divers on the loch in an inflatable boat.

Chapter 11

Vivien closed the bedroom door and went to the window. There was no boat visible, nothing out of the ordinary, but there wouldn't be. The crags concealed the shore and the police vehicles must be parked behind rocks.

The door opened and she turned guiltily. No one other than Rupert would enter a bedroom without knocking, but convention had been thrown to the winds since last Friday. The others mustn't see her watching the loch; she had agreed with Rupert that they must never show any undue interest in that half-mile section of road, must never glance down as they drove past that specific place. There were two passing-places on the dangerous section; the crucial one was that nearer Lair.

It was Rupert at the door; she had left him talking to the postie. She relaxed and moved away from the window. 'No sign of them,' she said, sitting on her bed.

He was puzzled. 'The postman's got the idea that Alastair walked off the road in the snow,' he told her. 'It's Mac who implied that. I can't think what's behind it but when the police come back let them make all the running; look blank, let them come up with a time of death.'

'When did the snow start?'

'That's the point: after we went to bed, hours after – it happened.'

'If Mac suggested it he could have got it from Aileen. Would it be more likely to incriminate me if he died after the snow started?' She stood up. 'This is a waste of energy. Let's wait and see what the police come up with.' She winced. It was a bad choice of words. At this moment they could be coming up with a flaccid corpse: pushing it into the boat or hauling it up to the road.

Rupert took the mail to the office and she turned back to the window. This situation was a world away from crime fiction. In a murder story you had to think yourself into the minds of your characters, which was easy because you had created them and you knew the plot in advance. In her experience characters didn't diverge from their creator's story-line to follow their own courses. The big difference was that this did happen in reality. Here she was, trying to get inside the heads of real people, and they were totally unpredictable, and the penalty for a mistake didn't bear thinking about. If you made an error in fiction it could be remedied with a few hours' re-writing; if you made a mistake in the real world of murder it could result in life spent in a cell.

Who had suggested that Alastair walked off the road after the snow fell: Aileen? Mac? The police? If the theory were deliberately misleading, what was the purpose? What was Drummond's thinking – or, more likely, the CID, because if Drummond had relayed Aileen's accusations, detectives might be on the road now, literally. They could be on the loch shore, watching the divers.

A vehicle turned off the road and crossed the snowy cattle grid: a Mountain Rescue Land Rover. Someone had telephoned earlier to say that a few people might be spared from the big operation on Cairngorm and if so, her local knowledge would be much appreciated. It was now eleven o'clock: five hours of daylight left... She shook herself; he wasn't on the hill – but then, she thought excitedly, I was getting into the skin of the innocent rescuer who thinks her neighbour is missing on the mountain – or in the glen: anywhere but floating in the loch.

How should she organize this futile search? How would she have organized it had it possessed a goal: that is, the goal of finding a body, not of making the police think she expected to find a body? The rescuers would ask her which were the most likely places to search, where she thought he might have gone – at three thirty on a winter's afternoon. She shrugged; they should start from Lair.

There were five men and no dogs; all the search dogs were on Cairngorm. She told them that there were no crofts or bothies in the vicinity, that Alastair had to be in the open, and in the circumstances that meant under the snow.

Everyone from Alder turned out. If they weren't mountaineers they could trudge through snow in the bottom of a glen. They took Thomas, the Alder collie, but not Flora's cairn (the drifts were too deep) and they all piled into the Volvo, the Mountain Rescue truck leading the way to Lair.

Vivien was driving, Rupert was in the back. As they turned out of the drive she wondered who would make the first comment on a subject that she felt was almost tangible, like ectoplasm connecting her with Rupert. She glanced in the mirror and saw that Flora's face was turned to the water.

'Is there any point in going on the hill?' Flora asked.

There was a silence in which Vivien floundered, fumbling for the right response.

'I suppose we have to look everywhere,' came Rupert's doubtful observation: the stranger to the Highlands in winter, dubious about his inclusion in the party.

'Shows willing,' Danny grunted. 'Maybe we won't go. They should have found him by now if he's in the loch.'

'Will you stop and speak to them?' Flora asked.

'I'm not climbing down that lot.' Vivien nodded at the crags ahead, wryly remembering the agreement not to evince undue interest in this section of the road.

Both passing-places were empty. A crow flapped out of the trees.

Una spoke for the first time. 'He could have been shooting.'

'I'm not with you,' Vivien said, her brain reeling.

'He'd be unlikely to fall here in the normal way but if he was climbing down' – Una peered over the drop – she was sitting on that side – 'or even standing on the edge, the act of firing could have unbalanced him.'

'I wonder if the police have thought of that,' Vivien breathed. 'Any sign of them – yes, here they are!'

Police vehicles and uniformed men were on the road at the Lair end of the crags. The Land Rover stopped and she saw Sergeant Drummond approach the driver's window.

'Shall I go and see?' Rupert asked, diffident again. This wasn't his show.

'I'll go,' she said, taking the hint, but Drummond was walking back to the Volvo.

'Ah, Mrs Lasco! Good morning, ma'am.' He peered inside, taking casual note of the occupants. 'I was just telling the man there that the divers are moving down the loch. There's nothing under the cliffs so if the body floated clear it will have gone eastward, is what they're thinking, the current setting that way. Would he be wearing bright clothing?'

Vivien stared at him. 'I've no idea. If he was wearing his anorak, that's a dull blue, but if he was shooting he'd probably be wearing an old drab thornproof.'

'Shooting? This is the first we've heard of shooting.'

'Someone suggested it only this minute.'

'We all shoot crows,' came Flora's earnest voice. 'It seems a likely possibility.'

Drummond was not unduly concerned. 'If he did shoot himself or overbalance he's not in the water, not here anyway. I'll be leaving you to search the glen.' He looked over the roof to the slopes beyond Lair's woods. 'Sooner you than me.'

At Lair they picked up Mac and two collies. The man greeted them with an appearance of grim resignation, not exactly willing but not unwilling either. It was a job; if someone was missing on your patch you turned out to look for him. Highlanders were dour folk; if it had been his son instead of his son-in-law Vivien thought he would have been equally phlegmatic – and Alastair wasn't even a son-in-law because Aileen wasn't his daughter. A stray thought flicked through her mind and was gone; Mac was looking at her, not with his sly grin but with a certain intensity. He nodded, acknowledging something – in her mind? In his? And she remembered skins: the difficulty of getting inside people's skins.

The blizzard had lifted a lot of snow off the tops and dumped it in the glen, the glen that they had ridden up so easily in October. After a mile Rupert was shattered, but no one was going well. Vivien had hoped to organize a sweep search: eleven people advancing up the trough in line abreast, but in these conditions controlled movement was impossible. Boulders big enough to conceal a man were drifted so deep they were revealed only when the searchers fell over them. She thought then that they would concentrate on the burn which, like the stream at Alder, ran in the bottom of gorges. But when they looked down into the first ravine they saw only unbroken snow, and the drifts reached the top of all but the highest waterfalls. These were draped with ice.

After a mile she sent Rupert back with Una. He didn't protest, he recognized the expert on her own ground. He wondered how Alastair could have dared to attack her – but Alastair was confused, mistaking a chance moment of exuberance for commitment. There were times when he felt sorry for this guy whose basic fault was that he couldn't read signals. He wondered how many murderers felt pity for their victims – and then he reminded himself that he wasn't the murderer, he had merely disposed of the body. All the same he knew he had been capable of killing the man. He hadn't tried very hard to find a pulse. It was possible that there had been a pulse, that Alastair had been alive and merely concussed when he was pushed off the road. Maybe he was a killer after all.

'You're very quiet,' Una said as they wallowed down the glen.

'Oh, my dear! I need all my concentration for this bloody progress. No one could call it walking.'

She stopped. 'Let's have a hot drink.' She took off her pack and found her Thermos. His eyes gleamed at sight of steaming coffee. She smiled ruefully. 'I can't cope with this fresh snow, and if you ask me, the others will turn back shortly. We just jumped the gun.'

'How gallant you are. I thought this was normal winter conditions, that I was the odd man out. One has to do something; I couldn't have sat indoors while all the rest of you were searching.'

'It's only a gesture.' She looked back at the wastes of snow where the others had disappeared. 'Vivien knew that,' she murmured. He shot her a glance. 'The body won't be found until the thaw,' she went on. 'We're doing this only for the sake of the family.'

The search party pushed on doggedly, taking turns to break the trail. They were following the line of the path, reasoning that if the man had come up this glen he would most likely have been taking the easiest route – and a search had to start somewhere.

At three o'clock they stopped at the foot of a rise, having progressed less than three miles. Vivien saw that two of the men were slumped over their axes oblivious to their surroundings. They were searching for a dead man who wasn't even here; she'd certainly put her back into the subterfuge, she thought bitterly, she'd taken these chaps to the brink of collapse.

'It's hopeless,' she said, and met Mac's eye. 'What do you say, Mac?' He could say what he liked; they were turning back.

'We'd only find him by luck,' he agreed. 'And I'm thinking we'll no' be lucky today. And it'll be dark shortly.' The glen was already in shadow and there was a touch of gold in the light on the high snowfields.

'We'll take a different line on the way down,' she said. 'And watch your ankles. Carrying a loaded stretcher through this lot wouldn't be funny.'

It was past six o'clock when they returned to Alder. There was a strange car outside the front door but Flora and Danny were too tired to speculate on the identity of the visitors. They went in the house by the back door to collapse on chairs at the kitchen table, making no move to unzip their gaiters.

Una had been preparing dinner but the whisky bottle was on the table and in no time she'd set a dram before each and a pint mug of tea. She stood back and surveyed them.

'We're fit,' Vivien assured her. 'No bones broken, but a fine crop of bruises between us. You should have seen a couple of those guys from the team; they can't go out in these conditions again, it's asking too much. Of everybody,' she added, then: 'How's Rupert?'

'He recovered,' Una said. 'We had baths as soon as we got in. There are a couple of police in the drawing room. One of them's a girl.'

'Oh. Did they find anything in the loch?'

'No.'

'You must be exhausted!' Rupert stood in the doorway, flushed and smiling, exuding admiration at their fortitude.

'I'm sorry' – Vivien ignored a shadow in the passage behind him – 'I didn't realize how bad it would be. Everyone's worn out.'

'But no sign of him?'

'None. We'll keep trying. We'll find him eventually – if he's on the hill, that is.'

'Not necessarily.' Flora, her back to the door, was pouring herself a second dram. Only Vivien was aware that there were people behind Rupert. 'There was that lad on Ben Nevis,' Flora went on: 'He's never been found, and never will be now – not whole, I mean. That was way back in the forties; even the bones will have disintegrated.'

'There are people all over the Ben in summer.' Danny was intrigued. 'How could they miss him?'

'He'd be in a gully where no one goes—' She stopped short as she realized they weren't listening. A man and a woman had appeared beside Rupert. Neither was in uniform.

Vivien stood up, politely expectant but haggard with the strain of the day. Rupert glanced at the whisky bottle but there was no way he could signal to her to go easy on the drink. He introduced the detectives; the man was an inspector called Binnie, the woman was Detective Sergeant Forsyth. Vivien asked them to take a dram. Binnie declined for both of them. 'Could we have a word?' he asked.

She looked round the kitchen as if wondering if it were suitable for 'a word'. Flora stood up, flustered, and glared at Danny who started to struggle to his feet.

'Sit down,' Vivien ordered. 'We'll go to the drawing room. Take your time. We'll eat when we're ready, Una.'

Rupert turned and shepherded the detectives along the passage. Vivien started to work her gaiters loose.

'You have a bath,' Flora hissed indignantly. 'Don't let them push you around.'

Vivien grinned and winked at her.

She padded upstairs and washed her face, noting with grim satisfaction how ravaged she looked: tough as old boots, with sunken eyes, and never in a million years seductive. In the bathroom she hesitated, eyeing the bath. No, that would be going too far, to make them wait while she soaked. It would be natural behaviour for a person who had been fighting drifts for five hours, but not prudent for a potential murder suspect about to be interviewed by the CID. She pulled on bulky cords and an old brown jersey and went downstairs.

'Here you are,' Rupert exclaimed facetiously, standing as she entered her drawing room, not turning a hair at what he knew was a deliberate attempt at dowdiness. 'Come to the fire and get warm.' He went to the sideboard.

Binnie had stood up and she smiled approvingly. Good manners. She sat down with a sigh and Rupert brought her a Scotch and water. She always drank her Scotch neat. She turned her tired smile on him and he smiled back. No signals that the police might recognize: only an adulterated whisky which meant: watch the alcohol, these two are trouble. And, she reflected, he'd already talked to them and she had no knowledge of what had been said; she'd have to play this one very carefully.

They faced her, sitting at opposite ends of the big sofa on the other side of the fire. Rupert had taken an easy chair at right angles to them. Binnie allowed her to savour her drink for a moment during which she regarded them across her glass; the man: lean and dark, wasted like a jockey; the woman: very young, she saw now; she looked eighteen but she must be older, must be experienced to be a detective sergeant. She was a blonde with short, well-styled hair, a snub nose, full mouth and intent grey eyes: nothing startling, just a fresh-faced kid. Which is what I'm meant to see, she thought, smiling encouragement as she might with a youngster who was a little in awe of her surroundings.

Binnie said, as if feeling his way, 'I understand you were friendly with the missing man.'

She nodded. 'We climbed together.'

'He'd been your partner for a long time.'

'That's right. Climbing partner,' she added after a fractional pause.

He blinked. There was no sign from Rupert. She didn't take her attention off Binnie but she knew that Rupert was physically relaxed, alert but not anxious. She felt sure he'd kept to the original story. ' "Partner" has come to imply an intimate relationship,' she explained.

'But that stopped after you married Mr Lasco,' Binnie said.

'No way!' She laughed. 'If there'd been any question of me giving up climbing I'd never have married. Of course I continued to climb, and sometimes with Alastair.'

'And the – more intimate relationship?'

She shook her head. 'You've been listening to his wife. Alastair and I weren't on those terms. I said he was a climbing partner but even that's a distortion. I climbed with him when there was no one else around. He wouldn't have been my first choice.'

'You chose him?'

He was talking in innuendoes and it annoyed her. 'Figure of speech,' she said impatiently. 'I meant if there had been some good climbers around I'd have gone with one of them. Alastair was a steady second—' She stopped. Climbing shop: they wouldn't understand. 'He couldn't be relied on in a tight place,' she said, knowing that was too vague, seeing the perplexity in Binnie's face, feeling the familiar onset of boredom when forced to explain climbing to laymen. Binnie glanced sideways and the girl spoke for the first time.

'What would a tight place be?'

'An emergency. But it never occurred.'

'What kind of emergency?'

She suppressed a sigh. 'If he had to take the initiative; if I fell, or couldn't get up a pitch – a piece of rock, a wall – if it was too hard for me, that kind of thing.' A wave of exhaustion hit her. She sounded sullen.

'Couldn't he pull you up?' Binnie asked.

She stared and blinked, then spluttered with laughter.

Rupert started to speak. 'I don't think—'

Forsyth said, 'That's not how it's done—'

Binnie bore them down angrily. 'We're not here to talk climbing techniques!' He rounded on Vivien. 'The man visited here.'

She sobered abruptly. 'Yes.'

'Often.' It wasn't a question but she responded: 'Not lately. Not much since we married.' A glance towards Rupert.

'But the relationship was resumed after your marriage.' He had a one-track mind.

'I climbed with him since I married, yes.' She was cool now.

'And they resumed visiting?'

They? What was this? 'No,' she said.

'Why was that?'

Rupert broke in. 'I objected. I disapproved before we were married but obviously I couldn't say anything about fellow guests in someone else's house. Alastair was drinking heavily and the atmosphere between him and his wife was – awkward: embarrassing at a party. After we married we didn't ask them any more.'

'He came on his own though,' Binnie said.

'Once or twice,' Vivien said tightly. 'The last time was when everyone else was out and he – approached my housekeeper. He was drunk.'

'Why did he come?'

'He wanted to climb and I kept turning him down. He was virtually an alcoholic by then and who wants to climb with a drunk?'

'If he wanted to climb with you why did he approach your housekeeper?'

She hesitated. They watched her steadily. Rupert was still, too still. 'It sounds silly,' she admitted, 'but the only reason seems to have been to annoy me: to inform her that *I* had wanted to climb with him rather than the other way round. And to call me names.'

'Such as?'

'Oh,' she spread her hands: 'the usual. Bitch, whore, the standard macho abuse.'

'Sexual abuse.'

'Obviously; he's a man.'

'And you resisted his advances,' the girl said, a spark of admiration showing.

'He didn't make any.' Vivien turned to her. 'You don't have sexual harassment on rock. How could you?'

'So what you're saying,' Binnie broke in, determined not to revert to technicalities – as he saw them, 'is that he kept coming here to persuade you to go out with him—'

'He telephoned,' Vivien interrupted loudly. 'He didn't come here after that occasion when he saw my housekeeper. And the idea was that I should *climb* with him. There was no one else around, you see, I was the only chap for the other end of the rope.'

'Inverness and Fort William are crawling with climbers,' Binnie said. 'Why couldn't he take one of them? What made you so special?'

It was a loaded question and she rose to it smoothly. 'He wanted to do the harder routes and no one would take him – for the same reason that I wouldn't: no one wants a drunk handling the rope and he wasn't much cop anyway: a reliable second when he was sober, but he couldn't lead anything of a high standard to save his life.' It was an unfortunate choice of phrase but she couldn't retract now.

There was dead silence. Then Forsyth said, 'You always led?'

'Of course.' It occurred to Vivien that the girl might actually know what she was talking about. 'The point is,' she told Binnie earnestly, 'he couldn't climb at all unless I took him. No one else would go with him. Now do you see? He was a *climber*, he lived for it.'

'I see,' Forsyth said, adding, with a glance at Binnie, 'Some people put climbing before everything else. It was Mrs Lasco who took him climbing, not the other way about.'

And what are you going to make of that? Vivien thought, watching him.

He said slowly, 'Mrs Semple says her husband told her you were his mistress.'

'I know.' She was equable. 'It's common knowledge. She'd want to believe that. Wives prefer to think that other women are having an affair with their husbands rather than climbing with them. They know that climbing is more important, that it makes for a stronger bond than sex, and they can't handle that. Sex is comprehensible; climbing's another world.'

Binnie looked from her to Forsyth, who nodded at him. 'Mrs Lasco's right,' she assured him. 'Even hikers think more of going on the hill than staying with their families. I scramble a bit,' she told Vivien shyly.

Rupert stirred. 'Perhaps I can get you that drink now,' he suggested.

'Thank you.' Binnie was ungracious but Vivien felt that Rupert had scored a point, implying that the interview was approaching its end. But Binnie's acquiescence could be a feint. She was tense in anticipation of the next question.

'So you think Mrs Semple is lying,' he said.

'Not necessarily' – an easy one – 'she could be quite sincere, merely repeating her husband's lies.' She added expansively, 'You can understand him: men do boast about mythical conquests.'

'Hypothetical,' Rupert murmured from the sideboard.

Binnie shot him a glance. 'You reckon he fancied you?'

Vivien snorted. 'He's never shown it.' Her mouth drooped. With her sunken eyes, unkempt hair and bulky clothes she looked dull and, to Binnie, faintly repugnant. He didn't understand any of this. Forsyth, on the other hand, was thinking laterally. She had absorbed the atmosphere of this house: big and luxurious (central heating as well as the fire), with its competent staff and elegant furniture, everything speaking of wealth and security – and its mistress: shabby, plain, middle-aged. Forsyth had read the expedition books and appreciated that they were written some time ago, but not that long ago. She'd been wrong, of course, to visualize Vivien Reid as her contemporary, but she was still bewildered that the woman should turn out to resemble a bag-lady. And that gorgeous picture in the *Scotsman*: that must be decades out of date. Forsyth was intrigued. The woman didn't fit her frame. Certainly she must be very tired, and she'd had no time to get dressed up but the anomaly went further than that; her behaviour seemed out of kilter. This was a celebrity, a media personality; she should be volatile, impulsive even, attractive. She was none of these. Her drink was large and pale: well-watered, like Forsyth took whisky when she was working, to keep a clear head.

'You must have some idea as to what happened,' Binnie said, tasting his single malt.

'We've talked all round it,' Vivien admitted. 'But we're still no nearer. Presumably he's in the loch or on the hill but as to his motive for going there in the first place, no one has any idea.'

'Except Aileen,' Rupert reminded her.

'That's not an idea,' she retorted. 'It's retaliation: for all the times he climbed with me.'

'Retaliation,' Binnie repeated.

'No, I don't – I'm not suggesting – retaliation against *me*, of course, that's what I meant.'

He smiled and held up a hand. 'I didn't think you were accusing Mrs Semple,' he said indulgently, giving the impression that he was mellowing under the influence of the good whisky, an impression that was immediately contradicted. 'Let's get this straight: when was the last time you saw Semple?'

'Ages ago. It must have been when we came back from Skye in September. I started to write a book then so I hardly left the house. And when I walked the dogs I went in the opposite direction from Lair. When I finished the book we went to London so I haven't seen him for months.'

'Where do you go in the evenings?'

'We don't. Occasionally we go to a concert or something in Inverness and then we stay the night there.'

'And when did you see him last, Mr Lasco?'

Rupert looked startled as the spotlight turned on him. 'I think it must have been after she started the new book – yes, it was, I had to stop him barging into the study. He was insisting she should climb. It was shortly after breakfast! She'd just started work.' The memory obviously irritated him. 'That would be the last time he came here – except when he made sure I was away and our housekeeper was alone in the place.'

'How did you stop him barging into the study?'

'Why – er – manners? I said something to remind him of his position, you know. He's the laird. The kitchen wasn't a suitable place for neighbours to argue.' The tone was vague, the sense explicit, conveying to Binnie that gentlemen didn't make a scene in front of the servants. Binnie shied away like a horse.

'It seems unusual,' he said, 'to be living almost next door: only two miles between you, and seeing virtually nothing of them for months.'

'My husband didn't move here immediately after we were married,' Vivien pointed out. 'By the time he did arrive I was ready to start on the new book and when I'm writing life at Alder contracts: everything revolves round the book. Even if our neighbours were congenial we wouldn't do any entertaining at those times, and as far as the Semples were concerned we were avoiding them.'

'Yes,' Binnie said. 'You would. And the MacDonnells?' he asked idly.

Vivien looked blank. 'You see much of them?' he asked innocently.

'No. We ride occasionally and we see the MacDonnells then. That was when I was at Lair last: before today, I mean. It was when Aileen accused me of seducing Alastair.' She shrugged. 'Jeannie MacDonnell said it was a combination of drink and tranquillizers. Alastair was driving her up the wall.'

Chapter 12

Binnie lit a cigarette, exhaled with gusto and leaned back, prepared to enjoy the drive home. Forsyth was a good driver. 'What did you make of that?' he asked. She was good with women too, knew how their minds worked.

She was peering down the headlight beams; the drive was clear but no one had troubled to mark its line. 'No foul play,' she murmured absently. 'None that she was involved in anyway.'

'What makes you so sure?' Why did she always make his hackles rise, and just when he was relaxed, tasting the first cigarette for over an hour? 'You can't tell me they weren't having an affair: spending nights together last autumn. Only an affair could make Aileen so vicious. She knew what was going on all right.'

'He was a creep! He was knocking her about too.'

'His wife?'

'It certainly wasn't Vivien!' She saw the frame of the cattle grid in time and eased carefully on to the road. 'Aileen had a nasty bruise on her jaw.'

'I didn't notice it.'

'She'd tried to cover it with make-up.'

'So he was beating his wife and having it off with the woman next door and you're saying there was no foul play?'

'I said Vivien wasn't involved. Sleeping with him isn't important.'

'Of course it is. You've got two jealous spouses. Aileen's jealous as hell, and he's possessive: it sticks out a mile.'

'There's no way I can imagine Rupert being violent, and as for Aileen: all the spirit's been knocked out of her. Still – battered wives... But not Vivien.' She was adamant. 'She didn't kill Alastair.'

'Oh come on! They had a relationship, he was pestering her and she wanted out. We see it all the time: playing around while the old man's away, trying to end it when he comes home – but Alastair couldn't handle rejection.' He beamed in the darkness, pleased with that last bit.

Trees showed on the right and Forsyth drove as close to the left as the snow bank allowed, conscious of that unprotected drop to the water.

'I really can't see Vivien interested in a bit on the side,' she said, and Binnie stirred impatiently. 'She wasn't speaking the truth when she said Alastair was mad to climb; if a guy's an alcoholic and pesters a woman he's after *her* in my book. Drink has to take the edge off this craving to go on the hill. When she said climbers care for nothing else she was speaking for herself. And that's why Alastair isn't important; she probably slept with him but she wouldn't think anything of it. It doesn't have any bearing on his disappearance.'

'What about Rupert? Didn't you see the way he looked at her? You reckon he wasn't interested in her goings-on?'

'That's your department. I observe the women. You know how men react.' That was below the belt; Binnie knew how some men react to their wives having it off with the neighbour but Rupert was a different kettle of fish. However, he tried. 'And then there's the financial aspect,' he said thoughtfully. 'She's not the least bit sexy but she's rich. Did you see that stereo in the lounge? Bang and Olufsen: cost thousands, they do. He's landed himself a cushy billet there: no job, lives on his wife's earnings – what did the housekeeper say he was? Her manager and agent! That's a tax dodge if ever there was one. That man's not going to queer his pitch by making a fuss because his wife's screwing the neighbour, and him the laird.'

'You're agreeing with me, in a sense. He's not violent.'

He ignored this. 'But you're wrong about her living for climbing,' he mused. 'What about the writing? She's a workaholic.'

'I thought she laboured that a bit.' Forsyth eased round a bend, the headlights sweeping the snow, glinting off water. 'She's a very intense woman: single-minded.'

'The only thing she cares about is work. And money of course. Yet she dresses like a tinker, looks like one too. Definitely not a *crime passionnel*.'

She winced. 'I'd like to go back there when they're not expecting a visit from the police.'

'You reckon we missed something? I saw the shotguns in the

kitchen but everyone has guns in the country, and Drummond says they shoot crows at Alder. So they were having an affair: what's new? What we have here is a drunken accident; he was an alcoholic, it was a nasty night, he walked off the road. Aileen's accusations were just getting her own back: at her old man as well as Vivien. For all we know he's done a runner. Whatever, we're finished here. If he's under the snow he died of hypothermia. You won't be coming back.'

After the police left the Lascos went up to change, and Vivien's first question concerned what Rupert had told Binnie before she came home. He reassured her. He'd been vague and nothing he'd said had contradicted the information she'd given them. As they talked she soaked in her bath while he sat on a stool beside her.

'At the end it sounded as if you were accusing Aileen,' he mused.

'So what? She would have done it if I hadn't. As far as Binnie's concerned she's a more likely candidate anyway.'

'You can say that again! You looked as alluring as a bin-liner.'

'I tried.' She was smug. 'D'you think they suspect?'

'Whether they do or not seems immaterial – although we must never relax our guard when we're with them, or with our own people, come to that.'

'Your timing was perfect when Binnie asked if they continued to visit here after we were married. It was so natural: the way you came in there.'

'But it was natural. Don't you remember me telling you we really couldn't have them here again?'

'I'm sure you did. God, I'm tired.'

'Early night for us, for everyone, soon as we've eaten. A good way of avoiding questions too. You did splendidly with Binnie, my love. I was proud of you.'

'It was the girl who frightened me.'

'Ah. Yes, perceptive little thing, wasn't she? But she admires you. Unless she was acting . . . However, you said nothing incriminating, nothing she could get hold of.'

'Or Binnie. But we left out a lot, Rupert. I hadn't *seen* Alastair since Skye but I'd spoken to him on the phone. And we said nothing about him watching the house – and no one even touched on him being violent. I played the whole thing down, as if he were no more than a nuisance; all the heat was taken out of it. What happens when they find out? Will the others tell the truth? Flora could dramatize it, make it worse. I don't want to tell her to keep quiet about Alastair threatening to kill her, but that demonstrates his violence if anything does. And from there it's only a step for Binnie to guess that force might have been used as a defence against him: violence breeding violence.'

'Quite. But he battered Aileen, remember.'

'She's not going to tell the police. Jeannie might,' she mused. 'Or Mac.'

'Viv! They don't suspect murder, not seriously. They had to come here because Aileen told them you were Alastair's lover, and for my money they don't believe your denial' – he paused. Vivien was expressionless – 'But there's nothing they can do without a body—'

'Oh yes there is—'

'Not without evidence, and that has to be circumstantial—'

'Suppose Mac did see you?'

'Forget him. He didn't. He's bluffing. There's nothing to show, Viv; no smell in the study' – he dismissed the possibility of glass splinters in the carpet – 'there's nothing to show there is a body.' Another thought occurred to him. 'Why hasn't anyone suggested he might have disappeared of his own volition: to escape debts, his wife, the whole shebang? He could be with distant relatives in South America right now.'

She looked at him blankly. 'You forget he didn't take a vehicle,' she said, sinking lower in the bath, wondering where Alastair was: still under the snow, caught in roots where the divers hadn't searched, or somewhere out in the North Sea where he'd sink quite quickly and be eaten by the crabs?

Christmas came and went, and the New Year: festivals made more exciting – and more secure – by fresh snowfalls, the Lascos knowing that the more time that elapsed before the body was found, the fewer clues would survive to point to the killer.

The big searches in Glen Coe and the Cairngorms had ended with the students discovered alive in a tent by Loch Avon and the Glen Coe walker found dead below a waterfall. There was some discussion concerning a renewed search for Alastair but it was decided to accept Aileen's version of events (or the first part of it): that he had set out for Alder. So it was assumed that, by accident or design, he had fallen from the road into the loch. The police divers were agreed that the body wasn't floating in the loch itself so now the only course of action that remained was a general request to farmers and others to keep a look-out for it along the banks of the river that left the loch at its eastern end.

At Alder Rupert and Vivien held anguished discussions about Texas; they were due to leave shortly. If they left, did that look like a guilty action? On the other hand, if they cancelled the trip and the body was found and Binnie came back, would he think they wanted to be on the spot, the better to coach their employees if they were subjected to police interrogation? Which was exactly what the Lascos were afraid of: the body being found while they were abroad. However, as speculation about Alastair's fate receded, Texas became the focus of attention. Una and Danny planned to stay at Alder but Flora had booked a skiing holiday in Norway. If the Lascos cancelled the police might wonder why their plans were changed after Alastair disappeared.

'We have to go,' Rupert insisted. 'We must carry on as usual. It's going to be fraught, always wondering if the body's been found, but we'll keep in touch with Una. We'll compromise: come back after two or three weeks, and then we can go again later, when it's all blown over.'

So they simulated a mood of excitement, letting it be widely known that they were going to the States on a working trip, Vivien wondering if there would be a call from Binnie suggesting they remain in Scotland, even telling them to surrender their passports. But there was no move from the police. 'You're thinking like a guilty person,' Rupert told her. 'I am a guilty person,' she reminded him. And, 'That's what you have to put behind you,' he said.

Texas was different: spacious, bleak but thrilling; for long periods Vivien forgot those snowy northern wastes. Texas was immediate: the Rio Grande and its fords where the mule trains crossed, loaded with drugs, where the Lascos forded, splashing through the river on horseback to primitive Mexican villages where they were regarded with suspicion by the adults and eagerness by beautiful children, too proud to beg, who offered them coloured chips of rock in exchange for a few cents. They were agreed that, in fiction, the children would be look-outs for the drug gangs.

They rang Alder. At first Vivien pretended to be curious about the contents of the mail but they knew that frequent calls would be suspect, if the police ever had cause to check, because their business contacts knew they were abroad. So she let several days go by and when she rang again nothing had changed: Danny and Una and the animals were well, there was a card from Flora, it was snowing again.

She waited a week, becoming increasingly absorbed in the new and savage country. It was Rupert who called home next time. They were in a spartan hotel in a tiny town called Presidio, lounging on their beds, a bottle of bourbon on the night table between them. After a brief conversation Rupert replaced the phone. 'Everything's fine as usual,' he said. 'The weather's changed. The snow's starting to thaw.'

They exchanged speculative looks. 'It's not what they'll find,' she murmured, 'but what they won't find.'

'They didn't expect to find anything – if they're assuming he walked off the road. If the river hasn't taken him away already it will now. Think of all that snow melting; Una says it's sleeting already. That will soon be rain. There'll be floods.'

'And a body left in someone's river meadow.'

'But no clues, Viv. All washed away after so long.'

'So we just carry on here, collecting material?'

'Of course. A thaw in Scotland has nothing to do with us.'

Rain and gales swept northern Scotland. At Alder Una toured the lofts looking for leaks. A tree fell on the deer fence and one morning Danny, hitting a patch of old ice under water, drove straight off the road. Unfortunately he'd chosen one of the few spots where the trees were wide apart and the Land Rover went all the way to the bottom, a twenty-foot drop in that place. He jumped clear and escaped with a few bruises but the 'Rover was a wreck.

Una set the insurance claim in motion and next time Vivien called she said Danny was to buy another Land Rover (secondhand, in good nick) and she was thankful he hadn't been badly hurt. Not a word of reprimand.

After two weeks Flora came home from Norway, tired but fit, and looking forward to starting work on a new book. The Lascos returned in February to find their staff had coped very competently with the ravages of the gales. The deer fence had been repaired yet again and the tree sawn up for logs. The new (second-hand) Land Rover was in the yard and the old one had been sold to a breaker to be baled as scrap. Alastair's body had not been found.

Life resumed the kind of tempo that revolved round a Work in Progress. There was the seemingly aimless period when Vivien showed slides for herself and anyone who wandered into the study: not speaking, merely looking, letting her ramble on, and then came days when everyone was excluded from the study and she ate her meals in a trance. Finally the evening arrived when she appeared in the drawing room before dinner. Rupert was seated by the fire listening to *Aïda* when she slumped opposite him, exhausted but with feverish eyes, and told him she was on the second chapter.

The solid work started. Flora was admitted to the study, Rupert saw to it that his wife took daily exercise, although he allowed her to walk alone unless she specifically asked for company. There was a smell of spring in the air now and the afternoons could be balmy when the wind came soft from the southwest. There was still snow on the tops and the burns were full but down in the glen the grass was starting to show green and Vivien watched south-facing banks for the first celandines. One morning, on her way to the library in Inverness, she met Aileen.

They met on the single-track road east of Lair. Both were driving Land Rovers. Vivien pulled into a passing-place and waited tensely, feeling as if a claw were clamped on her guts. She had recognized the Land Rover and for one moment had thought that Alastair had returned from the dead, then she remembered that Aileen could drive.

The other vehicle drew level and stopped. The drivers regarded each other without expression, although Vivien had difficulty in hiding her surprise. When she'd last seen Aileen – on that momentous afternoon when they came back from their ride – she had been a travesty of her old self: bony and bruised and full of spite. She had been an arresting woman, although always too thin, and her clothes looking as if they'd been picked up at jumble sales. She was still wearing the old Icelandic jersey but now she wore it with the poise of a model, and her face had filled out and altered. At the same time that Vivien deplored her own stiffness she identified the change in the other; Aileen wasn't only relaxed, after her first blank stare she was amused. Another bloody sadist, Vivien thought: she's going to haunt me like he did, but she rose to the occasion.

'You're looking well,' she said, as if they'd never exchanged a cross word.

'But you look tense,' Aileen said – and sweetly: 'Is anything wrong?' At that she looked away and very deliberately: along the line of the road to the trees above the loch.

She knew. Vivien swallowed and her lips tightened. Aileen turned back and regarded her, waiting for a response. Vivien breathed deeply. 'You never said what you were doing that Friday evening,' she said.

Their expressions were duplicated: tiger eyes, tiger minds circling each other.

'What were *you* doing?' Aileen asked.

'Binnie asked me that.'

'But you didn't tell him the truth.'

'Did you?' Aileen was silent. 'You don't want him found,' Vivien said.

'I was wondering when you'd say that.' The fine eyes widened and the lines in the face smoothed out. The predator was gone and Aileen was a striking woman again. 'Don't waste your time pretending to look for him any longer,' she said. 'You must have better things to do than put on a show for my benefit.'

'I'm writing a book.' It was inane: an acknowledgment that Aileen had scored, but two could play this game. 'You're better off now.' Vivien's tone was like treacle. 'And you're showing it. I've never seen you look so well. And unmarked.'

'I have you to thank for that.'

Vivien thought wildly: there are no witnesses – but could she be wired? Is this a set-up? She said coolly, 'If you mean he was drinking because of me, that's ridiculous; he always drank heavily. No way can you blame me because he fell in the loch when he was on his way to Alder.'

Again their eyes locked and again they were calculating: trying to discern the extent of the other's knowledge – and intentions.

'What are you going to do?' Vivien asked, knowing the question could be read in two ways.

Aileen accepted it in the innocent sense. 'I can't claim the property until the body's found,' she said easily. 'Or until seven years have gone by: a hell of a wait. I shall carry on the business; Mac's teaching me to ride so I can help with the trekkers. Don't look so surprised. I'm fit and healthy. I had a breakdown but that was a long time ago.' Vivien wondered if this was intended as some kind of apology. 'Otherwise,' Aileen went on, 'I'll inherit debts. That's why I have to continue the trekking: to keep us going until we can sell.' She shrugged. 'But look at it' – she motioned to the mountains – 'the estate's no good for anything except deer and who's going to buy a Highland estate in a recession? The house is just a pile of stones.'

'Rich Arabs? Japanese?'

'Maybe. When they find the body. I don't suppose you could help in that direction?' It was said winningly, as if she were trying to persuade her neighbour to run a stall at the Highland Games.

'You told me not to waste my time searching.'

'True, but if you could just give me a hint as to where he might be?'

Vivien grinned while the claw squeezed her guts. 'You've positively bloomed,' she said admiringly. 'Widowhood suits you. You've even recovered your sense of humour.'

'Are you repeating this word for word?' Rupert was looking at her askance. 'She actually asked you where the body was?'

'She implied it: could I give her a hint as to where it might be, but she said it with a smile, making a joke of it. Everything was implication: it was in her eyes, in her expression, filling the gaps between the words. She told me as plainly as if she'd said it that she knew I'd killed him and disposed of the body. She didn't mention you; no doubt she'd have got around to you eventually but I pushed on, I couldn't take any more. As it was, you can imagine what kind of day I've had. I never even went to the library, I couldn't concentrate. I drove along the coast and walked on the sand.'

They were in the garden, ostensibly planning the summer's vegetables. This was Danny's department but they couldn't keep going to their bedroom when they needed to talk privately. As they talked they considered the turned earth and made appropriate gestures, aware that they were in view of the upper windows of the house. From the top of the wood came the tapping of a hammer where Danny was putting up a new nest-box.

Rupert had listened to her story with mounting unease. Now he took a grip on himself. 'It's an echo of Mac,' he said: 'suggesting that Alastair's in the loch. He'll have talked about it at home and Aileen's following his lead, that's all. She's guessing. Did you give her any cause to think she'd guessed correctly?'

'I don't know. She said I didn't tell the truth about the night Alastair went missing, but that was probably retaliation because I asked her what she was doing then.'

'What made you ask her that?'

'It just slipped out. It was after she accused me of being tense and she deliberately looked at the place – you know: the trees? She meant there to be no doubt what she was looking at. I suppose subconsciously I thought she'd seen you push the body over the edge, and in asking her where she was I was accusing her of leaving Alastair to drown.' Her voice rose. 'But he was dead,' she added. 'I wasn't thinking straight.'

'All I'm asking is did you admit anything?'

'No–o. No. I even controlled my expression – and I'll swear she was controlled too. She's clever when she isn't drinking, or drugged – and when she's free of Alastair. She's a different woman now.'

They looked at each other, remembered the possibility of watching eyes, however friendly, and looked away. 'Asparagus,' she murmured, moving up the garden. 'We must have asparagus.'

Danny came down through the wood thinking that if only she'd taught him to shoot he could have an accident with a gun and shoot Mac instead of a crow. Perhaps it wasn't too late to learn, despite his horror of guns, or perhaps he could think of something else – but it had to be good.

She was with Rupert in the vegetable garden, both of them pretending to study the soil. Something else had happened; he could sense it. Flora said they were amazing: at their age, always sneaking off to their bedroom, but Danny knew that the Lascos were preoccupied with more disturbing matters than sex, and he wasn't sure that they could handle all of it on their own, especially now.

'Are you all right, Danny?' Vivien asked as he came down the garden. 'You look pale.'

'I'm fine.' He wondered how he could get her on her own; he couldn't decide whether Rupert should be involved in this.

'We were thinking about asparagus,' she said, her eyes searching his face.

'Aye, why not?' He continued down the garden, his head bent, pondering. He didn't want to ask baldly for a word in private.

Vivien and Rupert exchanged glances. They strolled after him and when he went to the stable that he'd rigged up as a workshop, Rupert continued to the house.

'What's up?' she asked, following him into the stable, switching on the light.

He put his tool-box on the bench and faced her. 'Mac wants to see you.' She stiffened. He wanted to tell her not to worry, that she could rely on him, but the situation was unprecedented and they had always maintained a certain distance between them.

'What's he want to see me about?' she asked. He hesitated. 'He told you?' She was astonished.

'Some,' he croaked, and cleared his throat. 'He told me a bit – to persuade you to see him, I suppose, like bait.'

She wiped her face with her hand. 'Tell me.'

'He says he knows why I totalled the Land Rover, and why I didn't get myself injured.'

She gaped at him. She hadn't expected that, but then how could she? He said shyly, 'I thought it was a good idea: crash it and sell the wreck for scrap. It stank of whisky until I hosed it down. I thought there could be other traces.'

'Traces?'

'Of Alastair.'

She glanced at the door. It was ajar, people could see them inside – but they were only talking. She picked up a half-finished nest-box and asked weakly, 'How did you know?'

'Little things, and then the stink of Scotch – and Flora said you couldn't get the smell of it out of the study. The connection was obvious. Not to people outside, of course.'

'What about Una and Flora?'

'Not Flora. And if Una guessed she's not saying anything, no more'n me.'

She sighed and said softly, 'He attacked me and I hit him with a bottle of Scotch. He was very drunk and he passed out, so Rupert ran him home in the Land Rover, but he started to choke so Rupert stopped and put the tail-board down, but Alastair staggered out under his own steam – and then he just went over the edge – before Rupert could do anything to stop him.'

'I knew it had to be something like that,' Danny said evenly. 'Crashing the 'Rover was just to be on the safe side.'

She stared at him. 'I don't know what to say, except to thank you.'

He shrugged. 'The point is: Mac's guessed. He's up there now' – he nodded – 'at the top gate, waiting for you. I'll come too.'

She smiled fondly. 'No. My neighbour wants a word. It's probably about a boundary.' She looked meaningly at him. 'I'll go and see if I can bag a rabbit for the pot.'

He was appalled. 'You won't—'

'No, love. I've got more sense. But it's not a bad idea to be seen to be ruthless, is it? When you hear a shot that'll be me firing in the air before I meet him.' She paused in the doorway. 'Don't tell the others about Mac,' she warned.

He fiddled at his work-bench, watching her cross the yard and enter the house. After a couple of minutes she came out carrying a shotgun. On the back step she paused and loaded it. She crossed the yard to the garden gate without a glance in his direction.

She didn't hurry. In the middle of the wood she fired in the air, re-loaded and continued, hoping she hadn't scared him off; she wanted to attend to this thing now, not have it hanging over her head. The adrenalin was surging and she was eager for him to be there.

He was, but he was very wary. He hadn't liked the gunfire. She guessed he'd been sly and insinuating with Danny, and that riled her; the lad had been white as a sheet when he met them in the garden.

Mac was on the mountain side of the top gate, not on her property. She grinned as she advanced, appreciating his prudence. He liked the grin even less than the gun. She left the gate open.

'Yes, Mac? You wanted to see me?' He looked at the gun. 'I'm after vermin,' she said cheerfully.

He was silent, considering this development. He essayed a warning: 'Jeannie knows I've come here.'

'You've got a message from Jeannie?' But if she were to get this over, teasing was the wrong ploy. 'You were saying something to Danny about his crash,' she said. 'When he wrote off our old Land Rover.'

'Is that gun loaded?'

Quite. She had too much superiority; he wasn't going to talk to a killer who was holding a loaded gun. She ejected the cartridges and pocketed them.

'I know what happened to Alastair,' he said.

'Do you!' She looked interested.

'I know about the whisky and putting him in the loch. And Jeannie knows,' he added.

'Who put him in the loch?' she asked curiously.

He started to grin. Vivien thought of lifting the gun but she didn't. She had to hear the rest.

'Both of you,' he said.

She did move at that, shifting her feet impatiently. 'What do you want, Mac?'

'I want a new Land Rover too.'

She shrugged. 'You should know how to go about that.'

'I do, but insurance won't pay for a good second-hand one. I'd need a couple of thousand over the insurance money.'

'Get it from Aileen when she inherits.'

His eyes narrowed. 'There's no body. How can she—'

'That's what we were saying' – she bore him down – 'we were discussing it this morning, didn't she tell you? About having to wait until the body's found? It has to be somewhere, and if it's been washed out to sea it'll never be found.'

'What happens then? What happens if it's never found?'

'You have to wait seven years before you get any money.'

'I'm not after the money.'

'A moment ago you were wondering where you could lay your hands on two thousand.'

He glared at her. 'He was here that night,' he said fiercely. 'You took him away in the Land Rover and Danny sold it for scrap, destroyed all the clues: blood and whisky and the like.'

She smiled indulgently. 'You ought to have my job: making up stories – although you're not much good at it. People believe my stories; I don't think anyone would believe yours.'

'The police would.'

She considered this. 'Possibly. Why don't you try them?'

'They're not guessing any longer,' Rupert said, when she found him in their room. 'They know you hit him – and with the whisky bottle.'

'But they haven't told the police. Why's that? I'd understand it if we were all related and they were protecting one of their own, but when the CID came here, it was only because Aileen was making insinuations; they had nothing concrete like this: the whisky and using the Land Rover.'

'Perhaps Mac's only just found out – but how could that be? More likely they've been keeping it in reserve. Mac waited until it had all blown over and you're feeling secure, and then he moves in to blackmail you.'

'But how did he *know*? About the whisky, I mean. He had to have seen something.'

Rupert said slowly, 'He could have seen my headlights, saw me stop, and turn round after an interval – I had to put the lights on to turn – and then he came down to see why I'd stopped in that place.'

'And climbed down and found the body reeking of whisky, and the bruise on the head: all that in the dark?'

'It had to be something like that.'

'Unless he was watching me from outside the study window, had followed Alastair here.'

'No, the dogs would have alerted me when I came home. But I'll swear Mac wasn't close enough to see how Alastair went over the edge. He's bluffing. He doesn't have a shred of proof.'

'I thought he wasn't very competent as a blackmailer.'

'No wonder, when you turn up with a loaded shotgun. You must have scared him stiff. All the same, I wish you'd let me know you were going to confront him. Weren't you bothered about him turning nasty?'

'Never.' She shook her head vehemently. 'Mac's not a killer.'

'He's a villain.'

'Oh yes, I'll give you that; there's nothing he wouldn't do, in a small way: theft, blackmail, even knocking Jeannie about—' She stopped and thought about that, dismissed it with a gesture and went on, 'But murder? No. He's a runt, he won't come back; I called his bluff.' They were silent. 'Anyway,' she resumed abruptly, 'it's the one who's being blackmailed who kills, not the blackmailer. Mac's going to be looking over his shoulder from now on. Particularly when he remembers what happened to Alastair.'

Chapter 13

On a damp morning in April Danny was putting the finishing touches to a terrace when Vivien approached, carrying a package. She admired his work, which was impressive; he'd transformed a slope into a level bed held back behind a low wall of stones taken from a ruin in the wood.

'We'll have a long plot of asparagus,' he told her, 'and I thought we'd have rock plants in that wall, like different coloured aubrietias? They'd look grand from Rupert's office.'

'That's fine. These seeds have just arrived for you.' Her tone changed. 'Danny, you've got to stop worrying. Una was watching you last night at dinner. You kept staring at Rupert. He noticed it too.'

'I can't figure him out. He doesn't seem bothered.'

'We're not! I told you what happened: Alastair was drunk and he fell. He wasn't pushed.' She regarded him steadily. He licked his lips and looked away. She said firmly, 'There isn't a shred of proof that it didn't happen that way.'

'Are you absolutely sure?'

'Certain.'

'If the police come back they'll be asking why Rupert didn't pull him out of the water.'

'He'd fallen a long way. Rupert isn't familiar with drops. To him fifty feet is like a thousand, so he felt sure Alastair was dead. He heard him fall in the water too. In any case there was no way he could have climbed down, he's not a climber. He panicked.'

'Vivien! That's too much.'

'Well, I'd not roll it out so baldly for the police. The point is, we haven't told them the truth because we're scared to. If we're driven into a corner we'll come clean with what really happened.'

'That he was alive when he fell in the loch.'

'When he fell off the road, yes. Now you see why we're not concerned, and why you have to forget about it, because you're attracting attention.'

'What about Mac?'

'I sent him away with a flea in his ear. He suspects, but he's bluffing. He knows Alastair came to Alder, and he knows – or guesses – I hit him, but he doesn't know that the death was an accident. Basically we're in the clear. Mac can't blackmail us because we're not bothered about the truth coming out. You see?'

'He's also terrified of a woman with a gun.' Danny allowed himself a grim smile.

'That reminds me: there's a pair of hoodies building in the gorge. They'll be living on nestlings unless I get rid of them.'

'That's Lair property outside the wood.'

'So – Alastair gave me permission to shoot over his land.'

She went back to the house and left him staring at the dark soil that was waiting for the asparagus seed. He had a sudden flash of insight and as quickly dismissed it. They would never have buried the body because it was he, Danny, who looked after the grounds, and he'd have noticed. Besides, the Land Rover had been used to take him away. All the same, he thought with a tight grin, his mind jumping, Mac had better watch it; in the Highlands there were innumerable places where you could put a body and it would never be found.

Throughout April Vivien and Flora worked on the new book, and Rupert negotiated subsidiary rights in *Thin Ice* and *Cutthroat*, which was to be published in September. Outside Danny worked like an acolyte in a temple, serenaded by willow warblers and the crooning of a small flock of pullets in their wired pen. They were not to have their freedom until they were grown. A pair of buzzards nested on a crag half a mile away, and there were always the eagles. Vivien shot hoodie crows but there was nothing you could do about birds of prey – nothing anyone wanted to do – so the pullets had to stay behind wire, safe from the huge raptors who, every so often, passed down the glen and over Alder to patrol the loch shore looking for carrion.

Tourists started to make their appearance: motorists venturing westward, exploring the old road, the odd mountaineer who camped on the shore and climbed Garsven, bird watchers, botanists and, of course, the pony-trekkers who were quartered at Lair. Aileen could ride now and she looked good on a horse although she was always mounted on a quiet animal. All animosity seemed to have been forgotten and she waved cheerily to everyone from Alder, even Vivien, although no one stopped to speak. Una said she had met Jeannie in the supermarket and they exchanged a few words. Evidently the trekking business was doing well.

No one encountered Mac. He was glimpsed in the distance, on a horse or a tractor, but for the rest he seemed to be avoiding Alder and its people.

The Texas book was finished, entitled *Mexican Brown*, and taken to London by Rupert; Vivien refused to leave the Highlands in May. She pointed out that Rupert was her agent; she had submitted the book, her part was over until she was needed for promotion. She went to climb on Skye and when they were reunited at Alder it was to find that Rupert had returned from London with airline tickets and all the logistics finalized for a horse trip through the red rock canyons of Utah.

They were in Bryce Canyon Lodge when they telephoned home and Flora told them that a human hand had been found in the eagles' eyrie. At Alder Flora was bubbling with excitement. 'You're not going to believe this,' she told Vivien on the telephone, grimacing at Una who was clearing the table, 'but a man in Kent discovered it!'

'*Kent?*' The line was so good that Una heard the cry from the other side of the room, but then she'd been expecting it.

'It was like this,' Flora rushed on, sitting down, settling in for a long chat, regardless of expense, 'there was this bird-watcher who went up and took photographs of the nest – what? Oh, you know where they nest: on the crags above the lochan . . . why, up the back here, of course: behind the house. Anyway, he took a lot of pictures of the chicks in the nest and he went home – to Kent – and had them developed – they were slides – and then he projected them for his family, and his wife saw it immediately. She's a doctor. He hadn't noticed it when he was taking the pictures – he probably thought it was animal bones: hare, fox, whatever; he was in a hurry, scared of the eagles attacking him, and of course he was using a telephoto lens . . . It's been proved, Vivien! The Mountain Rescue roped down and recovered it and it's human all right, so now they're searching the loch . . . I know that, but the thinking is, the body must have been caught under some tree roots and it's come free and floated to the surface, or else it was there all the time but on the far side where they didn't search... Oh no, that's impossible; it's just bones, you see; no flesh left, so no fingerprints, and Alastair didn't wear a ring; anyway, a ring would have slipped off... '

'What did she make of it?' Una asked as the phone was replaced.

'Funny thing,' Flora mused. 'She said there could be other corpses lying around.'

'You didn't tell her the pathologist said it was comparatively fresh.'

'No, I forgot that bit.'

Danny came in with a bunch of greens. 'Thinnings,' he said. 'Any good to you? I've given the rest to the pullets.'

'Vivien's just phoned,' Flora told him. 'She said the hand could be from another corpse.'

He grinned but his eyes were intent. 'How many do we have to choose from?'

'Well, it's not a local person; it has to be someone who went missing recently so it could be one of the summer visitors. When they climb Garsven no one counts them back.'

'But they leave tents and cars down here. We'd notice if those weren't reclaimed after several days.'

'Not if they *were* reclaimed. Two go on the hill, one comes back and removes the tent and the car.'

Danny swallowed. 'You're talking murder.'

'Of course. It's my job.'

Una was silent but she was listening as she washed the lettuce thinnings.

'When are they coming home?' he asked, suddenly casual.

'Their flight is July the tenth. They come north on the twelfth. You knew that; someone has to meet them.'

'I forgot.'

'This doesn't make any difference to them,' Una said, not turning round.

'What doesn't?' Danny was sharp.

'The hand, or the body if they find it, but they won't.'

'Why not?' Flora was amazed. 'It has to be there if the eagles found a hand. Doesn't it?'

Una turned. She knew that Flora hadn't seen the significance of the hand but Danny should have – unless he was preoccupied with another angle. 'The body must be breaking up,' she said. 'Even if the bird took the hand from a corpse, by now the foxes and such will have been there too; that's apart from all the damage the water must have done. Even if they find the skull they'll have a hard time identifying it. How many teeth will be left?'

They were staring at her. 'Goodness,' Flora breathed. 'How on earth did you work all that out?'

'I've seen what's left after animals drown.' Flora winced. Danny's eyes widened. 'It's nothing to do with us,' she assured him. Her tone lightened. 'What did Vivien have to say about the trip, Flora?'

Flora tried to concentrate. 'I don't know that she said anything, and I didn't ask. She must have been bowled over by my news. I mean, it's not something that happens every day, is it? Do you realize that bird must have flown over Alder carrying the hand?'

'For God's sake!' Danny cried. 'Why the hell can't you—'

'Now, Danny!' Una broke in harshly. He stopped and gaped at her. 'That was in bad taste, Flora,' she said sternly. 'Alastair was Vivien's climbing partner. You should be more tactful about the – remains.'

Flora glared. 'But you were saying – you were talking about skulls and teeth . . .' She trailed off in the face of Una's hard stare.

Danny turned and stalked out of the kitchen. The two women regarded each other, the one bewildered, the other speculative.

'The police will come back,' Una said slowly. 'You're going to have to watch your tongue. You can control yourself: look how superb you were with Alastair, that time he forced you to give him a lift home—'

'I wasn't controlled when he threatened to kill me—' Flora broke off. She had gone pale. 'I haven't told the police about that,' she whispered. 'You're warning me to keep quiet about it, aren't you?'

'They didn't interview you so you weren't asked. But I'm not suggesting—'

Flora wasn't listening. 'Because,' she went on, her eyes huge and terrified, 'it could have been foul play, and if they knew he'd threatened to throttle me, they'd think he tried, and that I – I'm a suspect – for Alastair's murder?' Her voice rose. 'Is that what you're telling me?'

Una bit her lip and glanced at the door. She said carelessly, 'How could you be? You weren't here. And even if we were all suspects as far as the police are concerned, the body's breaking up so if it was foul play there's nothing to show it was, and certainly no clue to point to who was responsible.'

'Danny,' Flora whispered: 'he destroyed the Land Rover. It could have been used to—'

'Flora!' The warning was rough. After a pause Una went on tensely, 'You're too much involved with crime. You need a rest from it. Why don't you take a good long day trip with the dogs before Vivien comes back? It's a lovely time of year.'

'I suppose you're right. I don't seem to be able to switch off. It's the penalty of being in this kind of business: like policemen, or CID' – she shivered – 'you see crime everywhere.'

At Headquarters Binnie and Forsyth were discussing the next move. The loch had been searched meticulously. Instructors from an adventure school had paddled round the shore-line in canoes, while an RAF Mountain Rescue team had devoted a day to combing the crags below the road and studying the water through binoculars. Either the body had sunk again or broken up or it wasn't there.

'It's not there,' Binnie said firmly. 'So where is it?' Forsyth said nothing, the question was rhetorical. 'It's on land,' he mused, 'but not buried – unless the grave was shallow and the hand stuck out.'

He lit another cigarette. Forsyth stared at the wall, hating him; she had given up smoking two years ago. She tried to ignore the health risk and concentrate on the other problem. They were convinced that the hand had belonged to Alastair; no one else had been reported missing recently, no one who could be traced to the northern Highlands.

'You're going to get your chance,' Binnie said. 'That is, providing she does come back, and they don't make a run for it.'

'They've made no attempt to break off communication,' she pointed out. 'We know where they are.'

'If the staff are speaking the truth.' Binnie studied his sergeant and grinned. 'On second thoughts I think you should go back before the Lascos come home.'

'On my own?'

'Why not? It looks more innocent. A man's a threat. The Mountain Rescue are searching the glen tomorrow so you can get yourself kitted out with boots and a haversack, and go with them.'

'In what capacity? CID don't search for missing mountaineers.'

'That's why you go back before the Lascos get there. You find some excuse not to join in the search and you spend time in Alder's kitchen. You can pull the wool over their eyes, but you couldn't deceive the Lascos.'

'That housekeeper's a tough nut; she'll suspect me as soon as I appear.'

'Try it. You'll think of something. And if you don't, negative reaction can be as significant as the truth. There's the lad too, the gardener. He's a surly number, he might let something slip in a fit of temper.'

Forsyth arrived at Alder the following day in the company of the civilian mountain rescue team. Una allowed them to park in the stable yard and told them to come in for tea when they returned. No one seemed to notice Forsyth who kept in the background, the team leader accepting her as a police observer. They were accustomed to the police tagging along when there was the chance of finding a body.

Danny pointed the way through the wood and they started up the hill. Within the hour Forsyth was back, her shirt torn, her jeans soaked to the thighs. She stood at the gate that separated the wood from the vegetable garden and watched Danny hoeing between rows of young plants. He was wearing a shirt like a short smock and a straw hat with a wide brim. The scene: the old house and its outbuildings slumbering in the sunshine, the lush garden, the birdsong and the man oblivious to her presence, all this made her feel as if she had walked into a world totally unrelated to criminal investigation – but her lips twitched as she realized that she was overlooked by windows on the first floor of the house. They were open to the air and looked as innocent as the woods. And how innocent were those? Binnie had suggested a shallow grave.

Danny looked up as the latch clicked and leaned on his hoe, watching her approach.

'It's hot,' she grumbled. 'I couldn't take it; I kept falling off the boulders into the burn.'

He showed no surprise. Had he picked her out among the rescuers or had he not recognized her? He'd glimpsed her only fleetingly on their previous visit to the lodge.

'We drink that water,' he said.

She looked away, considering the remark, then came back to him. 'Meaning you'd know if he was in the burn? Of course you would.' She paused for a response. Danny chopped at a weed. 'They're wasting their time?' She made a question of it. Still no reaction. 'Where do you think he could be?' she asked.

He frowned and looked into the depths of the wood. 'He's not in the loch,' he said thoughtfully, 'and he didn't go down the river and out to sea because the eagle found him, so that means he's somewhere within range of the nest.' He regarded her with wide eyes and she was fascinated by the length of his lashes.

'How far does an eagle fly? Does it have a territory?'

'Oh yes, but territories can overlap; they can be taken over if the birds next door have been shot. Crofters shoot eagles. And there again, an eagle can have several eyries.'

'But they know where the hand was found. It was at the head of this glen, right?'

He nodded, pursing his lips.

'So – how big is the territory?' Impatience was creeping into her tone.

He shrugged. 'Could be as much as forty thousand if your pair had taken over neighbouring territory.'

'Forty thousand *what*?'

'Acres.' He smiled at her. 'That would be around sixty square miles, so if their patch was like an oblong, it could be ten miles by six, and if the eyrie was near one end that would give you ten miles to search in a straight line, then, of course, there'd be three miles either side. That's simplifying things a bit.' He sounded apologetic. His eyes were warm and friendly. This was the guy Binnie said was surly, said he'd likely let something slip in a temper.

'My,' she breathed. 'What's the use of searching?' His eyes flickered. 'Do you see any point?' she asked.

He looked down. 'Not really.' The smile had gone.

'And you're the local man, you should know. Have you always lived here?' She looked round vaguely, as if wondering where the family croft might be.

'No,' Danny said.

'How long have you been here?'

Deliberately he turned his back and resumed hoeing. She raised her voice. 'Where were you before?'

He stopped and faced her. 'Who's asking?'

She left him then, before he could think of an excuse to get to the house ahead of her.

'Where did *you* come from?'

Flora, emerging from the study, stopped short. She took in the soaked jeans and the boots. 'Oh, I'm sorry, you're with the team. You startled me. Did you want something...' She trailed off, staring. She recovered and laughed. 'I forget your name.'

'Forsyth. The door was open. I did knock.'

'That's all right. Have you found something? In the burn?'

'No. I gave up. Inspector Binnie sent me; he thought I'd make a better job of it than him, but all I've done is fall in the water. They told me to come down before they had to carry me back on a stretcher.'

'Just like a man,' Flora said, 'giving women the dirty work. Come on, we'll have a cup of tea. It must be baking hot in that glen.'

The dogs wandered in from the front garden, sniffing the visitor suspiciously.

'We always have cairns at home,' Forsyth said. 'My mother's got a bitch and her daughter. They're not as young as this one. He's all muscle, isn't he?'

'He's a hill-walker,' Flora said proudly. 'If I go too far for him I put him in my rucksack, and he's a load after a while, you wouldn't believe! Sit down, take the weight off your feet.'

Forsyth looked round the kitchen. 'How neat you are. My place is a dump.'

'This isn't my department.' Flora was warming the teapot. 'Una's the housekeeper. She's away shopping. I'm the secretary.'

'I see.'

'Full-time job,' Flora rattled on. 'I have been the housekeeper as well, back in the days when there wasn't as much money—' She broke off. 'Talking out of turn again.' She giggled. 'Una's been with us a while now; it'll be a year in September.'

'Where's your home?'

'This is my home. I wouldn't want any other.'

She put mugs on the table and a plate of shortbread. She poured the tea and sat down. 'Where do you come from?' she asked.

'From Wick.'

'Really. You couldn't get any farther north. Except the islands, of course.'

Small-talk wasn't getting Forsyth anywhere – and Danny could come in at any moment. She grasped the bull by its horns. 'You keep the house open while the Lascos are abroad? You don't have a holiday?'

'We can go away if we want to but we do just as we like anyway. Alder isn't like real work, not really. One feels attached.'

'You must like being alone—'

'But we're not! There are five of us here and we work as a team; the three staff aren't subordinate, not so's you'd notice. We eat together, we share all the rooms except the bedrooms, and they're really bedsits. There's a huge television in a room on its own but everyone's got a personal set as well; we can be private or sociable, depending on how we feel.'

'But it's so remote. I couldn't stick it. No store to pop out to when you run short of something – although I suppose you can always borrow from the neighbours.'

'Hardly. Not our neighbours. Oh, don't get me wrong, Jeannie MacDonnell will keep a good stock of food—' Flora stopped.

'But you don't want to run into Alastair.'

'Didn't,' Flora murmured absently, and changed direction. 'Do you think they'll find him up there?' she asked brightly, nodding at the window.

'Probably. How long had he been knocking his wife about? When did it start?'

Flora's eyes wandered. 'I don't know. Had he – did he knock her about?'

'Oh, come on!'

Flora swallowed. 'I hadn't noticed. I think – yes, she had a black eye once and – we assumed she'd walked into a door. So he did beat her. We – wondered.'

'He was a very violent man.'

'Really?' The tone was too high, too amazed. Evidently she realized it herself. 'Of course you'd be alert for that kind of thing,' she said. 'Domestic violence isn't – er – within our remit. Is that the term?'

'Actually I'd think it was.' Forsyth smiled. 'Violent as they come,' she went on, admiration in her tone. 'It was a curious relationship between her and Alastair.'

'I'm not with you,' Flora said, in a polite little-girl voice. 'You're saying Mrs Lasco is violent?' She was incredulous.

'Vivien Reid,' Forsyth corrected. 'The violence is inferred more than described. But it's there, and far more effective even than Puzo.'

'Puzo?'

'*The Godfather*. The horse's head in the bed. Wasn't Alastair frightened of her?'

'Of course he wasn't. He wasn't frightened of anybody. Alastair did all the frightening around here.' Flora was impatient, dismissing Alastair, furious with her own stupidity. 'I thought you were saying Vivien was violent herself. You mean the books. You're wrong; that's the impression the reader has, and there is horrifying violence but it's off-stage: implicit, not explicit.' She nodded gravely. Forsyth guessed she was quoting her employer. 'The writing's stark,' she went on: 'ruthless and cold. Cold passion, that's Vivien – her writing, I mean. I love it. I couldn't have a more exciting job.' She smiled warmly. She had put things right, recovered her equilibrium.

'Alastair threatened her?' Forsyth prompted.

Flora, reaching for the teapot, stiffened, her hand in mid-air. After a moment she completed the movement. 'What a strange suggestion,' she said. 'Alastair would never have threatened Vivien. I see what puzzled you about their relationship now; you think he was violent—'

'We know he was violent.'

'Yes, well, so you reckon that if he knocked one woman about, he'd behave the same to all women.' She laughed and shook her head. 'Not Vivien. You don't know her.'

She was pouring tea into Forsyth's mug.

'And you?' Forsyth asked. 'What did he do to you?'

The tea splashed on the table. Forsyth jerked back as the scalding liquid ran over the edge. Flora shrieked and leapt for the sink, rushing back with a wet cake of soap.

'Here, get your jeans off—'

'It missed me,' Forsyth said. 'Get my jeans off?' She looked shocked.

'Soap!' Flora waved it, blushing. 'For burns and scalds. There must be some ointment around but I wouldn't know where she keeps it.'

Forsyth laughed. 'I thought you were making a pass at me.'

Flora was speechless. 'Why did Alastair threaten you?' Forsyth asked gently.

'Because I – I don't know. I gave him a lift home.'

'That was risky.'

'His truck wouldn't start. He wasn't sober. He was all right then.'

This was shorthand. Forsyth didn't pause to interpret but seized on the salient point. 'He didn't threaten you then.'

But Flora had turned back to the sink and replaced the soap. She washed her hands slowly. Forsyth came and stood beside her, looking out at the yard. 'It was to do with Vivien,' she said.

Flora dried her hands with great care. She was pale and breathing fast. She returned to the table. 'I can make more tea,' she said, without enthusiasm.

'You haven't answered the question.'

'I lost sight of it. I can't believe that you'd think I was a lesbian. Do I look all that masculine?'

'It was a joke in bad taste. I think you're very feminine. Are you trying to tell me Alastair raped you?'

'Rape!' Flora shrilled. 'Heavens no! He wasn't interested in me. He treated me like a mother – a sister – just someone to confide in. Rape? He was a romantic.'

'And he poured it all out when you gave him a lift. Poor you. He was trying to enlist your support in the affair.' The guess emerged as a statement, and Flora didn't perceive it as a question. There was no flicker of denial in her expression. She looked miserable, cornered, unable to rally her reserves. Forsyth pushed her advantage.

'And then he regretted letting his hair down, and he came back and threatened you' – she caught the faint shake of the head but she persisted – 'he warned you to keep quiet' – a pause – 'or else.'

Flora was sullen. 'Why are you telling me all this? It's a scenario you dreamed up. He was violent to Aileen but he'd never dare behave like that outside his own home. He was the laird, after all.'

'So when you said everyone was afraid of him, that was a scenario too? Why did you buy the guns?'

Flora looked at the shotguns on their rack. 'We've had those for ages.'

'Not according to the certificates.' That was another inspired guess but it came near the mark.

Flora hesitated. 'We had them before—'

'Before?'

'Before that night – I gave him a lift—'

'And he confided in you, then threatened you. We've gone over that. So the Lascos thought him dangerous enough that they needed to arm themselves for protection.'

'Not at all.' Flora looked indignant but by now she was so confused that her reactions were incongruous. 'We've got nesting birds and a garden; Vivien shoots crows and pigeons, rabbits—'

'Why does she need two guns?'

'Una shoots—' Flora stopped, wide-eyed.

'And the guns were bought – when?'

'I don't remember.'

Forsyth thought rapidly. She might be pushing too hard and none of it could be used in evidence but it was knowledge that would surely guide their future actions. Binnie might – would bawl her out – nothing she did was right for him – but she'd been fantastically lucky to get Flora on her own; it could never happen again without her being forewarned. She might as well swing for a sheep as a lamb.

'Where were you the night Alastair was killed?' she asked.

'I don't know.' Flora was quick.

'Or the afternoon?'

'I don't—Ah!' – satisfaction, a breath of relief – 'we were all in town. We took Danny, the gardener, to the dentist.'

'So no one was here.'

'Vivien and Rupert—' She hesitated, then added shakily, 'They were here, of course. Alastair was supposed to have been coming to visit – according to his wife – but he never reached here. He fell in the loch, or so we thought. That doesn't seem to be the case now.' Her voice steadied as she was speaking; she was almost back to her normal self but still pale. 'He must have changed his mind,' she went on, 'or he was teasing his wife when he said he was coming here. He went on the hill instead and got caught in the storm.'

'That must have been what happened.' Forsyth stood up. 'Thank you for your time, and for the tea. Have you spoken to Vivien since the hand was found?'

'Yes.' Tension again.

'How did she take it?'

'How could she?' Flora looked bewildered. 'It's amazing, macabre. Of course she was astonished. We all were.'

'She's still coming home on – when is it?'

'The twelfth. Why shouldn't she?' It was defiant, and bitten off, as if she would have liked to add: She had nothing to do with Alastair's death.

'Or his murder,' Forsyth said to Binnie, back in the office. 'She knows – or thinks – he was murdered. She didn't turn a hair when I asked her where she was when he was killed.'

'Being killed needn't mean murder,' Binnie said. 'You can be killed in a car accident or a plane crash.' He turned back to her notes. 'No tape,' he murmured, 'no record, only your infallible memory. So what's your conclusion?'

'She suspects Vivien. I don't think she *knows*; they wouldn't trust her, she's too susceptible. But if she suspects, then the other two: Danny and Una, they probably know. I got nothing out of Danny.'

Binnie leered. 'Is he fond of his mistress?'

'He must be, he calls the place home. But all the staff were in Inverness that afternoon. They didn't get back till late.'

'We don't know when Alastair died.'

'I think it's murder. Flora was very touchy on the subject of violence as it related to him.'

'So I see.' He indicated her notes. 'You're suggesting that because he was violent the Lascos, or one of 'em, used violence against him.'

'They bought the guns recently. I checked the certificates.'

'They were bought as protection against Alastair?' He looked up at her. 'At the start of this business you said that Vivien wasn't a killer.'

'It could have been an accident. If he went to Alder drunk and she took down a gun, loaded it – and he was too drunk to care . . .'

He considered this. 'The body may be well enough preserved. A fox wouldn't make off with the skull, would it?'

'The wound could be in a soft part. That would be gone.'

'Where *is* that body?'

Forsyth's eyes were unfocused; she was remembering the garden and the wood. 'Like you said, it could have been buried, and then a dog could have started digging, exposed the hand, and the eagle came down and flew off with it. Then someone – Danny? – discovered the remains, or revisited the grave, and covered it up, but properly this time.'

'Is there any turned earth in that garden?'

'It would have been all bare in December. Now it's full of plants. Marvellous vegetables they grow—' She stopped.

Binnie grinned. 'Well fertilized? I think we're going to have to do some digging at Alder Lodge.'

Chapter 14

'Of course he was violent,' Aileen said. 'Everyone knew that.'
'But you didn't tell us,' Forsyth pointed out.
'You didn't ask, and who wants to publicize something like that?'

She didn't seem bothered now. It was the morning after Forsyth had interviewed Flora. She had found Aileen saddling up in the yard at Lair, a row of ponies tied to a rail. Slim and elegant in jodhpurs, her hair caught back in a black ribbon, it was hard to reconcile her appearance with that of a battered woman. She eased a bit into the mouth of a stubborn pony while Forsyth, always fascinated by other people's expertise, watched with interest.

Binnie had discovered that although Aileen stood to inherit Lair, there appeared to be no cash – only land and the house, for which it would be difficult to find a buyer during a recession. So Binnie, wondering who might benefit from Alastair's death, rated Aileen low on the list, but this morning Forsyth was struck by the difference between this poised woman and the neurotic slattern she'd met shortly after Alastair disappeared. His death might bring her no financial advantages but she was in considerably better health now that he was out of the way.

'How did you find out?' Aileen asked casually. 'Neighbours talking?'
'Hospital records; you had your skull X-rayed.'
'I thought hospital records were supposed to be confidential.'

There was no answer to that so Forsyth contemplated the trees, noting that the woods at Lair were more extensive than those at Alder.

'You're looking well,' she said deliberately, and had the satisfaction of seeing Aileen's eyes narrow.

'I'm doing the trekking,' she said, as if that explained her vitality. 'I learned to ride, and I like it. Isn't that amazing?'

Forsyth, probing for chinks in the armour, her gaze lingering on the buildings, said, 'He could be in this glen, or nearer home.' Her eyes returned to the trees.

'You think he could be in the woods?' Aileen asked. 'But then—'

'Yes?'

'He wouldn't have been lost. It couldn't have been an accident.'

'What else could it be?'

Aileen was distressed. 'Suicide?' she breathed.

'So you don't think he went to Alder after all.' It was sudden and crisp.

She shrugged. 'That's where he said he was going.'

She turned and went into the stable. After a moment Mac emerged carrying a blanket and tack. He nodded to Forsyth, tossed the blanket on a pony and settled the saddle. 'Have you questioned Danny?' he asked quietly.

'I've spoken to him.'

'Did you ask him why he put their Land Rover in the loch?'

'No.' Forsyth made an effort to stay cool. 'Why did he?'

'Because there were clues in it of course. It were used to carry the body. Danny jumped clear.'

'You saw this?'

'No, but Danny wasn't hurt so he didn't go down with the truck. When it was recovered he sold it for scrap.'

'When did this happen?'

'Not long after Alastair were killed. Around mid-January. *She* were in America.'

Aileen was standing in the stable doorway. Forsyth didn't know how long she'd been there. 'What did they do with the body?' she asked.

He leered. He hadn't seen Aileen. 'How would I know? I only guessed about the Land Rover. It's your job to find out where he is. First person to ask is *her* – if you ever see her again; she'll be sweating blood now the hand's been found.'

'MacDonnell's got it in for Vivien,' Forsyth told Binnie when she met him on the road. He had stopped in one of the passing-places above the crags and they stood in the shade outside the car, looking down through the foliage at the gleaming water. 'He's saying their Land Rover was used to transport the body,' she continued, 'and Danny crashed it afterwards to destroy traces, then sold it for scrap. D'you think there's anything in it? Any point in going back?' He had just come from Alder.

'Spite. Neighbour's spite. And young Danny's like an eel. When I got there only Una was around; Danny and Flora were "on the hill", she said. But she was rinsing three mugs. The others would have done a runner out the back and through the wood soon as they saw me coming up the drive. I got nothing out of Una except that the Lascos will be home tomorrow.' He turned and stared at the mountains. 'That body isn't in the water. It's up there somewhere or—' His gaze travelled westward, towards Alder. 'What's the rescue team doing? I haven't seen hide nor hair of 'em today.'

'They're taking the day off. Tomorrow they're going to go up the glen behind Lair and come back down the ridge. They say he could be high in a gully. People do that: find a remote place and take some tablets and go to sleep. In winter they don't wake up.'

'You're talking suicide!' He was incredulous.

'It's the way the rescue people are thinking; I spoke to the leader last night. It is just possible: he was unstable, drunk, his relationship with Vivien was in a mess. Suicide's a possibility.' She looked dubious but she went on, 'Aileen mentioned it too...' She trailed off.

Binnie scowled at the mountains, bleached and bare in the sun, then he smiled. 'Danny,' he said softly. 'Forget the Land Rover; what we do is wait till the Lascos get back and then we move in. Looking for the body close to home should produce some interesting reactions.'

The Lascos had arrived in London the previous morning and gone straight to Notting Hill for a few hours' sleep. That afternoon they devoted to discussion of *Mexican Brown* with Joss, and in the evening Vivien telephoned home. Una told her of the negative result of the search behind Alder, and that Forsyth had been questioning Flora and Danny.

'What did Flora tell her?' Vivien asked sharply.

'Not much. She says the police already knew that Alastair had threatened her with violence.'

Vivien was aghast. After a pause she asked weakly, 'Do they know why he did?'

'Not really, but they seem to know all about him making a nuisance of himself around Alder.'

Vivien reported Una's end of the exchange to Rupert. 'The police are going to think it suspicious that we said nothing about him threatening Flora.'

'Binnie wasn't with Forsyth?'

'I don't think so. Una would have said.'

'So he sent Forsyth deliberately, and Flora was alone in the house.'

'She must have been, or Una would have stopped her talking—' She checked, and went on slowly, 'They suspect. They were watching the house and they knew Flora was alone; they know she's the vulnerable one, the weak link. They know they'd get nowhere with Una.' She went to stand at the french window that was open to the patio. She regarded the backs of houses beyond the garden wall. 'D'you remember the Prospect of Whitby?' she asked.

'Of course I do.'

'I'm losing my marbles. I was wishing we could put the clock back.'

'If you did that, Alastair would still be alive.'

'But there'd be a way out. We could give up Alder and go and live in the States.'

It occurred to Rupert that her timing was wrong; when they were in the Prospect of Whitby she hadn't yet given Alastair cause to think he meant anything to her.

'You *are* losing your marbles,' he said. 'You'd never have left Alder to get away from a barmy neighbour.'

She fingered the curtain. 'What am I going to do, Rupert?'

'I can't make out whether you're still suffering from jet-lag or coming down with 'flu.' He really did look puzzled. 'What's this "I"? It's "we". What we're going to do is stick with our story, when it's necessary to tell it. I was running him home, he came round and fell over the edge under his own steam. Heavens, how many times—'

'You didn't climb down, Rupert, that's the clincher. If it had happened that way, you'd have gone down to pull him out of the water.'

'Oh no, I wouldn't.' He came and put his arm round her shoulders. 'I hated the fellow. That's why I didn't go down. Binnie knows that's in character. It's more plausible than saying I didn't go down because I'm not a climber. The truth is always more plausible.'

'Then I should tell it. It was me he was attacking, after all. And we did think he was alive when we put him in the Land Rover.'

'He was alive, Viv.'

'No, love. You've been protecting me all along. I killed him, you know it, and you tipped the body out at that place to simulate an accident.'

'He was alive. I felt his pulse.'

They stared at each other. 'We've got to agree,' she said at length. 'Otherwise we're going to get snarled up if they interview us separately. Now tell me the truth: did you feel a pulse?'

'Yes.'

He went to the sideboard and poured Scotch for both of them. She sat down and watched him. 'It puts all the blame on you,' she said morosely, then, 'Wait a minute! Forget about the fall and the splash; what happened was, you tipped him out on the verge and drove back to Alder. He was coming round, you didn't want him being sick in the back of our truck, so you helped him out and left him to get home himself.'

He considered. 'It might work. I'll think about it – but none of this concerns you; all you did was knock the chap out: finish. End of story.'

Later, when they were preparing dinner, she said, 'They haven't found the other body yet.'

'What body? Oh, the hand in the nest.'

'But eagles have a hell of a range.'

'No one else is missing.'

'Rupert! People go missing all the time; it's not impossible some should end up in the northern Highlands. It can't be Alastair; how long could he survive after the blow on the head and the fall? He must have—' She stopped, appalled.

'Drowned within a few minutes.'

'I can't shake you, can I? You insist on accepting responsibility.' She was slicing tomatoes at the sink. She put the knife down and turned. 'Did you ever wonder why I married you?'

'I assumed it was because you loved me,' he said stiffly.

'Rubbish. You might have thought that at the time but not since.'

His world was threatening to fall apart. A murder charge could be waiting for one of them at Alder – either or both, it was immaterial – and now she was examining their relationship.

'You thought I was grateful to you,' she said. He made a gesture of protest. She went on, 'I was on my beam-ends and you came to the rescue; you showed me a new career and how to make a fortune. I was able to hold on to Alder because of you. You made me over.'

'You're just a wee bit drunk, my dear.'

'*In vino veritas.* I did marry you out of gratitude; not quite true, I was fond of you as well. You were like a nice dog that I took in, gave a home to, and you gave me love and service and security in exchange.'

It was all past tense; he waited dismally for the body-blow.

'You've grown on me,' she said. 'I'd prefer to go to prison and leave Alder in your charge than the other way round. I can't bear to think of you in prison.'

'No one's going to prison,' he said explosively, lowering his voice to a harsh whisper as she gestured at the open window. 'What's this got to do with gratitude?'

'I'm not grateful any longer, I gave that up ages ago. I've come to love you.'

'Oh.' He blinked. 'I thought I was being given my marching orders.'

'Idiot! Equals don't give orders.'

Flora, meeting them at Inverness, was touched to see them holding hands as they approached. She greeted them warmly and tried to seat them in the back of the Subaru but was thwarted by Vivien's sliding behind the wheel and Rupert getting in beside her. It wasn't until they had left the city behind that she remembered to tell them that Danny had refused to meet them because he maintained that as soon as he turned his back the police would be digging up his vegetables. 'He says he's a suspect,' she told them. 'And that Binnie fellow thinks he buried the body in the garden—' She stopped, horrified at yet another demonstration of her appalling lack of discretion, but Vivien seemed to be amused; Flora caught her eye in the mirror and she was smiling.

Beyond Inch they came on two young girls standing beside a Land Rover and waving them down. They were from Lair and the Land Rover had packed up on them after they'd been to the bank. Could Vivien give them a lift? They were put in the back and they informed Flora chattily that they weren't riding today because of saddle sores, and they were worried about the 'Rover because it was Mrs MacDonnell who had given them permission to use it and they guessed Mac wouldn't be too pleased when he came home. He was away for the day with Aileen and all the other paying customers.

Vivien came to Lair's road-end and turned. Rupert glanced at her. The girls protested that they could walk from there but she continued, saying she wanted a word with Mrs MacDonnell. She stopped at the back door of the big house and the girls got out, thanking her profusely. Rupert didn't move, he was waiting for a cue. Flora was silent.

'I won't be long,' Vivien told them. 'If you like you can take the car and I'll walk home.'

'We'll wait,' Rupert said. 'I'll tell Flora about Salt Lake City.'

Jeannie was in the kitchen and the girls were explaining about the breakdown. They broke off when Vivien appeared.

'You couldna help it,' Jeannie told them. 'That old thing's always breaking down. Thank you for picking them up,' she told Vivien when they'd gone. 'Surely you've only just got back from America?'

'We're on our way home. How are things here?'

'We're fine. And we're fully booked till September.'

They might have been neighbours who had never been involved in a dispute. Jeannie had automatically pushed the kettle on the Aga's hotplate. She did it easily, one-handed, and it was an iron kettle. A powerful peasant-type, Vivien thought; the sleeves of her overall bulged over her biceps, her greying hair was permed in tight curls, her eyes were bright and watchful in the fleshy face. She would be watchful, she'd be wondering what Vivien was doing here – and Rupert and Flora waiting outside in the car.

'How is Aileen?' Vivien asked.

'She's well.' It was neutral.

'She wasn't always; she practically accused me of murder.'

Jeannie's eyes flickered; after all, relations between the two households had appeared normal for months. 'It was those tranquillizers mixed with brandy that did it,' she said. She placed tea bags in two mugs. 'I should have watched over her but there, you can't do everything.'

'And she'd been having a hard time of it.'
'Oh, aye. She's a sight better off now.'
'You think so?'
'I know. She's beholden to you, although of course she can't say that.'
'Actually she does. So why are you trying to blackmail me?'
'Blackmail?' Jeannie poured water in the mugs with a steady hand. 'That's an unpleasant word.'
'Two thousand was the figure quoted.'
'Who quoted it?' It was quick and angry.
'Mac wanted two thousand as the price for keeping quiet about Danny crashing our Land Rover. Mac said he did it deliberately.'
Jeannie sat down and Vivien took a chair opposite her. After a while the woman said, 'You mustn't take on. It was an accident.'
'Danny?'
'Oh, Danny's not important; what you did was an accident. I knew, soon as Aileen told me Alastair had gone to Alder, that there'd be trouble. He wasn't sober when he left here.'
'Did you know Mac demanded two thousand from me?'
'Of course I didna! You think I'd have allowed it? Listen, Miss Reid – Mrs Lasco, I should say: I've never seen my girl as carefree as she is now – and there's yourself to thank for it. Blackmail! Hah! I'll give that man a piece of my mind; you won't see him again, I can tell you that now.'
Vivien grinned. 'I know. I went to meet him with a shotgun; he showed his true colours then. There's another small matter. He says Alastair fell in the loch. What made him say that?'
Jeannie sucked in her cheeks and considered the question. 'Whatever happened,' she said slowly, 'I know you didn't mean no malice by it, except maybe he got the first blow in?' The small eyes queried Vivien's. 'You're a fighter,' she added with approval. 'Not like my girl who was never able to stand up to him. I think Mac was guessing. Or could he have seen something? I don't rightly recall how long he was out that night.'
'If he thought that Alastair was in the water why didn't he pull him out?'
'Ah.' Jeannie looked towards the window. Vivien sipped her tea, fascinated by the way the woman's neck was set on her shoulders, like a wrestler's. 'Mac's another one who's better off now,' Jeannie murmured.

'So he tried to blackmail me.'

'He was always one for the main chance, was Mac.'

'But this time he's queered his own pitch. You do see that if he heard Alastair fall in the loch: staggering along the road, drunk, walking off the edge, then if Mac didn't go down and pull him out of the water – which we know he didn't – it's a kind of murder by neglect?'

'How do you know he didn't go down?'

Vivien was immobile. 'And?'

Jeannie smiled. 'You'd have to ask Mac.'

'They're home, Danny.'

He was setting his slug traps. He looked up at Una's call and sighed with relief. He felt as if Alder had been under siege for days. He knew that Vivien had come home to trouble but she was more than a match for Binnie and Forsyth – he hoped; she'd be able to remedy his mistakes if he made any, would definitely stop them wrecking his garden: digging up the winter greens, the cherished onions, the new asparagus bed. He washed his hands at the yard tap, hearing raised voices in the kitchen, entering, grinning, and being hugged. He glowered then and sniffed and shifted his feet, treading on a dog's paw. She was as excited as a child, pulling stuff out of bags – 'Here, Danny, this is for you,' and – 'I must come and see the garden,' but it was ten minutes before she came out, to exclaim in delight at his handiwork. He wasn't interested.

'The police reckon the body's here,' he told her. 'I'm feared they'll start digging.'

'Over *my* dead body.' She was scornful. 'He's in the loch: held down by something, like tree roots.'

'What about the hand?'

'That's another corpse. Give over, love; I'm here now.'

The police were so close behind the Lascos that they must have had word of their homecoming. They arrived an hour later. Vivien and Rupert were in the paddock admiring the pullets which were now running free. They observed the approach of the familiar car without expression.

'No men with dogs and spades,' she murmured. 'Just another interrogation. At least we've silenced Mac; he probably wouldn't have made another attempt at blackmail, but Jeannie will make sure he doesn't. No one's going to talk; everyone's got too much to lose now.'

It was disconcerting to hear Binnie ask if the police could enter the wood. Vivien stared at Forsyth who was hanging back, a position which, a pace behind Binnie, suggested embarrassment, as if she wanted to dissociate herself from this development.

'Why?' Vivien asked. 'What's in our woods that could interest you?'

'You have a warrant?' Rupert asked.

'A warrant?' Binnie looked surprised. 'Why would we need a warrant?'

'In England you'd need one for a search of private property. Is Scotland different?'

'A warrant is needed when you have reasonable cause to suspect a crime,' Binnie said blandly.

'I asked you why you wanted to search our woods,' Vivien said.

'Because a man is missing, ma'am, and part of a body's been found. We need to find the rest of it.'

'What makes you think he's not on the hill – or in the loch?'

'We're searching everywhere, providing no one objects.'

'And if they do?'

'That's their privilege.'

'Right. I object.'

'May I ask why?'

'There are nesting birds in that wood: second broods, vulnerable to disturbance. There are small mammals, all kinds of wildlife; we keep it as a reserve. By going in there you could disrupt years of careful management.'

'We could go in with dogs if—'

'*What!* Never! I—'

'Viv!' Rupert's hand was on her arm. 'Come here a moment.' He led her out of earshot. 'Let them go in now, just the two of them,' he urged. 'That way you'll show them we've got nothing to hide, and it'll keep them from bringing in dogs.'

'Then I'll go with them.'

'Let them go alone. You have to do it, Viv, for all our sakes. The birds will come back,' he added desperately.

She turned back, furious. 'You'll make as little noise as possible,' she ordered. 'That's the most densely populated patch of woodland this side of the watershed. There are – oh shit!' She gestured helplessly and stalked away.

Rupert said quietly to the detectives, 'If you'll come with me—'

Danny was hoeing the onions and the first he knew of the arrival of the police was when they entered the garden, led by Rupert. He stopped work and glared at them.

'They have to go in the wood, Danny,' Rupert said.

'Not without her permission they don't.'

'She's given it.'

'Then why isn't she here?'

Binnie regarded the lad without expression. Forsyth's eyes were on the hands grasping the hoe. The knuckles were pale through the dirt. Once again she resolved to enrol for a course in karate – anything that would prevent this awful sense of insecurity when you faced a person with a potential weapon, even a hoe.

'She left me to do the honours,' Rupert explained, his back to the detectives, grimacing fiercely as he tried to signal Danny not to make the situation worse. But Danny had spent too long brooding over the threat to 'his' land. 'She'd never let 'em in the wood,' he stated. 'It's full of birds and – and more.' He frowned in his turn, trying to convey a message.

'What's more?' Binnie asked.

Danny turned on him savagely, then reverted to Rupert. 'That's the point,' he insisted. 'They can't go there; she don't know yet.'

Binnie stepped forward. It had worked with her, he'd try it here. 'We can bring in dogs,' he said.

'No, no, *no*!' Danny lunged towards him, bringing up his hands, brandishing the hoe.

'*Danny!*' came a shout like a megaphone.

He looked towards the buildings. Una was leaning out of his bathroom window waving a yellow duster. 'Vivien wants you,' she shouted. 'Right away, lad!'

He hesitated, torn between priorities. 'It's badgers,' he said tersely to Rupert. 'Don't let 'em go in there till I get back.' He ran down the path.

'Badgers,' Rupert said, smiling: 'they mean more to us than bodies. You'd better get up there quick before he tells Mrs Lasco.'

Binnie scowled at him but he set off for the upper gate, the one that opened into the wood.

Una had been alerted by Flora who had observed the arrival

of the police from the study. When Vivien stamped into the house swearing with frustration, Una had gone across the yard and up to Danny's bathroom to monitor the confrontation in the garden. When she saw him coming she met him in the yard. 'Into the house with you,' she ordered.

'Vivien—'

'Yes, she's there. Come away—' Her powerful arm was round his waist and he was enough in awe of her even at this moment not to resist.

'Vivien!' she shouted, pushing him into the kitchen.

She came running along the passage, followed by Flora.

'Danny attacked that Binnie,' Una said. 'You speak to him.'

'I didna!' he cried. 'I just had the hoe in me hand. I was telling them they couldna go in the wood.' His voice dropped. 'There may be badgers.'

Everyone gaped. 'Badgers?' Vivien repeated.

'I saw a big old one walking along the back road. If there is a set, or they're looking to make one, it'll be either in our wood or Lair's.'

'That's great, Danny!' Vivien was beaming. As suddenly her face fell. 'Sod them,' she hissed. 'Can we stop them?'

'No,' Rupert said from the doorway. He came in, holding their attention. 'Badgers aren't as important as us,' he told them. 'Think about miscarriages of justice. If we don't let them search, they'll get a warrant and come back with dogs and dig up everything; badgers' sets, the garden, nothing will be sacred. The more you try to stop them the more convinced Binnie will be that a body's buried there. Vivien and I could be arrested, charged, even convicted: both of us. Then what will happen to this place? And yourselves? Forget the badgers, Danny; the police aren't going to kill them.'

'He's right,' Vivien said miserably. 'You have to see that.' She was speaking to all of them.

'Of course Rupert's right,' Una said comfortably. 'And that girl – Forsyth – she's sensible; she'll see he doesn't make too much noise. Now sit down, all of you, and we'll have a cup of tea.'

They stayed in the kitchen for half an hour drinking tea and waiting for the police to come back, but it was a big wood and densely overgrown at this time of year. As Rupert pointed out, Binnie knew that if a body had been buried last winter, there could be few pointers to the grave in July. 'It's possible,' he said generally, 'that the suggestion was made only to see what kind of reaction it would produce.'

'Oh God!' Vivien gasped. 'So my protests' – she glanced at Danny and away – 'convinced them there is something there.'

'The trouble with all of us is that we're as much concerned about disturbing the wildlife as we are that they'd find "a shallow grave", as they say.' Rupert was smiling.

'They won't, will they?' Flora asked.

Danny swore. Vivien looked at her in amazement. Una's lips were compressed. Rupert said gently, 'Someone would have had to bury him, Flora. It couldn't be a drunken accident, like falling in the loch.'

'Oh, how stupid of me! Of course!' She stared at her mug and a slow blush suffused her face as she realized the import of a shallow grave in Alder's wood. As she struggled with the advisability of an apology Una said kindly, 'It's not all that improbable. The police could be thinking that he was so drunk he got lost in the wood, or fell and knocked himself out. There must be lots of deep holes in there among the rocks. The body could have lain all winter without discovery.'

'I never thought of that,' Vivien said. 'If he came along the back road – that is, accepting the premise that he did come here, as Aileen says – he had to come through the woods.' She avoided Danny's eye and turned to Rupert. 'Perhaps he is there after all.'

'That's—' Flora began, and stopped, biting her lip.

Rupert glanced at her and said, 'That would be sinister only until the autopsy showed no sign of foul play. You could be right, Una; Aileen said he'd been drinking when he left Lair.'

The others looked at Vivien who grinned. 'So stop worrying; we're all of us in the clear.'

'It would explain the hand,' Danny pointed out, picking up his cue. 'I don't think an eagle would come down into the trees but a buzzard would, and then the eagle could have robbed the buzzard.'

No one contradicted him, no one knew if eagles did attack buzzards. They drifted away to self-appointed tasks; Una to the back bedrooms from where part of the garden and the fringe of the wood were in view. Danny went back to his hoeing, alert for the slightest alien sound. He didn't hear the police but he guessed they were still in the wood; a blackbird was yelping nervously from the northwest corner.

Rupert, Vivien and Flora went to the study to unpack bags of brochures and books but their attention was on the empty police car and the drive. When the phone rang, Vivien answered. A man asked to speak to Binnie; it was urgent, he said.

There was an argument, and when Vivien started to get heated it was Rupert who went to find Binnie because, he said, she would lose her temper. Flora bent over a brochure, wondering how they would ever have managed without Rupert, remembering how once she'd resented him and now she cast him in the role of their saviour.

In the garden Rupert had a word with Danny who said he'd go with him. He was told to stay where he was. 'I can keep my cool,' Rupert said. 'You and Vivien can't. Understand?'

Danny did. He nodded unhappily, resenting their dire need of direction. Vivien would fight to the end: over my dead body, she'd said, and she meant it. But Rupert was clever: sneaky like an old fox; he'd fight dirty.

Rupert found the police sitting on a log at the top of the path by the gate on to the mountain. He didn't shout as he approached, no one shouted in the wood. He plodded upwards selfconsciously, aware of their scrutiny, his face as expressionless as theirs. He delivered the message, didn't trouble to ask for the result of their search – if they had searched – and the three of them returned to the house.

The caller had hung up and Binnie used the kitchen phone to recall him. Una, kneading bread at the table, sensed rather than saw him stiffen as he listened, heard him bark 'Where?' and saw the flare of excitement in Forsyth's unguarded face.

'What's the state of it?' Binnie asked, and listened again. '*What?*' He was breathing heavily. Una turned her dough with a slap, seeing Forsyth's hand creep out to the back of a chair as if for support.

'How far is that from here?' Binnie asked, then, 'Alder Lodge, where d'you think— Well, look it up; you've got maps. Christ!' He glared at Forsyth. 'Where's the access?' he snapped. 'This side or . . . Then get a chopper laid on and put people in there right away. Have it come back for me; I'm on my way right now.'

Rupert was standing in the doorway, blocking Vivien's attempts to push past him. 'They've found the body?' he asked pleasantly. 'Where?'

Binnie sucked in his cheeks, looking past him to Vivien. She was alert as a pointer. 'Miles from here,' he said. 'Does Corrie Ba mean anything to you?'

They were bewildered. 'It's over the back,' Vivien said weakly, waving a hand. 'Beyond the ridge.'

'Some shepherds found him under a cliff,' Binnie said coldly. 'He's got a hole in the skull: small, like a bullet wound.'

Chapter 15

Flora spoke for all of them. 'How on earth did he get there? Was he found right under the cliff?'

Binnie looked at her sourly. 'He seems to have been climbing,' he said, adding, 'except for the wound.'

Rupert said, 'You must have something to eat before you leave. You've had no lunch.'

'We have something with us, thanks.' He was curt. 'We'll be off now. Good day to you.'

Rupert shouldered Vivien out of the way and accompanied them to the door. He lifted a hand as Forsyth drove off but Binnie appeared not to notice. He was staring ahead, his mouth a thin line. Rupert turned back with a sigh. There was silence from the kitchen.

Vivien had sunk into a chair, realizing that her shock had been misplaced, the body couldn't be Alastair's; there was no way he could have walked seven miles on a winter's night, injured as he was, and climbed a cliff in a snowstorm. This was coincidence; it was the body of a solo climber whom no one had reported missing. The hole had to be some injury from a sharp rock. They were back to square one, just as soon as his dentist confirmed that the teeth weren't Alastair's.

Una, absently setting her dough to prove by the stove, was deeply relieved; she had thought that Vivien killed the fellow, that Rupert disposed of the body, and that Danny had got rid of the Land Rover because it might contain traces.

As for Flora, she'd reached the conclusion that Rupert had fought with Alastair and killed him by accident but now, on reflection, sitting opposite Vivien and staring at the shotguns, she saw that this was impossible. A neat hole was, as Binnie observed, from a bullet, not from a load of shot, and there were no rifles at Alder. She smiled warmly at Vivien, willing her to look less stunned.

Rupert, entering with a bottle of Martell, said, 'What a hell of a day! We all need a stimulant.' He poured a modest measure for each of them. Vivien lifted hers and sipped it. She hadn't spoken since Binnie's announcement.

'I'm so sorry, my dear.' Rupert put a hand on her shoulder and sat down beside her. 'What can Alastair have been doing up there?' he asked clearly, ignoring Flora and Una, looking into her face. Her eyes came round to him and she frowned. 'Climbing alone,' he went on. 'Or do you think he fell from the top? We did wonder about suicide.'

Poor thing, thought Flora, she's in deep shock; she never really faced it till now. He could have been alive: just disappeared abroad because of debts, or he had another woman or something. It could have been an insurance swindle, we wouldn't know. Now Vivien had to face the fact that he was dead. 'Whatever happened, it was sudden,' she said. 'He didn't suffer.'

Vivien stared at her and made to speak but she could only croak. She cleared her throat. 'Fell from the top?' she repeated, turning to Rupert. 'I suppose that's more likely.' She sounded lost. 'Even drunk, he'd hardly have started climbing at night in a blizzard.'

'He needn't have been that drunk when he left Lair,' Rupert said. 'If Aileen thought him sober enough to walk here, he was sober enough to walk over to Corrie Ba. Remember it was still daylight when he set out.'

'So it was,' Vivien said. 'So he was on the hill all the time—'

'I don't think they searched the wood—' Danny interrupted from the passage. He didn't finish but advanced slowly, studying their faces. 'What happened?'

'They found Alastair's body,' Vivien said. 'Under Creag Dubh.'

'Fallen?' He gaped at her. 'It was a *climbing* accident?'

'It could have been deliberate,' Rupert said gently.

Danny couldn't hide his excitement but even Flora pretended not to notice it. After all, she thought, Alastair could be cruel and no doubt he'd been horrid to Danny, he was to everyone. Now he turned and strode across the yard to his flat.

He sat behind his locked bathroom door and hugged himself. He didn't regret that business with the Land Rover; nothing could mar the overwhelming relief that Vivien was no longer in danger. He'd been terribly alarmed when Rupert pointed out that both of them could be convicted and sent to gaol, but the alarm had been more for her than for Alder and what would happen to the staff. Now the worry, the wasted energy, were nothing compared with the exhilaration of knowing she was safe. All that time when she'd been protesting that Alastair was alive when he left Alder, she'd been telling the truth – and of course the guy was alive after Rupert tipped him out of the Land Rover. Rupert hadn't committed any crime either.

He dashed cold water on his face and grinned in the mirror. At that moment he heard her call from downstairs. He opened the bathroom door and she started up, giving him a wry smile in response to his obvious elation. She walked into his living room and turned to face him.

'You didn't hear all the conversation back there in the kitchen,' she said.

The elation died. 'Something's wrong?'

'It's just a wee bit complicated. Flora and Una still don't know that Alastair came here that night, so Rupert put forward the suggestion to them that he went straight over to Corrie Ba from Lair. I went along with that, Danny.' It was a warning.

'But you don't have to say that now! He had to be alive when he left here. I mean' – he blushed and stammered – 'I m–mean if the police . . . but you didn't tell them—'

'He *was* alive,' she said gently. 'The trouble is, that may not be Alastair's body. It could be a stranger. You see? So we still have to keep quiet about him being here.'

'Oh' – a heavy sigh – 'yes, I see.' In the silence the chirping of sparrows was loud in the eaves. 'I'll not tell a soul,' he assured her then, desperately, 'but it will be him, won't it?'

She echoed his sigh. 'I expect so, Danny.'

'It's a bastard,' Binnie exploded. 'And just as we were getting so close!' If he'd been driving he'd have hammered the steering wheel.

Forsyth tried not to smile but risked a light touch. 'Like someone said when Adelaide Bartlett was acquitted: "Now she should tell us how she did it." '

'Who the hell was she?'

'A woman who stood trial for the murder of her husband.'

Binnie looked past her to the trees above the loch. After a while he asked, 'How did she do it?'

'Adelaide Bartlett?'

'Don't play games with me. This woman. Vivien Lasco.'

'It doesn't have to be Alastair's body.'

He didn't turn a hair. 'It would be a very odd coincidence if it wasn't him. There's no identification on him but his wife should recognize the clothes, not to speak of his dentist; the jaw's still intact. Assuming it's him, what do we make of that hole? I've only seen shotguns at Alder.'

'It could be that something pierced his skull on the way down: a broken branch for instance.'

'Trees? Up there?'

'Stunted hollies, rowans, yes. We'll know after the autopsy. Isn't it odd that shepherds should have seen the hole? You'd think with hair, a balaclava—'

'Animals have been at it, and maggots; it's been a hot summer. You never answered the question: assuming it's him, how did she do it?'

'Climbing? There has to be gear—'

'Climbing? That night? He was last seen around three thirty and by next morning he was missing. They went climbing on the night of the blizzard? Or did she lure him up there just as it was getting dark?'

She nodded. 'It can't be him. We're back to square one.'

'With a wound in the back of the skull. Let's hope you're right and it's an accident – and to a stranger. A second mystery death is all we need.'

'How long do we have?' Vivien whispered.

Rupert calculated. 'Presumably the dentist hasn't seen the skull yet because it's surely only a matter of minutes to compare the teeth with his records. If – *if* we assume working hours on his part we may have until around nine tomorrow morning.'

'And as soon as Binnie discovers it's not Alastair, he'll be back. Someone's going to break; one of us, I mean. They all know.'

He didn't contradict her; the profound relief of the others had been obvious. He knew that, without exception, they'd come to suspect that one or both of their employers had been responsible for Alastair's disappearance.

They were sitting on the sofa in their bedroom. The room was lit only by the moon and the house was quiet. They sat close, the better to hear each other's low voices as they plotted tomorrow's action.

'I'm not going to confess straight away,' Vivien said. 'I'll lead Binnie towards me: leave avenues open for him to exploit. Finally I'll tell the truth: that it was an accident. I'll probably get around two years for manslaughter.'

'You can't do that because the one who hit him has to be the one who disposed of the body, otherwise we'll both be in gaol, and then what happens to Alder and the others?'

'In that case I drove the Land Rover and tipped him in the loch. I can cope with prison better than you, and you'll be better at running the business while I'm inside. But the clincher is that I'll get a lighter sentence than you would; he was known for beating up women.' Rupert was silent. 'With good behaviour I could be out inside two years,' she insisted. 'I can write several books in that time.'

A fox barked down by the loch. From the far shore came an answering call. She closed her eyes in anguish, anticipating the dreadful loss of two years of freedom. 'It's common sense,' she urged. 'You're being sentimental.'

'What!'

'Chivalrous, if you prefer. My way's the best for everyone. Now this is the situation: Binnie comes back tomorrow and eventually I shall break down and tell the truth. You can't stop me. Then I'll say I drove the Land Rover, and put the body in the loch. No one can prove I didn't. You had to help me get him in the back of course, but you thought he was alive and I was merely running him home. Anyway, they're not going to be bothered who put him in the truck, even about dumping the body, what Binnie's concerned with is who killed him. So there you are: you're left in the clear to hold the fort until I come back.'

'They haven't got a body yet.' He seized on the one chance to stop her confessing. 'Not Alastair's body, if that's a stranger on Creag Dubh.'

'I think they'll go ahead without a body. It's been done. And Binnie's after blood.'

Breakfast at Alder was a fraught affair. The Lascos were preoccupied and Una and Danny watched them covertly, concerned about her obvious tension, about Rupert's pallor. Flora, sensing a problem, tried to convince everyone that they were now back to normal: Alastair had fallen while climbing and any suspicion of foul play had evaporated. She chattered brightly and made everyone selfconscious. In the end Una snapped at her, she came back with a retort concerning her seniority, and Vivien got up and walked out of the kitchen.

Rupert tried to smooth things down and followed, to find her sitting in front of her desk. 'Come on,' he urged. 'We're going to go and look for traces of the badgers.'

The phone call came at nine thirty. Vivien's presence was requested at police headquarters. There was a ghastly humour in the phrasing. She had her overnight bag already packed and it included her notes of the Utah trip and a book on American deserts. The bag went in the boot of the Subaru and she left with Rupert without saying goodbye, pretending to the last that she would be back for tea.

Neither was surprised when Binnie suggested he should see her alone. Rupert said he'd do some shopping and meet her in the Caledonian for lunch. He was putting a brave face on it, implying that his wife was merely filling in some gaps for the police, almost a kind of consultant. As for Vivien, she entered Binnie's office feeling cold and empty but well prepared. She was surprised that the interview should be in an office rather than the kind of room she thought they used for criminals but she assumed that this was a ploy, part of a softening-up process. In any event she had no time to dwell on it: Binnie was seating himself behind a desk, Forsyth sat at the side – with a notebook. No tape recorder? It must be behind her – or hidden—

'Now, Mrs Lasco,' Binnie was saying. 'We want you to tell us when you last saw Alastair Semple.'

Very formal. Starting all over again at the beginning, but she was, as yet, the innocent witness.

'When we returned from Skye,' she said. 'In September.'

'Did you see him on the Friday when he went missing?'

'No.'

'Did he come to Alder Lodge that day?'

'Not to my knowledge.'

'Could he have come without you seeing him?'

She hesitated. Could the answer involve Rupert? 'It's possible,' she admitted. She wondered whether to say she had been in her study most of the day, and thought better of it. Give them no more than is necessary.

'Can you offer any explanation for the wound in his head?'

She was silent for too long. As she became aware of this she said no, sharply, then added on a lighter note, 'If he was climbing – winter climbing – he'd have an axe. Was an axe found?'

'A pickaxe?' A pause. 'What's funny about that, ma'am?'

'A pickaxe is what you dig up the road with. Climbers use ice axes, axes for short.' There was no response. 'Was he carrying one?' she asked.

'One was found nearby with the – attachment broken.'

'The wrist sling. Yes, it would be after that fall.'

'You've seen the spot?'

'Not where he fell. I know the height of Creag Dubh.' Why were they concentrating on this strange body when they knew— She looked down at the desk. Had the jaw been crushed so there was no way of identifying him after all?

'So you think the pick – the ice axe made the hole in his head,' Binnie mused.

'I can't say. It's possible.'

'The back of the skull.' He indicated the position on his own head.

She allowed herself to be side-tracked by this problem, regarding her own wrist, raising her arm, elbow bent, to behind her head. 'At first,' she said, 'the axe would still be attached to him by the wrist sling, but he'd release his grip on the shaft as he fell, and you'd have this vicious point whirling round – like having a dagger attached to your belt in a long fall; every time he hit something on the way down, he could be stabbed by his own weapon – his axe.'

'There were no other wounds of that type.'

'There didn't have to be. He could have been stabbed on the first impact. At the second the wrist sling broke.'

'Ah, you'd know, you're the expert. The axe was certainly the weapon that was used. It fits that hole as if it was made for it. What was he doing up there?'

'I've puzzled over that—' She checked. It was too chatty. 'I can't think,' she said, recalling that this wasn't Alastair they were discussing, so Binnie was playing with her. She reminded herself that she had to pretend it was Alastair, for a little longer anyway, so that the confession would seem to be dragged out of her. If it came too easily they could think she was shielding Rupert.

'How long would it take him to walk there from his home?' Binnie asked.

'Seven miles from Lair?' She calculated, going along with the cat-and-mouse game. 'He'd do it inside three hours.'

'As much as that?'

'There's a lot of uphill work.'

'And he fell from the top, not from low down.'

She didn't question it, he'd be familiar with bodies that had fallen a long way; from high-rise tenements, for instance.

'So,' he said with a sigh, as if he were working down a list of tiresome questions, 'what was he doing up there?'

He'd just asked her that. Suddenly, after only a few minutes, she was tired. 'How the hell would I know? Aileen said he'd been drinking; I wouldn't climb with him... Perhaps he went up to Creag Dubh to prove something, to prove he didn't need—' She stopped.

'Didn't need you?' Forsyth asked quietly.

Vivien transferred her attention to the girl. 'Didn't need a climbing partner,' she corrected.

'You were more than a climbing partner,' Forsyth said.

'Not in my book,' Vivien flared. 'And I wasn't even his climbing partner; I took him when no one else was around, that's all.'

'You got tired of him.'

'I was always tired of him.'

'Because he was dependent on you.'

'What's wrong with that? Who wants a man who wants a mother?'

'A *mother*!' Binnie was incredulous.

'A boss then. Alastair wanted to be bossed around. He was spineless on his own. That's why—'

'Why he knocked Aileen about?' Forsyth suggested.

Vivien glared at her. 'Did he knock you about on the rock?' Forsyth asked.

'Don't be daft.'

'Or any other time?'

'You're out of your mind. He never touched me.'

'Never?' Their eyes locked. Vivien grimaced and turned back

to Binnie, pointedly waiting for a sensible question.

'That wound in the back of the head could be murder,' he said. 'Made with the pickaxe certainly, but someone was wielding it.'

'Oh yes.' She had a grip on herself now. 'Someone he was climbing with? In the dark, in a blizzard? *Two* madmen on the cliff?'

'Not climbing with, but someone he was with, yes. In the dark certainly, but the snow didn't start till after midnight.'

She didn't deign to reply to that, had already realized that, if someone had gone up to Corrie Ba with Alastair, they couldn't have been home again before seven thirty at the earliest, by which time all her people had come back from Inverness. There were four witnesses to swear she was at Alder when they returned. But then, it wasn't Alastair...

Forsyth said carelessly, 'It could have been a stranger.'

Vivien raised an eyebrow; at last they were conceding it wasn't Alastair. 'The body? You're saying a stranger was pushed—'

'No,' Binnie said. 'No one pushed a stranger off that cliff. It was Alastair.'

She frowned. 'I'm not with you. You're saying Alastair was with a stranger?'

'That's Alastair's body.'

'Yes, well, why bring a stranger into it?' What twist in the game was this? Some ploy to force her to confess? She'd lost command of the situation; she felt she was losing control of herself.

'We weren't sure until we'd seen his dentist,' Binnie said. 'Dentists keep charts of their patients' teeth. It's a positive identification. The body is Alastair's.'

'You're shocked,' Forsyth said kindly. 'I'll fetch a cup of tea.'

'I'm not shocked,' Vivien countered, trying to keep her hands out of sight. 'I'm bewildered. We knew it was Alastair. You told me it was. Weren't you sure?'

'What made you so sure?' Binnie asked.

'Why, because you said so!' They didn't rise to that. She looked from one to the other; she was gathering strength, working back to the role of innocent neighbour. 'We assumed— We didn't question— After all, he had to be carrying identification. Everyone does. Like, a wallet?'

'All identification had been removed,' Binnie said.

She blinked, alert to the phrasing but making no comment on

it. 'So you didn't really know until this morning?'

'And when did your husband last see Alastair?' Binnie asked.

She picked up her handbag. 'I can remember for myself, but I couldn't tell you when my husband last saw a man around a year ago. You must ask him, but you'll have to come to Alder. We're running a business and none of us can spare time to drive here and repeat answers to questions you asked months ago.'

They made no attempt to stop her leaving. She found a cab and drove to the Caledonian where she discovered Rupert ostensibly reading the *Scotsman*, a stack of newspapers beside him. His initial delight at her appearance died with her greeting.

'Have you been waiting long, darling?' she asked in a loud county accent.

He grunted and collected his papers. 'I suppose you want to go straight home?'

If anyone were watching them (which she was afraid of) this churlish familiarity clashed with his initial joy. That couldn't be helped. She didn't speak until they reached the car and then she waited until they were inside and the doors closed. Then, 'It's Alastair,' she told him. 'The dental records check.'

'How can it be?'

'I know. It means he had to be alive. We didn't kill him.'

They stared at each other, speechless; for months neither had been sure which of them had killed Alastair, but both were ready to assume responsibility.

Rupert broke the silence. 'Mac *was* there; he went down and pulled him out of the water and some time afterwards Alastair went over to Corrie Ba and jumped off the top of the cliff.'

'I think we stick to our original story,' she said.

'Why? Well, I know it wasn't a very nice thing to do: tipping a drunk out of the Land Rover on a night like that—'

'Not for that reason, but because we don't know what happened. There's that wound in the skull.' She gave him the additional information culled from Binnie. 'And there was no identification on him,' she pointed out. 'Binnie said it had been removed. Taken with his suggestion that Alastair could have been murdered, it points to someone at Lair.'

'Why would Mac pull him out of the water, then murder him? And how would he get the body to Corrie Ba?'

'Perhaps Mac wasn't there – and Alastair reached home on his own. Suppose he was only concussed and by luck he didn't hit a tree on the way down, not with his head anyway. The water revived him and he managed to stagger home. It wasn't far.'

'Then what?'

'Aileen? No.'

'Why not? It's classic: the battered wife finally rebelling.'

'No, she couldn't handle a horse then. That's how Alastair was taken to the top of the cliff: on the back of a pony. They're used to bringing stags down off the hill, and a stag weighs more than Alastair did.'

'But that was the night the snow came.'

'It didn't start till after midnight. Mac had plenty of time.'

'You're suggesting we keep quiet to protect him?'

'No, I'm merely suggesting we keep quiet. I can see how Binnie's mind's working: it's a murder rigged to look like a climbing accident; that, and the location of the body point to another climber as the killer. We'll wait and see what Mac's next move is.'

Rupert frowned, pondering. 'What did Binnie actually want to see you for?'

'You think he does suspect me – still? It's impossible, Rupert; I have an alibi: four alibis.'

'He could be thinking in terms of collusion. He must have had some reason for wanting to see you.'

'The wound: he was asking me how it could have occurred by accident. But Forsyth did ask me – again – if Alastair knocked me about – ah!'

'What?'

She grimaced. 'She suggested he beat Aileen because of me – sort of.'

'She's not the first to suggest that,' he said meaningly.

She glowered. 'Let's get home. Whatever happened, it's nothing to do with us.'

Chapter 16

In the days that followed the residents of Alder Lodge withdrew inside their boundaries. The press, realizing that the celebrated author, Vivien Reid, was a neighbour of the dead man, sought her out, assuming that they'd climbed together. They claimed they needed the expert's comments on the likely circumstances of the accident. By now the media had discovered that some victims of long falls did suffer terrible injuries from their own axes but the repetition of bizarre facts did no harm to a newspaper's circulation figures. However, reporters who visited Alder were disappointed, never getting any further than Rupert or Una. They might hear sounds from the open windows of the study but its closed door (and her protectors) barred all access to Vivien – and to Flora, whose loyalty was less in doubt than her discretion.

The inquiry into Alastair's death concluded that it was accidental, a verdict which put the seal on any doubt remaining in people's minds, with the possible exception of the police, but the police were keeping a low profile. At Alder preliminary work started on the Utah novel, Vivien going through the familiar stages of purdah and slide shows to hard writing. In the outside world there were rumours concerning the sale of Lair but if the others discussed them in Vivien's presence she ignored them. So when, several weeks into the novel, she emerged exhausted from the study one afternoon, not only was she still preoccupied by red rock canyons, she wasn't conscious of the latest developments in the real world.

She put on her sheepskin and called the dogs but there was no response. No one seemed to be about and she wandered up through the wood and without thinking turned right on the back road to Lair.

The simplest of sensations recalled her to reality. First, she was too warm and she removed her coat, then she found it bulky to carry and wondered why she'd worn it. She drifted through the shade of some hollies and her feet scrunched ice. She stopped, bewildered as a wakened sleepwalker; she'd thought it was summer and here it was autumn. She walked on, amused and thankful that she could afford staff to run her house; as an author she'd make an appalling housekeeper. She remembered now that she'd sent Flora out to take advantage of the glorious afternoon; no doubt they were all walking – and why was she walking towards Lair which they had avoided for so long? Alastair was gone of course, but there was Mac. Had someone said Mac was absent – just a mention, something that went in one ear and out the other, something about Aberdeen and oil rigs? As the Utah world receded, Lair and Mac bulked larger; her nature couldn't accept a vacuum.

When the woods of Lair came in view she worked up the hillside on a long diagonal and sat down on a boulder. Lair was quiet and there was no movement except a couple of ponies grazing in a paddock. It occurred to her that she'd seen no sign of the bullocks that were usually on the slope above the back road. She frowned; she couldn't see Aileen or her mother looking after cattle. A Land Rover was parked at the side of the big house, another by the cottage. Suddenly the cottage door opened and Jeannie's solid figure emerged, a coat over her pink overall and gum boots on her feet. She was carrying a basket. She opened the garden gate but she didn't go to the big house; she turned left, threading her way through weeds and old farm implements to another gate and the entrance to the woods.

Vivien stood up and started to make her way down the slope towards the trees. Those at the top of the wood were mostly birch and oak, as at Alder; the lower section held the legacy of nineteenth-century lairds who had followed the fashion for sequoias and exotic pines to create that dim Victorian ambiance so typical of large Highland houses.

Jeannie was picking blackberries in a clearing among the birches. Companionably as they talked, Vivien picked with her. She was surprised to learn that Aileen was on the hill with some riders, but this was the last booking, Jeannie told her.

'Until next season,' Vivien murmured.

'No.' Jeannie was equable. 'The very last. Aileen's selling, didn't they tell you?'

'I'm working on a new book. If they did, I didn't notice. So – she has a buyer?'

'I hope she has because now's the time to sell so that the new people can do the house up before next summer. There's a couple who want to carry on with the pony-trekking. They're talking big: buying more stock, building a couple of bungalows, employing folk from Inch.'

'That's great. But what about you and Mac? Will you stay on to help with the business?'

'I reckon we've worked through this lot.' Jeannie extricated herself from the brambles and looked up towards the mountain. 'Mac walked out on us,' she said calmly. 'Our cottage is included in the sale of course, so Aileen and me'll be leaving together.'

'Yes, well, at least you won't be destitute.' Vivien was at a loss for sensible comment. 'I'm sorry to hear about Mac.'

Jeannie was quite happy to talk. Perhaps mother and daughter had talked the subject into the ground and she welcomed a fresh listener. 'He knew Aileen would sell soon as the body was found, and there was no love lost between 'em so no money would be coming his way. Nothing to keep him here, so off he went.'

Nothing to keep him except his wife, thought Vivien; evidently no love lost there either. 'When did he go?' she asked.

'A couple of months since. Not a word to me except he'd said something about finding work on the oil rigs when Aileen sold up. I came downstairs one morning knowing he hadn't come home the night before, never come to bed, and he wasn't on the settee like he is when he comes in drunk. His Land Rover wasn't in the yard but I didn't think much to that. He drank hard when he was in the money. But he never come back.'

Vivien thought of the second Land Rover she'd seen outside the cottage. Jeannie started to stroll downhill, following a path. 'Then when Aileen went to her truck,' she continued, 'there was a note on the seat telling her his'n was at the station.'

Vivien gaped. 'Which station?'

'Why, Inverness of course. We had to go and fetch it.'

'Didn't the note say anything else?'

'Nothing. But he phoned. Said he was in Aberdeen—' The rest of this was lost because they were walking in single file and Jeannie was leading, talking to the air.

Vivien pondered, staring thoughtfully at the solid back and a gaping shoulder seam. It was an old tweed jacket: one of Mac's, she surmised.

They came to the conifers and a grassy ride where they could walk abreast. 'Is he working on the oil rigs?' Vivien asked politely.

'I doubt it, he's too old. I doubt he was in Aberdeen at all. He had to say he was somewhere but he's not going to tell the truth, is he, with the police looking for him?'

'They are? Why?'

'Well, it won't be because of the money.' Jeannie was smiling.

'You said he drank when he was in the money. Did he sell the bullocks?'

'No, we sold those after he left. The day I'm talking about Aileen had just been to the bank. A hundred and fifty pound disappeared from her bag.'

'*Mac* stole it?'

'Well, I didna.'

'Good lord, Jeannie! No wonder you don't seem to be missing him much.'

The woman shrugged meaty shoulders. Vivien shivered. Despite her sheepskin she felt cold under the sombre pines. A damselfly that had escaped the frost darted through a ray of sunshine, bright as blue enamel. 'Where's the water?' she asked.

'What?'

'Oh, of course: the pool. That damselfly came from the pool.'

Jeannie wasn't interested. 'He's a clever bugger,' she said, with a touch of pride. 'Binnie won't ever catch him.'

'Binnie?' Vivien repeated stupidly. 'Catch who?'

'Mac, of course. Run rings round the police, will Mac. Aileen doesn't care. It's like you all over again, isn't it? Remember? It was me made her see she should be grateful to you – but I was wrong all the time! Well, part wrong. Alastair came to Alder that night but you didn't kill him.'

Vivien regarded her stonily. 'Is this an apology?'

'For what?' Jeannie was amused. 'I never harmed you, and I soothed Aileen down. Didn't I always say it was an accident?'

'When did you change your mind?'

Jeannie stopped walking. She sighed heavily and looked round as if seeking help among the pines. Water showed between the reddish trunks where a pool lay unruffled by any breeze, a short wall of rock on the far side sliding into depths like black treacle.

'The riders were climbing out of Corrie Ba,' she said. 'And they realized there were men among the rocks under the cliff. They stopped and Aileen says she knew what had happened immediately she saw them 'cause they were police, see, in uniform. What else would they be doing up there? Then she looked at Mac – and he looked like he'd given up; he'd been holding out on her, said he'd tell her where the body was if she'd go halves on the sale of the estate.'

'Why didn't she turn him in?'

'Because he'd say she killed Alastair and took him up there on a pony.'

'She couldn't manage a pony at that time.'

'The police wouldn't know that. It was after the body was found that Mac left.'

'Why then?'

'We all knew, didn't we? No way the body could be got up there 'cept on a pony, and only Mac had the ponies. Funny thing though, it truly was an accident. Alastair, he got out of the water and came home, no trouble at all.' Vivien frowned. Jeannie went on reproachfully, 'And that was a very nasty crack on the head you gave him—'

'Hell! He asked for it!'

'Maybe. He was hot-blooded, like all the Semples.'

'So how did— Why did Mac clobber him?'

'It was an accident.'

'Not stabbing a man in the back of the head with an ice axe.'

'I don't know.' Jeannie regarded her helplessly. She looked defeated. 'They were fighting over something, Alastair wasn't himself: drunk, suffering from the blow you gave him; all I know is Mac said it was an accident. As for the axe, Mac put the tape thing round Alastair's wrist so that stabbing happened in the fall – I think.' She looked away. 'And the inquiry brought it in as accidental. Least said, soonest mended. It's my family, Mrs Lasco; leave it be.'

'After that,' Vivien told Rupert when they were changing that evening, 'I felt I was dismissed. My questions had been impertinent anyway although at the time I felt that she was leading me on, that she wanted to talk. Then she warned me off. Perhaps she regretted what she'd said.'

Rupert sniffed: the faintest sign of derision. 'More likely it was because you came too near the knuckle by questioning the ice-axe wound. Obviously Mac stabbed him and set it up to look like an accident. As you said, a pony was used to get the body up there. And Jeannie knows everything.' He was thoughtful.

'But the case is closed. We don't know the police thinking but the inquiry brought the death in as accidental. So why did she tell me at this stage?'

Rupert walked into the bathroom: not rudely because he came back; he was pacing. He stopped. 'She had to tell you. You knew Alastair could never have walked to Corrie Ba that night. He was drunk and concussed so badly I thought he was dead – but he wasn't; he got home and he told them you'd hit him and that someone, he wouldn't know who but they'd know it had to be one of us, had tipped him in the loch. So they knew all along that once his body was found, we'd know he couldn't have gone out again that night on his own feet. That meant someone had to take him to Corrie Ba. In fact, someone else killed him, not you – or me. Jeannie told you who it was, otherwise you might have thought it was Aileen. Probably she'd been waiting for weeks for an opportunity to tell you.'

'I wouldn't have thought of Aileen because she couldn't manage a pony at that time. D'you think Jeannie wants me to pass this on to the police? I'm not going to of course' – as he made an impatient movement – 'it's her family and her business.'

Binnie was like an old lion baulked of his prey. He was well aware that one of the easiest ways to commit murder is on a remote cliff; there are no witnesses, in this case there was nothing to show that anyone else was present. Method was suspect, opportunity difficult, the motives: legion. Any or all of them could have had a motive. He'd favoured Vivien initially of course but he was forced to dismiss her, at least officially. Even if everyone at Alder was lying: saying she was home that Friday evening when the staff returned from Inverness, the problem of how she got the body to where it was found was insoluble. As Forsyth pointed out, going for the jugular as women did, if there was so much friction between these former lovers, how did she manage to lure him seven miles into the mountains as dusk was falling on a threatening winter's afternoon? Forsyth favoured suicide, as did most people except Binnie, but since no one knew, and Aileen was working hard to keep her head above water, Authority, bearing insurance claims in mind, turned a blind eye, and officially Alastair died an accidental death. Binnie still thought it was murder and he was eager to find Mac but so far there was no word of his whereabouts. He didn't think Mac was working on an oil platform, it was more likely that he'd found a job in some stables. In that case he could be anywhere: Newmarket, Ireland, even abroad. At the very least the fellow must know something, Binnie thought; Jeannie wasn't telling the whole story. She was covering for Mac – who could even be the killer – but that woman was stolid as an ox, he'd never got anywhere with her. Her husband had walked out on her and that was that.

At Alder people settled to the familiar but exciting routine of autumn: Vivien and Flora engrossed in the book, Rupert negotiating rights and considering where would be the most stimulating destination – colourful and evocative – for the New Year. Danny prepared his garden for winter, strengthened his fences against marauding deer, built up the log pile and, in the evenings, listened to Mozart, his latest discovery.

The sale of Lair was agreed in early December and the Lascos were forced to discuss the question of how they should say goodbye to Aileen and Jeannie. To allow them to leave without a word would be unneighbourly but to have them to dinner could prove embarrassing for everyone, horrifying if Flora were to come out with some outrageous remark in a misguided effort to put people at their ease. However, to ignore their imminent departure would imply that the Lascos held the Lair women responsible for the sins of their menfolk. 'Maybe not responsible,' Vivien stated. 'But there was collusion.'

'And Aileen did have a breakdown,' Rupert pointed out. 'Her hostility was mainly hysteria.'

Vivien wasn't so sure about that but they settled on a compromise and invited Aileen and Jeannie for drinks.

The women arrived one evening, Aileen looking marvellous in a cream trouser suit, Jeannie solid in navy wool. They brought an elegant decanter, unwrapped to show it wasn't a Christmas present, explaining that they were afraid it would be broken in store, asking Vivien if she would give it a home. She was touched and wished she'd invited them to dinner.

The visit went well. Aileen was open about their plans; they were putting their few possessions in store (the grim old Victorian furniture was to be sold with the house) and they were going to stay with friends in the Borders: friends with horses. Aileen confided that with tuition she might improve her riding; she could now cope with any of the ponies at Lair and she thought it would be exciting to see just how far she could progress. Vivien, observing her, thought she'd go a long way, not perhaps in a horsey career but married to a rich countryman. She couldn't see Aileen flying over stone walls but she'd grace any meet, mounted on a sleek hunter. In the last year the woman had blossomed, her beauty enhanced by good health and the way she carried herself, conveying superb confidence. Even her voice had softened but it was firm, part of the new image. There was no stridency now, and no diffidence. Vivien recognized that the nervous breakdown had been an isolated incident, an aberration between the battered housewife and the integrated personality she'd become. She warmed to her and wished she weren't leaving. She said so, quietly, as they sat apart from the others – and so it was Vivien herself who led up to the subject which she and Rupert had been afraid that Flora might introduce inadvertently.

'I envy you,' she said sincerely, 'setting out on a new life and a new activity: horses. It's like starting at the bottom in climbing: all those different experiences ahead – new climbs, new horses. You look as enthusiastic as I used to feel.'

'We've come full circle,' Aileen said. 'You've no idea how I used to envy you. You didn't give a damn for security, or danger, or men, and me – I was scared of horses! Now, would you believe it, I want the wild ones – well, not quite yet, but I like the awkward beasts best. I love the challenge, the uncertainty: who's going to win this time, you know? It's the danger, isn't it? I've caught up with you.' She was excited, her eyes flashing. 'You were my role model,' she confessed.

'Then why on earth—' Vivien checked, aware of Rupert on the other side of the room, his sharp eyes on her. 'You didn't have much time for me at one point,' she said carefully.

'What did you expect? The battered wife, the other woman treated like a goddess.'

Vivien flinched. 'You must have loathed me.'

'I suppose so. I don't remember loathing – but it would have been the natural reaction after Skye. Don't look so surprised, it was obvious. Before Skye he just taunted me; afterwards he was telling me the truth.'

'He told you a lot of lies: like me leaving Rupert to go away with him.'

'I discounted that as trimmings.' Aileen was dismissive. 'I knew Alastair pretty well.'

'Then you knew we weren't having an affair.' Vivien was indignant. 'And yet you told everyone we were. Why?'

Aileen's eyes flickered under the intense stare. 'You're right,' she conceded. 'I did hate you at the time. But don't forget' – momentarily the clear eyes were flat, implacable – 'life wasn't easy for me. You saw the damage.' Vivien licked her lips. 'What I thought,' Aileen went on, more easily, 'was that if you turned on him, if he infuriated you . . . ' She trailed off. 'Not very neighbourly of me, was it?'

'You were expecting me to kill him?' Vivien's voice rose. She paused, looked away and saw Danny and Flora staring at her. She shook her head as she turned back, a reluctant smile forming. 'You weren't drugged, you were setting me up! And afterwards you had the bloody nerve to ask me where I'd put the body!'

'Did I? I may have implied you knew where he was, but you did ask me what I was doing that Friday night.'

'Tit for tat? And all the time you knew that Mac was the one you should have been gunning for, you and Jeannie together.' Vivien glanced across to where Una and Jeannie were in earnest conversation.

'We weren't gunning for anyone,' Aileen assured her. 'We knew that when the body was found they'd bring in a verdict of accidental death; it was natural for me to have suspicions of you until then, at least so far as the police were concerned. It would have been unnatural *not* to appear jealous.' There was a long pause. 'It was better that he should have an accident,' she insisted.

They regarded each other steadily. Hanging in the air was the observation that Aileen had continued to voice suspicions of Vivien when they were alone, that they had both accepted the verdict of accidental death without a murmur, at least without any public expression of doubt. Vivien looked into the lovely eyes and remembered that it was seven miles to the top of Creag Dubh and all of it uphill and over rough country. Aileen couldn't have led a pony that distance, let alone loaded a corpse on to its back. It had to be Mac. And yet— 'I suppose we all share the responsibility,' she murmured with an air of defeat.

Aileen smiled. 'Does it matter?'

Lair stood empty while negotiations progressed. Mac's dogs had been given away, the ponies shipped east to spend the winter on good pasture; Vivien took the cats and a few hens. In the New Year the Lascos spent a month exploring the Western Ghats of India and by the time they returned the sale of Lair was completed and the new owners were hoping to move in during the spring. Their name was Barstow: Edward and Angela. Edward was a banker who had taken early retirement.

During the latter part of the winter the Barstows came north several times, flying to Inverness from their home in East Anglia and hiring a car. They seemed to have money to burn and they weren't short of energy either. They stayed at the hotel in Inch but they spent all the daylight hours at Lair, accompanied by surveyors, builders, water engineers, even foresters. They were the right age to be settling in the Highlands: old enough to appreciate the problems but still young enough to have enthusiasm. Angela was plain and plump but fashionably green; she was going to grow her own produce organically, to fell most of the conifers and replant with native species; she was going to establish new wetlands and drain the pool in the wood – which their advisers said was responsible for damp in the cellars, something that Edward would not tolerate. He was a wine buff and told a story of a friend whose cellar had flooded, floating all the labels off his bottles. Their pool seeped, it didn't flood, but it smelled, and that was unacceptable.

With the snow level at two thousand feet the Barstows chartered a helicopter and, taking Vivien along as the local expert, they had a fascinating morning exploring the deer forest from the air. Vivien was enchanted by the view of familiar terrain from this unfamiliar angle; she was appalled by the drops under ridges which she traversed so casually, surprised by the deceptive level of the snowy plateau which she knew wasn't level at all and – 'Where did Alastair Semple fall?' asked Angela Barstow.

They were flying round the summit of Garsven. Under Vivien's direction the pilot turned back and flew along the face of Creag Dubh. Vivien stared expressionlessly at the snow-banked ledges, at the ribbons of gullies draped with ice, at black overhangs. Below, the boulder field looked like a floor of white cobbles.

Snow covered the stalker's path but she knew where it was and could trace its line through Corrie Ba and up the side of the cliff to the ridge. From that point it was less than half a mile to the top of the crags: a few minutes for a loaded pony – and on that night over a year ago the snow hadn't come till after midnight. She wondered where Mac was now.

The Barstows moved into Lair in March and very shortly the place came to resemble a construction camp, something which the residents of Alder accepted good-humouredly in view of Angela's abject apologies. They had brought their own builders from England whom they housed in trailers, but people from Inch supplied all the labour, and earth-moving equipment was hired from Inverness. The conifers came down, leaving only three sequoias; a series of ponds was scraped out below the house and a rash of pink tubes appeared on their margins protecting tiny willows. They started to drain the black pool.

At Alder they were finishing lunch one day when the telephone rang. Una answered it. 'It's Mrs Barstow,' she told Vivien. 'She wants to speak to you.'

Vivien, who had been arguing about monsoon times with Rupert, took the phone carelessly. Angela was always ringing to ask for information. She listened, first blankly, then shocked. 'Are you sure?' she breathed. 'There must be – it could be a log... Yes, I – we'll come right away.'

She put down the phone. Four faces were turned to her. She felt for a chair. 'They drained the pool,' she said. 'They let all the water out.'

'Well!' Rupert barked, appearing angry in his concern. She'd gone white. 'What's there?'

She looked past him to the window. 'A body,' she said.

Edward Barstow was a mild-looking man but Rupert maintained that this was a mask, the man was sharp. The sharpness was in evidence when the Lascos arrived, accompanied by Angela who had been waiting for them in the yard. Angela needed a strong woman with her at this moment; she needed support and an explanation. Edward, standing on the margin of what had been the pool, in conversation with men in hard hats, needed only an explanation.

Vivien was momentarily disconcerted by the open space where

the trees had been felled but then she realized that she and Rupert were the focus of attention. She looked from Edward to the waste of grey mud: indecent in its exposure to the light. At the far side, under the rock outcrop and half-submerged in the ooze, was the unmistakable outline of a body: the back encased in slimy folds of clothing, the legs sprawled, one arm outstretched. The head wasn't distinguishable; it must be lower than the trunk.

'Who is it?' Angela whispered.

'I've no idea,' Vivien said.

'I phoned the police,' Edward told them. 'They'll take a while getting here. Let's go to the house and have coffee. You stay here,' he told the man who was evidently the foreman. 'Nothing's to be touched.'

They sat in the kitchen drinking coffee laced liberally with brandy. There were faint sounds of builders elsewhere in the house.

'Who do you *think* it could be?' Edward asked.

Vivien frowned and sighed. Rupert said, 'There's no one missing as far as we know – ' He hesitated.

'You have someone in mind,' Edward said, addressing both of them.

'MacDonnell,' Rupert admitted. 'Aileen's step-father. But he was heard from after he left. He telephoned more than once—'

'Once,' Vivien corrected dully.

Rupert glanced at her. 'Also he'd driven away; he took his Land Rover to Inverness. Aileen and her mother had to go there to retrieve it.'

This was followed by dead silence; no one wanted to say what was in their minds. Vivien guessed that Edward was wondering whether the sale of Lair was legitimate, and she didn't have to look at Rupert to know he was recalling that the only information they had on Mac's leaving had been supplied by Jeannie.

'He could have staged his own suicide,' she said doubtfully.

'*What?*' Rupert stared at her.

'Oh, for Heaven's sake!' She gulped down her coffee. 'Let's leave it to the police.' She looked at Angela. 'I hope this won't make any difference to you,' she said in a high voice. 'You know—'

'Know what?' Edward prompted.

'That we're in the clear.' Rupert smiled. 'We didn't put him there. If we had, we'd have scarpered long ago. She'd like to emigrate to Montana.' He regarded Vivien amiably.

Angela got to her feet. 'We can't do anything until the police arrive,' she said brightly. 'Come and see what we're doing to the house.'

The police arrived in force, even frogmen, which wasn't so ridiculous as it appeared at first sight; the mud was deep and could be negotiated only by men suited up for it. Binnie and Forsyth were there, exhibiting sharp interest in the presence of the Lascos but quickly distracted by the body. There were men taking photographs and a police surgeon.

The frogmen hated it. The bed of the pool was uneven and they had difficulty reaching the body. When one lost his footing he couldn't get up again without help from his partner.

When they reached the body they started to scoop mud away from where the head should be. The people on the banks followed every move with absorption. The civilians had stayed on the near side of the depression, only the police were at the outcrop.

The frogmen conferred with Binnie. They abandoned their efforts to clear the mud away and sank their arms deep in the ooze.

'What are they doing?' Angela asked.

'It's probably caught up in something,' Vivien said. 'People dump old fence posts and wire in water.'

The curious movements continued for what seemed a long time, punctuated by orders from Binnie who was now squatting on the edge of the rock, gesturing, conveying a sense of urgency. Forsyth moved up and gripped his shoulder. It looked familiar but he didn't brush her away.

The frogmen straightened slowly and both faced Binnie. 'Then get it up!' Vivien heard clearly, and saw him stand and step back, pushing Forsyth aside. He took a few paces and swung round to glare at his men who were sliding and straining with the body and with something else, trying to coordinate their efforts.

Suddenly they were still; they must have been getting a grip because after a moment they started to move again: a slow and slippery progress to the bank, the one sliding the body through the mud, the other struggling beside the head end – the head now visible as a large grey bulb – but it wasn't that which riveted their attention; it was what the second man was carrying: something heavy – and seemingly attached to the body.

Binnie looked across the dead pool and met Vivien's eyes. He said something and Forsyth left the group and came round, straight to Vivien. She said pleasantly, 'There's a concrete block chained to his neck. Who is it?'

By ten o'clock that evening Binnie, who had kept going on coffee and cigarettes, was slumped behind his desk and staring blearily at Forsyth. She looked so fresh he reckoned she must have been cat-napping whenever she was out of his sight. He realized that for the past few minutes he had been rambling, even nodding off; what had brought him to his senses was her sharp question: what was his opinion? She meant now they knew that the body was that of MacDonnell. A dentist had again furnished proof; he had fitted Mac's dentures. The remains had been hosed and washed, along with the concrete block and the chain. It was, in fact, two chains: ties from a cow-house.

The police, anxious to contact Aileen and Jeannie, had discovered that they'd vanished. And here was Forsyth asking Binnie for his opinion. He didn't appreciate that she was trying to prod him into action, preferably to go home.

'You can't have an opinion,' he protested. 'Mac was murdered: that's fact. Who did it, which of 'em – if it isn't someone from Alder: that's opinion.'

'There's that pile of concrete blocks in the yard—'

'The Barstows took delivery of tons of concrete blocks.'

'Those old ones have been there years. Vivien says so.'

'Vivien! She's involved. I can smell it.' He glowered. He'd almost added, 'Everyone's involved,' but that could sound paranoid. He needed his sleep. Roll on retirement.

'Why would Jeannie and Aileen disappear?' Forsyth asked. 'It's obvious.'

They had traced the women through the solicitors involved in the sale of the estate. From Lair they had gone to Kelso in the Borders where they stayed with a married couple who trained racehorses. When the sale was completed they left for a tour of Australia. The people at Kelso had been surprised not to receive a card from Australia but they weren't worried. Aileen and Jeannie weren't friends, merely paying guests. The trainer's wife had been augmenting her husband's salary.

'They needn't have disappeared,' Binnie mused, lighting one cigarette from the stub of another. 'They could have moved on to another hotel, guest house, whatever. Why did she choose racing stables? Funny choice.'

'Research?' Forsyth suggested. 'She's building an image. She's got some money, she's going to play the rich widow and catch a really wealthy husband.'

'All she had to do was stay at a posh hotel.'

'Maybe she likes horses.'

'What we want to know is what they did with the cash from the sale of the house. That would help in tracing them.' He had an appointment with the manager of Aileen's bank first thing tomorrow.

'Why should they murder him?' he asked suddenly.

'Who?'

'Mac of course. Who else?'

'There was Alastair.'

He gaped at her, then looked away. To introduce Alastair at this stage, at this time of night, was almost too much for him. 'You reckon they're connected?' he asked weakly.

'Say Aileen killed Alastair, she couldn't have got the body to Corrie Ba, she had nothing to do with the horses until after he died; Mac must have taken the body over there on a pony.'

Binnie opened his desk drawer, retrieved a half-bottle of Scotch and a couple of plastic tumblers. He drank appreciatively, Forsyth sipped like a sparrow. He sighed. His brain started to work again. 'Why would Mac do anything for his step-daughter?' he asked. 'You think there was something between 'em?'

'There is that.' She had obviously considered such a relationship. 'But money's the most likely motive. She could have promised him a cut when she inherited.'

He nodded. 'Then he got too greedy.'

'Right. When the body was found he demanded more. We came round again asking questions and they were afraid he'd break: wouldn't be able to stand up to interrogation.'

'We interview, we don't interrogate.'

'So they hit him over the head and dumped him in the pool.'

'First putting a chain round his neck and the other end through a concrete block. You think they were in it together: mother and daughter?'

'They're together now; that is, they vanished together.'

'Jesus!' Binnie breathed. 'I'm sorry for the poor sod they latch on to next.'

Vivien and Rupert were sitting above the burn watching a grey wagtail catch insects round the pool at the top of a waterfall. It was a week since Mac's body had been found and the people at Alder had been interviewed yet again, this time about Mac. Everyone was vague, maintaining that they knew nothing about his relationships with the rest of his family; they even had difficulty recalling when they'd last seen him. There were those distant glimpses of a person on a tractor who must have been Mac, because Alastair was dead and the women didn't work in the fields, but when pressed no one could remember seeing him for a long time.

Vivien was the vaguest, he'd been a gillie, she said; he was the fellow who looked after the ponies and delivered the peat, she couldn't say she knew him at all really. She said nothing about attempted blackmail, nor about her conversation with Jeannie in the wood.

Binnie told them that Aileen and her mother had disappeared, but most of the Lascos' information since the day the pool was drained came to them by way of the Barstows. So they learned that not only had the two women vanished but so had the money from the sale of the estate, merely passing through Aileen's bank en route to a Swiss account. As for the autopsy on Mac's body, his skull had been fractured by something like a hammer. All the hammers that had been at Lair before the arrival of the Barstows were sent to the forensic laboratory but none showed any sign of having been used as the murder weapon. The public inquiry had been adjourned but it was most likely that the outcome would be murder by person or persons unknown.

'Did you ever have second thoughts about not coming clean with Binnie?' Rupert asked, his eyes following a dipper that flashed upstream, startling the wagtail.

'No.' She was definite. 'There are the Barstows to be considered; if they bought Lair from a person who inherited because she murdered the former owner, their legal position as current owners has to be in doubt. And I like the Barstows. But the main reason for keeping quiet is a matter of ethics. Look' – as he raised a quizzical eyebrow – 'we know now that Aileen killed him – right?'

'Killed Alastair, yes.'

'Killed Mac too: either her or Jeannie, they were both involved. We all were, that's the point. Jeannie told me part of the truth: about Alastair managing to reach home that night, but it wasn't Mac who had the fight with him, it was Aileen, and the reason why she killed him, why she was able to do it then when always before he'd been the powerful brute battering *her*, was because I'd disabled him first.'

'Oh.' He hadn't thought of it like that. 'So you're saying that you were implicated in his murder. Then so was I.'

'You're agreeing with me. We were all involved.'

'So we were. But not in Mac's death. That was nasty, Viv.'

'Be reasonable. He was dead when they put him in the pool; his skull was fractured. The block was used just to keep the body down.' He said nothing. 'You mean,' she went on, 'he didn't have to be killed? But we're agreed it was Mac who took Alastair's body over to Corrie Ba, aren't we?'

'It had to be him; he had the ponies.'

'Mac tried to blackmail me. He must have tried it on Aileen, he'd have thought she was a sitting duck – particularly when you remember how – defeated she appeared to be at that time. He'd have wanted something for getting rid of the body in the first place; being Mac he wouldn't have agreed to do it otherwise. When it was found he could have pushed the price up. Jeannie said he was clever, that was a red herring; he was stupid: unbelievably stupid; fancy trying to blackmail a woman who'd killed already – and one with a mother like Jeannie! He would have blackmailed Aileen for the rest of her life, she'd never have been free of him. Besides—'

'Besides what?'

'Nothing. He asked for it. Is that an eagle or a buzzard?'

Besides, she thought, I've no regrets, there's more to this than being a role model – whether or not by that statement Aileen was trying to strengthen some kind of bond. I'm approving, not condemning, and in my book that gives me a share in their deaths; I have no *right* to go to Binnie. She smiled, wondering if Forsyth had guessed the truth.

She wondered too where Aileen and Jeannie were now; it would have to be a country with lots of beautiful horses and rich men.

Unlike Binnie, Vivien had no qualms concerning the man Aileen took for her next husband. She wouldn't do it again. 'And she won't feel guilt,' she said aloud.

He turned to her. 'Aileen? Do you?'

'I'm not sure I know what guilt is. I do accept responsibility but I don't feel bad about that. Negative emotions don't matter, it's reactions that count. Why did she *let* him beat her?'

'Why does anyone? You think she felt guilty, that she deserved punishment?'

'If she felt inadequate – and battered women do: they've failed at their marriage, they have to bear the consequences – like martyrs, you know? But not Aileen; I've changed my mind about her. It could have been the danger that attracted her.'

'That could have had something to do with it.'

'I think she enjoyed the fights,' Vivien said. 'No: she was compelled to confront him—'

'That's better.'

'—and now the compulsion's been diverted; it's still there: this lure of danger. She needs to ride wild horses.'

'Needs. Women. I'll never understand them.'

'Don't under-estimate yourself. You do very well.'

A shadow crossed the pool as the eagle passed, silent as a cloud, and turned, coming back in a slow circle.

'Youngster,' she said. 'She's not familiar with us yet.'

'How do you know it's female?'

'I don't, but there were two chicks and it looks as if only one survived. The bigger often kills its sibling, and females tend to be bigger. Among raptors, I mean.'

After a pause he said wryly, 'I see your point. Suppose both chicks were female?'

'Eagles don't have sisterly feeling, my love.' She stood up and held out her hand. 'Time we went home, there's honey cake for tea.'

They started to stroll down the path through the bracken. The eagle followed them a little way and then sheered off towards the great wilderness below Cape Wrath where the last wolf was killed, and ghosts of shipwrecked sailors haunt an abandoned village and a street of turf and ruins and green mounds above unhallowed graves.